Passion of the Streets

Also by A'zayler

No Loyalty (with De'nesha Diamond)

Published by Kensington Publishing Corp.

Passion
of the
Streets

A'zayler

KENSINGTON PUBLISHING CORP.
www.kensingtonbooks.com

DAFINA BOOKS are published by

Kensington Publishing Corp.
119 West 40th Street
New York, NY 10018

All Kensington titles, imprints, and distributed lines are available at special quantity discounts for bulk purchases for sales promotion, premiums, fund-raising, and educational or institutional use.

Special book excerpts or customized printings can also be created to fit specific needs. For details, write or phone the office of the Kensington Sales Manager: Kensington Publishing Corp., 119 West 40th Street, New York, NY 10018. Attn. Sales Department. Phone: 1-800-221-2647.

Dafina and the Dafina logo Reg. U.S. Pat. & TM Off.

ISBN-13: 978-1-4967-1806-8
ISBN-10: 1-4967-1806-2
First Kensington Trade Paperback Printing: May 2018

eISBN-13: 978-1-4967-1812-9
eISBN-10: 1-4967-1812-7
First Kensington Electronic Edition: May 2018

10 9 8 7 6 5 4 3 2 1

Printed in the United States of America

I would like to dedicate this book to my readers . . . I love you all.

Acknowledgments

To have a dream larger than anything you've ever imagined come to life and maximize into wonders that you've spent a host of nights praying for is not only an accomplishment but a blessing as well. I can't count how many times I've doubted myself and my capability to succeed in a realm of talent much larger than my own, but because of God and the support team that he's placed in my corner, I've not only become established but dominant as well.

All praises to the most high for blessing me with a continuous flow of love, passion, and surplus of inscriptive ideas. My mother, my siblings, my husband, and my granny . . . to all of you I'd like to say thank you. Thank you for believing in me when I didn't believe in myself, for pushing me to be better than I've ever thought possible, for being my sunshine on the cloudiest days, and lastly, for recognizing the plans that God had for me were much higher than the ones I had for myself.

Through all of the criticism, lack of support, competition, and any other adversity I've faced, you all have been there, and for that, I thank you and I love you.

—From the hearts of Jamil "Milli" Rock and Gianna "Gee" Ellis

"I love him from the inside out. He's the beat to my heart and the man who awakened feelings in me that run deeper than anything I've ever felt. Milli is the one person who I cannot—will not—live without. The love he gives me is like my oxygen. It's received in the deepest part of my soul, and he knows that. He knows the type of control he has over me, and though some days that's not always a good thing, I'll never leave."
—Gia

"Gia . . . Gia . . . Gia . . . Gia, what can I say about my Gee other than she's my muthafucking heart? Not only is she my heart, but she's my soul and my rib. Being from where I'm from and being the nigga that I am, shit ain't always been sweet, but she doesn't care about that. These days it's hard out here to find a real woman who's going to make you better, but Gia makes that shit easy. Hell, Gia makes life easy. My backbone, my homie, my lover, my friend, my fucking life, that's Gia. My baby, and the key to my muthafuckin streets."
—Milli Rock

Prologue

*"Had I known this one moment would change my life forever,
I would have just stayed at home."* —*Milli*

"Why you always being so bad, Jamil?" Lauren licked the orange ice cream that was melting over the side of her Flintstones push pop.

"I'm not bad. Why you always saying that?"

Lauren smacked her lips and looked over at him. "Because you are. You always be doing bad stuff."

Jamil sucked his teeth. "Like what?"

"Like how you just stole me this ice cream, and how you beat that boy up yesterday at the park." Lauren continued to swirl her tongue around the top of her ice cream. "My daddy said I shouldn't be with you because your parents ain't raised you right and that you're always getting into stuff."

Jamil turned his nose up at the mention of her parents and the things they'd said about him. "Man, fuck your parents."

"See? You be cussing and stuff too." Lauren shook her head as they turned the corner, headed for the playground.

It was Saturday, and Jamil and Lauren had just come from the corner store getting ice cream and were about to chill at the park. School had just let out for break, and it was already starting out to be a boring summer. Jamil, not one to stay in the house much, had woken up bright and early and headed to the basketball court. He'd bumped into Lauren along the way.

Lauren was cool and he liked her a lot. The only problem was that she was one of the privileged girls at his school, so she wasn't allowed to hang out much, nor was she allowed to hang out with boys from the hood such as himself The only reason she was probably in the hood right then was because she'd spent the night at her best friend Jessica's house the night before. Jessica had been living right up the street from Jamil since elementary school. She was just as hood as he was, if not worse.

"If you would stop being so bad all the time," Lauren said, "you could probably come over my house like everybody else does."

"Nah, I don't really want to come over your house. Your parents already don't like me."

"But they could learn to like you."

Jamil was about to say something else when he noticed a large crowd near the basketball court. He could tell by all of the noise and pushing and shoving that it had to be a fight, which wasn't very surprising. Growing up in downtown Columbus, Georgia, there was always a fight, especially in the Booker T. Washington projects, which were commonly known as BTW.

"Come on, let's go see what's going on." Lauren took off walking down the hill.

"Lauren, no. Let's go. We don't need to go down there."

With a quick smile in his direction, Lauren continued on her way. "I know big bad Jamil isn't scared to watch a fight."

Jamil sucked his teeth and jogged up beside her. "I'm not scared. I just don't run to fights. It's not smart."

"It's not like we're the ones fighting." Lauren craned her neck so that she could look around the people circling the brawl.

Jamil was standing to the side watching Lauren stand on her tiptoes when he heard shots ring out.

Jamil grabbed a screaming Lauren's hand and pulled her in the opposite direction. The crowd began to disperse rapidly and he wanted to get out of the way as fast as possible. He may have been into a lot of "bad things," as Lauren had put it, but a bullet wasn't one. Bullets didn't have a name, and he didn't want to be the one to give them one.

While still holding Lauren's hand, Jamil ran as fast as he could with Lauren tagging along behind him. The wind was blowing in and out of his ears as he breathed harder and harder. People were everywhere around them, all trying to run to safety, stumbling over one another, some even falling over each other. Screams could be heard at the same time that another few shots were let off.

"Come on, Lauren, run faster," Jamil screamed over his shoulder as his arm got heavy.

Unsure of what it was that had him dragging a little more now, he turned to look over his shoulder. Lauren was running slowly while clutching her chest. Bright red blood oozed between her fingers and down her wrist. Her eyes were watering and she looked like she was only moments from falling.

Jamil rushed to her immediately and tried to catch her before she could hit the ground. Lauren's body fell limp into his arms, causing him to stumble.

"Lauren!" he yelled.

"Call—" She coughed loudly. "Call my paren—" She began coughing again.

"I don't know their number. Where's your phone?" Jamil was frantic as he tried to figure out what to do next.

He was dragging her and trying to run for cover all at the same time, being that shots were still being fired. Afraid and not sure what else to do, Jamil pulled Lauren to the side of the building they had just come around a few seconds ago and crouched over her. She was making gurgling noises as he covered both of their heads with his arms.

He stayed hovered over her for a few more minutes, waiting for the gunshots to stop. When they did, he hurriedly searched her pockets for her phone.

"Hold on, Lauren, I'ma call 911." Jamil finally located her phone and dialed the police. "Hurry up my friend just got shot! We're in BTW. Hurry up and get here." Jamil stayed on the phone with the operator trying to tell her what was going on, but he made sure to keep an eye on Lauren.

Her eyes looked glassy and she wasn't making any more noises. Jamil rubbed her head softly as he held her cell phone to his ear. Her caramel-colored body and black hair lay across his lap as warm blood soaked through her light pink shirt. People had begun to gather around them saying things that he could barely make out due to the shock of what was happening.

"I think she dead," was the only thing Jamil heard, and probably only because it was true.

Lauren's once vibrant and lively body was now still and lifeless. Her eyes were cast onto him and unmoving. Jamil stared down at her as she stared back at him. In his heart he knew she was gone; she had been for a few minutes, he just didn't want to believe it. It hadn't even been ten minutes since they'd been laughing and talking, and now she was gone.

Jamil held her close as he waited for an ambulance to come. With his back against the wall and her body cradled in his arms, he sat as still as he could until he heard sirens. Even then, he barely moved. He turned his head to the side to see where they were coming from, and that was it. He watched the paramedics as they ran over to him and attempted to pull Lauren's body from his grasp.

So many lights, so many people, so much commotion, but all he could hear was Lauren's voice from when they'd talked on the sidewalk moments prior. He was lost in a world of his own until he heard a male voice.

"Get her away from him. Get that hoodlum away from my daughter."

Jamil looked up to see a man who looked a lot like Lauren marching toward him. He was pointing his finger and frowning deeply at Jamil. He probably would have gone right up to Jamil had the police not stopped him. Jamil sat lost and shattered forever as the paramedics finally pulled Lauren away.

A loud scream from a lady serenaded throughout the area as she dropped to her knees in front of where Lauren had been placed on the ground. Though Jamil had never seen them before, he knew they were Lauren's parents. Someone must have recognized Lauren and called them. The man was the spitting image of her while the lady had the same hair and a darker skin tone than Lauren.

The two of them leaned over their child sobbing and saying a lot of things before the man jumped up and lunged toward Jamil. Quickly, Jamil tried to scramble to his feet but didn't move fast enough and got punched in the face. He grabbed his nose and held his head down as blood leaked into his hands.

"You little bastard. I know it was you. I know you had something to do with this." He tried to break free from the police officers that had just grabbed him. "She would have never gotten into any shit like this if it weren't for you." He was yelling and hollering all types of stuff as Jamil turned and walked away.

On any normal day Jamil would have fought back, forgetting the fact that the man was twice his size and old enough to be his father, because that's just the type of person he was, but not today. Today he would give the man a pass. Today he would allow Lauren's father to take his frustrations out on him because he knew he needed to. He was hurt about something he couldn't change and needed to place the blame somewhere.

No amount of yelling, screaming, or hitting, for that matter, would bring Lauren back, and until her father accepted that, Jamil would take the blame. Jamil could hear all of the loud talking as well as whispers as he walked from his spot against the wall to the squad car in the middle of the street.

"Son, can I talk to you for a moment?" a black lady in a brown business suit and badge asked him.

Jamil nodded and followed her to the backseat of a blue Explorer. Once he and she were both comfortable inside, she began asking questions such as his first name and address. She then, of course, asked him to tell her his version of the shooting. Jamil answered everything to the best of his ability, telling nothing but the truth. Once she'd jotted down everything she needed to know, she leaned over and wrapped her arms around him, squeezing him tightly to her chest.

"It's going to be okay, sweetie. Don't let him or anyone else make this your fault." She squeezed him a little tighter before letting him go. "Tell me your full name, sweetheart."

"Jamil Rock."

"Well, Jamil Rock, I'm Detective Keating. I'm good with names, so that means I'm going to remember you. You stay out of trouble, you hear me?"

Jamil nodded.

"Okay, baby, head on home. I'll stop by later to check on you."

"Yes, ma'am." Jamil opened the door and got out.

The crowd around Lauren and the other dead body that he would learn about the next day had grown larger. Jamil could still hear people talking and crying as he made his way back down the sidewalk. As much as he hated to go home right then, he needed a bath and his mama. It wasn't even twelve o'clock in the afternoon, and he was more than ready for the day to be over.

Chapter One

"It's funny how the first time I ever saw Gia I had no idea how important she would be to me. Not for one second had I given my chocolate baby a second thought. Had a nigga known then what I know now, I would have stepped to her a lot sooner."
—*Milli*

Six years later

"Didn't I tell you one time to stop sweeping over my got damn feet?" Jamil's dad, Owen, yelled at his mom, Zanetta.

Zanetta was in the middle of the living room sweeping up the bag of Doritos that Owen had just wasted, and he had the nerve to yell about it. Jamil sat at the dining room table eating his food and watching his parents prepare for yet another argument. One he wasn't in the mood for at all, and one he wasn't even about to watch.

"Owen, you asked me to clean up the chips, and now you want me to stop? Make up your mind, please."

"What you say to me?" Owen hopped up, and before his feet could even become sturdy beneath his tall frame, he'd slapped Zanetta clear across the living room.

She yelped in pain when she slammed against the television stand. Crumpled into a heap on the floor, Zanetta held her lower back. Jamil could hear her moaning in pain as Owen walked over to her and kicked her in the stomach.

"Get your ass up and get out of here. I need to watch my game, and I don't want to hear all that damn crying while I'm trying to do it."

Jamil looked up from his plate of roast beef and potatoes and watched as his mother hobbled from the floor, still clutching her back. On her way out of the living room she picked up the broom and dragged it with her. All Jamil could do was shake his head. Why did she choose to put up with that kind of abuse? He would never know.

Once Jamil was finally done with his food, he took his plate into the kitchen and grabbed a Gatorade from the refrigerator. Without a word to either of his parents, he left the apartment. Jamil took the flight of stairs two at a time until he was at the front entrance of their home. He got hot the moment he stepped out of the door and headed for the gas station across the street.

It was summer and nearly a hundred degrees outside, and just like any other day, he was in the heat. There were only two things on his mind that would have him moving around in the sweltering heat: his money and his parents. Twenty-four years old, Jamil was a young hustler on the grind to get it by any means necessary.

He'd long ago stopped trying to intervene in his parents' cocaine-induced fights. Anytime they got high they would tear at each other physically, mentally, or emotionally. Before he understood the cause of their fights, Jamil would mediate and try to keep his father off his mom's ass, but that impulse had died years ago.

They would fight at any time of night or day, not caring who was around, and he would always be tossed in the middle trying to defend Zanetta. It only took one time for the two of them to jump on him together for him to leave that situation alone.

His mother and father had beaten him so badly outside of one of their regular crack houses that he'd needed stitches across his left eyebrow, a splint on one of his fingers, and a cast on his arm. Putting it mildly, they had beaten his ass like they hadn't birthed him.

From that moment to this one, he hadn't offered to help his

mother again. All of his stitches and casts had come from a quick high and hard shove to the ground. Had he known his mother was okay with being pushed down by his father in front of a crowd of people, he would have left her ass right there.

Just like had he known his "Uncle Money" was really a drug dealer and his father went there every day to buy him and his mother their fix, he would have minded his business, but he hadn't. Instead, he waited to say something as his parents went inside and got high, came outside, picked a fight, and his mother got knocked to the ground.

The whupping he took that day at the hands of Owen and Zanetta rang through the hood for months, but once it had finally died down and was over, he'd vowed to stay to himself and let his parents be who they were.

"Milli Rock, what's good, my nigga?" Omar held his hand out for a pound as Jamil passed him.

Milli Rock was the nickname he'd been given by his homeboy Shock, who was also a dealer from the hood. Jamil had been working with him for years, and they were really beginning to make a name for themselves. Though Jamil had always held a tad bit of clout in the streets simply because he was solid and would put in work for the older dudes, he was now coming into his own.

He would soon be a lot bigger if the opportunity he'd been waiting on finally came through. Working the blocks in Georgia was cool, but Miami was the place to be. He was so hungry for that promotion he could feel it at his fingertips, but he had to be patient, continue doing what he was good at, and in due time he'd get what he'd been working for.

Initially it hadn't been something he was too fond of because he knew Columbus like the back of his hand. He could move around the entire city with his eyes closed if necessary, so the idea of starting over brought about some apprehension, but he forced himself to shake it.

If he wanted to win, he had to stop being so scared to take

risks. Especially since serving his own weight and moving his own products was starting to make niggas take notice, which on his part was a good thing. Many watched while others worked, but they all respected him.

Jamil took a sip from his Gatorade. "Shit. Headed to the gas station real quick. What's the block looking like?"

Omar was one of the only other niggas that Shock had put on Jamil's team, and he was cool. He worked hard and always had Milli's money on time, which was all that Jamil really cared about. That was basically as far as it went. Neither Shock nor Jamil was a fan of dealing with a lot of people, so they kept their circle small.

If it wasn't Shock, Jamil, and Iverson, then it was no one. The only other nigga that knew anything about them was their supplier, and he only dealt with Shock, which was totally fine with Jamil. He wasn't a big fan of people anyway.

They worked so well together as a team that there was no real reason to add anyone else. Shock distributed everything that they were supplied, while Iverson was over the paperwork side of it and Jamil became the money man. Where one was weak the other was strong, and it made their bond even tighter. Never looking down on the other about anything, just doing what they could to make it work.

In Jamil's mind, Shock and Iverson were the brothers he never had. For years they'd been grinding together day and night, putting in work, fighting, living, struggling; anything you could think of they'd done together. The love Jamil had for the two of them was priceless.

They were the only two who had always had his back and always kept his secrets, and for that they would forever have his loyalty. Omar wasn't as close as the other three were, but he was cool too. Jamil fucked with him the long way.

"It's hot, as always." Omar referred to the drugs being distributed on the block.

Jamil nodded and held his hand out to dap Omar up again. "Bet. Keep it up."

After Omar told him that he would, Jamil continued on his way to the store. The BP gas station was right across the street from Jamil's block and one of the only spots he visited regularly.

The cool air welcomed him when he pulled the door open and stepped inside. He nodded at the cashier before walking to the potato chip aisle to grab a bag of Tom's salt and vinegar chips. They were his all-time favorite and had been for years. Once he grabbed those, he moved to the other side to grab a Twix and some SweeTarts.

"Oh my goodness, it's too hot out there." A female voice came from the front of the store.

Naturally, Jamil looked up. There were two girls standing in line looking to pay for their gas, he was assuming. They were both pretty, but the darker one caught his attention. She was the average female height, with skin that resembled a piece of milk chocolate candy and bright round eyes. Her face was bare minus the light coating of gloss across her lips.

She had a small earring in her nose and a sexy-ass mouth. Her lips weren't big, neither were they small, but the smile that illuminated from them had Jamil staring longer than necessary. From where he was standing, he could see she had a pretty decent shape under the purple Nike biker shorts and matching sports bra, even though he couldn't understand why she would have something like that on in the middle of the day.

Thirst trapper.

The large gold hoop earrings dangling from her ears stood out and brought an extra small light to her beautiful skin, but that wasn't what had caught his attention. The long, black dreadlocks with the red and dark purple ends was it. The moment he'd noticed them, his interest was piqued.

He'd always had a thing for dark-skinned women, but the fact that she had locs like him heightened her sex appeal even more. Jamil stood on the aisle watching her for a few moments longer before walking over to join them in line. When he got to where they were standing, both she and her little friend gave him the once-over. Her friend stared a little longer than she had.

Behind her, with only one person separating them, Jamil took in her stance from behind. She had nice toned bowlegs that rose from a pair of lime green running shoes up to a handful of ass and hips. He could tell by the way she was standing that she was an athlete of some sort, which drew him to her even more. That also made him rethink his earlier thoughts about her attire.

He watched as some of her locs swayed against her back when she moved her head. Women were the one thing Jamil took no real part in unless he was horny and needed a quick nut. However, that didn't mean that he didn't want to, because he did, he just wanted to do all the right things with the right kind of woman.

All of the women in his hood were scandalous, so he did his best to steer clear of them. Whenever he found one who was different, he'd change his opinion on them. Plus he had too much other stuff on his plate most of the time, but baby girl right there was nice to look at.

"Is it always this hot down here?" She looked at the brown-skinned girl she was with.

"Yes, Gia, damn." She giggled while the dark-skinned beauty just shook her head. "You act like you ain't never felt no heat before."

Gia.

"I don't know how I'm going to make it all summer. I think I'm already ready to go back home."

Brown skin smiled and looped her arm through Gia's as they turned and proceeded to walk away from the gas station. They both looked over at him again before brown skin waved. Jamil didn't even bother to acknowledge her.

Not a head nod, a wave, nothing. That wasn't his speed. He'd admired, and that was all there was to it. No need to be friendly because that was something that he wasn't when it came to strangers.

Once he'd paid for his things, he exited the store headed back in the direction of his block. The little black BMW truck was parked near the pump with a gas nozzle hanging from it as both of the girls stood near the trunk talking. Jamil found it amusing how their conversation ceased slowly as he walked past.

"Hey, what's your name?" brown skin asked him.

Jamil looked her up and down and kept walking. He didn't do pleasantries, and he especially didn't do overeager females. That was like a stalker waiting to happen.

"Well, excuse me, then," he heard her say from behind him.

Not missing a step, Jamil walked coolly across the street and back to his building. He took a seat on their stoop and opened his chips. It didn't matter how full he was, he could always stomach a bag of Tom's chips. Twenty-four and a middle school dropout, Jamil's life was pretty boring.

Outside of slanging at night and chilling during the day, he didn't do much. He'd been living the same life since his seventh-grade year when he'd dropped out of school. With no complaints from his parents, Jamil pretty much did whatever he wanted. He came and went as he pleased and stayed out when he got ready. He had pretty much been living an adult life ever since he was a teenager, so there was no point in changing.

His parents never really had much to say as long as he was serving them on the regular, which had recently come to a stop. He'd thought about it long and hard one night and decided he would no longer contribute to their inability to be good parents. Ever since then, they'd been at his throat even harder.

On most days he ignored them because he didn't give a fuck, but what irked him the most was that even though he wasn't giving them drugs and had warned everybody on the block not to either, they still ended up high. That shit was a mystery he couldn't wait to solve.

Over the years, the streets had turned Jamil into a hard-core loner who only dealt with people when it was necessary. Anything outside of that wasn't his forte. The only people that he dealt with personally were his best friend Iverson and his OG Shock. Nothing further.

"Hey, Milli Rock." A bucktoothed little girl rolled past him on her scooter.

"What's going on, Tia?" Jamil smiled.

She smiled back at him before pushing herself on up the street. He watched her playing and enjoying herself with not one care in the world. It was cute for now that she had no idea her mom was selling all of their food stamps for crack. He almost felt bad thinking that maybe he was taking food from Tia and her younger sister's mouth but quickly shook that thought.

How her mama chose to feed her kids was none of his concern. All he cared about was that she had his money whenever she showed up at his doorstep in the wee hours of the morning. Jamil sat on the stoop for a few minutes longer before going back into his house. Hopefully Owen and Zanetta had gotten their share of drug-induced fighting out of the way and he could get some sleep.

It was going on six o'clock in the evening, and he needed to get some rest before it was time to hit the block.

Jamil looked up once again and dusted the scattered pieces of sand and Sheetrock from his dreads. From the moment he and Iverson had walked into the basement of the club, fragments of the ceiling had been falling into his hair and eyes.

Maybe if they'd cut all that loud-ass music down and put out half of the people they had packed into the club, then the floor wouldn't be falling apart. He'd seen the line as he and Iverson passed the entrance and knew there were entirely too many people there to begin with, but that had nothing to do with him.

Now all he wished was that they would hurry up and get to the room they were supposed to be meeting in so that he could go.

They had been walking for almost ten minutes and still hadn't made it to the bottom of the club.

One flight of stairs after the next. After the first flight Jamil had already begun to wonder why in the hell they hadn't installed an elevator in such an expensive club, but once again that wasn't his business.

"Aye that's it right there." Iverson pointed to the last room down the hall.

The black door at the end of the hallway was closed with a red light hanging above it. Jamil's first thought was to be glad they'd finally gotten there, but now he was wondering why it was so ducked off. If it had been up to him they would have met upstairs at a table, exchanged money, and kept it pushing.

Jamil skeptically looked around the hallway again before turning toward Iverson. "They know we're here?"

Iverson nodded as he continued down the hallway. "Yeah, I hit that nigga up once we got outside."

"Bet." Jamil touched his back to make sure his gun was secure before sticking his hands into his pockets.

When they were in front of the room, Iverson opened the door and walked in with Jamil directly behind him. Stone, the guy they were meeting, was seated at a small table in the center of the room smoking a cigar.

The room was dimly lit by the hanging light fixtures in each corner of the room. There was just enough light to see everyone's face and hands, which was enough for Jamil. As long as he could watch everything happening around him, he was good.

A broad smile crossed Stone's face upon seeing the guys. Before rising to his feet, he took a long pull from the Cuban hanging between his lips and set it in his clear ashtray. With his arms outstretched, he walked toward Jamil and Iverson.

"My niggas, what's good?"

Iverson dapped him up first while Jamil chose to nod his greeting instead. Stone looked at him a little longer than necessary, clearly not liking the way he chose to handle things, but was smart enough to keep it moving.

"So what can I do for you boys?" Stone took his seat back at the table while Iverson took the one across from him. Jamil chose to stand.

Jamil looked at him as he puffed heavily on the cigar some more. "Shock told us that he already called you with the specifics."

Stone nodded. "Yes, yes, he did. Let's get down to business, shall we?"

Jamil tried his hardest not to frown at Stone. He was so fake, and that was the main reason Jamil hated him and didn't care to deal with him. It never failed, every time they did business with him, he would act as if it was their first time meeting. Pretending not to know what was supposed to be handled.

It irritated the crap out of Jamil, but he had to ignore it for business purposes. The most he could do was be the bigger person and disregard that nigga's immature antics.

"Two shipments for one month, and I'd like to double that amount next month." Stone fixed his suit jacket as he spoke.

"We'll give you that this month to see how you handle it. If it works, then you can do the same next month. But as of now, no guarantees." Jamil didn't bother sugarcoating anything. This was business.

It was clear by the way Stone was staring at Jamil that he wasn't too fond of what he'd just said, but Stone had no other choice but to respect it, so he nodded.

"You have the money and paperwork?" Iverson asked Stone.

Stone nodded at the same time he pulled the black briefcase from the floor and sat it on the table. He removed a brown envelope and turned the briefcase around so that it was facing both men.

After seeing Iverson and Jamil both nod, Stone pushed the envelope and money toward Jamil.

"You two can look this over and let me know if it's what you asked for."

Jamil took the briefcase full of money and pushed the envelope toward Iverson. "You can look over those. I got this."

Iverson pulled the paper from the envelope and read it over while Jamil thumbed through a few of the bills. When he was satisfied, he closed the briefcase and tapped Iverson lightly on the back.

"What's it looking like?" Jamil asked, referring to the contracts.

"It's straight," Iverson replied.

"Cool. Let's bounce."

Jamil stepped back and allowed Iverson room to stand up from the chair. After saying their goodbyes, they left the room and headed back into the club. Jamil was headed for the exit until he noticed Iverson was walking in the direction of the crowd.

"Aye, Iverson, what you doing, man?" Jamil asked.

"I was about to chill for a minute. See what some of these hoes talking about."

"Nigga, don't you think we need to drop this stuff off first?"

Iverson looked at Jamil with a sly smirk on his face. "Man, we can chill for a minute."

Jamil wasn't feeling that one bit, so he shook his head. He was too well known to be walking around with a briefcase full of money on him. Furthermore, he would be purposely making himself a target walking through a club with a briefcase. There was no place for it, and he was not about to risk losing his money or his life about it.

"Nah, you can stay. I'm about to dip."

Iverson looked like he wanted to reject but changed his mind. "Bet. Just take these with you, then." He handed Jamil the envelope, and Jamil turned away.

Jamil was happy he'd decided to drive that night because had he ridden with Iverson, he would have been past angry. If Iverson wanted to be left alone to party, then so be it. That was his business. Jamil just wasn't about to do it. That was stupid as hell.

Once Jamil was in his car and headed back home, he called Shock to let him know about Iverson's behavior. He'd thought that was very sloppy, but Iverson was grown. Once inside his house, he hid the money and contracts before hopping in the shower.

When Jamil finally made it to his bed, his eyes closed immediately. Hopefully Iverson had enough sense not to get himself into anything he would need help getting out of.

Chapter Two

"It was unnerving for me that even after only seeing Milli once, I wanted to see him again. There was just this weird feeling in the pit of my stomach every time I pictured his face in my head. I should have known then that once I actually spent time with him, that he would become unforgettable."
—Gia

Lying beside the pool with her shades covering half of her face, Gia scrolled through her Snapchat looking at all of her friends from back home. It was only her second day in Georgia, and she was already ready to go back to Hawaii. For some reason or another, Oni and her mother had thought it would be a good idea for her to fly to Georgia for the summer and visit.

Although she loved Oni like a sister, her house was boring. All they did every day was wake up, swim, and go to the mall, which wasn't much fun because all Oni ever wanted to do was look for men, and that was only when she wasn't laid up with her sugar daddy, Isaac.

Men were cool, and looking for them even proved to be a good time, but Oni just went overboard sometimes. Not that Gia didn't happily indulge occasionally; it was just never anything serious for her. She never saw any dudes worthy of her time. Some were cute, and some were just all right, while others were downright ugly.

Gia had a certain type of man that she was interested in, and not one of the dudes she'd seen since landing at Hartsfield International Airport in Atlanta the day before had caught her attention. Well, almost none of them. The light-skinned dreadhead from the gas station was cute enough to be bae, but there was something about him she didn't like.

On top of him being one of the rudest people in America, he looked bad. Not bad as in something was wrong with him, but bad as in bad as hell. Bad like he'd steal your grandma's purse and try to sell it back to you for half the price. He was handsome as ever with his tall ass, and those burnt orange dreads and facial hair. Then that one arm full of tattoos, and pigeon toes were an added bonus.

Gia had never once in her life seen a black man with orange hair, and it was definitely something to pine over. Since he had been dressed simply in a pair of gym shorts and a tank top, she'd gotten a good view of his tattoos and physique. It wasn't as defined as a man who went to the gym regularly, but he was far from fat.

His shoulders were broad, his chest was hard, and his arms had muscles, but that still wasn't good enough for her. If nothing else, Gia took her fitness and health seriously. She'd been a track star all of her life and did everything she could to maintain her speed. She was so good she'd just gotten selected as a hopeful to represent the United States in the following year's Olympics.

With the Olympics and men on her brain, Gia scooted down farther onto her chair and rested her hands behind her head. Once again thoughts of the grandma purse snatcher crossed her mind. His small slanted eyes, full pink lips, and the well-lined beard along the bottom of his chin had her daydreaming something terrible.

The light brown irises that looked somewhere between evil and sad, paired with the tough-guy demeanor and thick burnt orange eyebrows, made Gia wish she had paid him a little more attention. She had been so focused on getting out of the heat that she hadn't really given herself time to enjoy such a unique-looking man.

"Oni, you remember the guy from the gas station?"

Oni swam from one side of the pool over to the side that Gia was on. "How could I forget Mr. Rude Ass?"

Gia snickered at Oni. She could be so comical at times. "You stupid."

"Girl, I'm for real. His mean carrottop-face ass."

Oni and Gia giggled uncontrollably until Gia sat up and removed her sunglasses.

"Okay, for real, man, stop playing."

Oni was still laughing but she ran her hand over her face, pretending to be wiping her smirk off.

"What about him?"

"You ever seen him before?"

Oni shook her head and kicked her legs slowly beneath the water. "Nah, I don't think so. I never really be on that side of town until it's time for me to get my truck cleaned. I love the detail shop right next to the gas station that we went to."

Gia nodded and put her shades back on.

"Why? You must want to see him again."

Gia shrugged. "No, I don't think so. He was just the cutest thing I've seen since I've been here, that's all."

"Listen, just because our men down here ain't all big and fine with all that long-ass hair you're used to doesn't mean that they ain't fine. You're probably only thinking about him because he was relatively large in stature."

Gia rolled her eyes. "That's not what I'm saying, crazy girl."

"Yes, it is too, because I know I've seen some cute ones since you've been here, which hasn't been but a couple of days." Oni was being sarcastic.

"Well, maybe we simply have different taste in men."

"No, we don't, because Carrottop was cute. You and I both think so."

Gia got quiet, not really thinking that needed a response.

"The fair starts tomorrow. We can go back down there if you want. It's normally in that parking lot right across the street from where we was at. I'm almost positive we'll see him again."

"I don't know . . . is it safe down there? Those apartments didn't look like they were the best place to be hanging around in."

Oni sucked her teeth and scooted backward in the water. "Girl, it ain't. BTW is the projects, and neither you nor me was raised like that, so you better believe we won't be over there."

"It's bad like that?"

"I mean, I don't hear much about it on the news, but then again I'm always busy, so I can't really say."

"I guess that's cool. I ain't trying to go over there anyway. I really only want to go to the fair."

"Okay, well, I'll clear my schedule for tomorrow and we can spend the day out there." Oni swam away for a second but turned around and came right back. "Isaac wants me to come see him tonight. You don't mind, do you?"

"Isaac? You mean your other daddy?"

Oni smiled brightly, showing all of her teeth. "Don't do that. He's not that old."

Gia rolled her eyes. "Says who? All of the ladies who play bingo with your mama?"

Both girls laughed, because Gia was always making age jokes when it came to Isaac. From the moment Oni had told her about him and how old he was, Gia hadn't stopped clowning him. Though other girls might have taken offense to it, Oni didn't.

One of the main reasons was she knew it was all fun and games. The other was because even though Gia might have been being silly while making some of her jokes, they were all very true. Isaac was indeed old enough to be Oni's father. Even with him being sexy as hell, he was still old.

"You better be glad that old nigga is fine or I wouldn't let your ass live."

"I know you wouldn't because you barely do now."

Gia scooted down a little lower in her chair. "You know I like to play. Go see your old man if you want to. Just make sure you get some money out of that nigga." Gia held one of her hands up in front of her face, admiring her acrylic nails. "I think I need a fill-in." She smiled even bigger when she noticed Oni was smiling as well.

"You know I'm hitting him up for some cash. Right after I bust this young pussy open for him."

Gia squealed dramatically while covering her ears. For one of the most ladylike females she'd ever met, Oni could be downright awful at times. After a few more laughs with each other, they went back to doing their own things.

Hopefully living in Georgia for the next two months wouldn't take too long to get used to. Life in Hawaii was all Gia knew. She had lived there since the first grade, when her father got stationed at Schofield Barracks. Her father was a colonel in the U.S. Army and had decided to retire in the sunny state.

Being an only child, Gia had spent all of her free time making friends, and now she was missing them like crazy. Living the high life in Hawaii had become the norm for her, and now that she was back on the mainland she felt incomplete. All of her life her parents had been her entire world, and not having them there right then was making her sad.

Growing up alone, her parents made it their business to keep her involved in sports, and they were there every step of the way to support Gia. Her father was her biggest supporter. Since her mother had gotten sick and was forced to get a hysterectomy, her father never had the chance to get the son he'd always wanted, so Gia was that for him.

They did everything together. Anything Gia could do to make him proud she did, which was why she'd been training for the Olympics in Hawaii instead of flying to the mainland to do so. She had been offered numerous opportunities from accredited track coaches all over the United States, but she couldn't fathom leaving her parents like that. They were both in their late fifties and not getting any younger.

Baseball and track had been two of her father's favorite sports growing up, so of course Gia took an interest in them as well only excelling in track. She was currently the second fastest female runner in the nation, only coming second to a white girl from Denver, Colorado, named Stacy Dunlap.

Though the two had never met each other, they had this on-going competition between them, and Gia couldn't wait until the day came where they would race each other. Many newspapers and magazines had been trying to sponsor a race between them since the beginning of their junior year in college, but it hadn't happened yet.

The main reason was that Gia's father didn't want her to, and the second reason was because there was no real purpose for that type of race to take place, other than the fact that the media wanted to see it. Initially it had been something small between both girls and their track coaches, with a few small-time media sources. That was up until last month when *Sports Illustrated* had run an article on them suggesting the race.

That had set Gia off. A magazine that large featuring little ole her had her super hyped and ready to leave Stacy in the dust, but her father had said no, and what the Colonel said went. Though in her heart racing Stacy was something she desperately wanted to do, she could wait. When the time was right, she would run against her and win.

"I know you ain't still thinking about Carrottop?" Oni was standing next to Gia, wrapped in a towel.

"Nah. I was actually thinking about track."

"Girl! Enjoy your break, please. Running track is all you do with your life. Let loose and have some Southern girl fun."

Gia smiled at Oni as she rolled her eyes every time she talked. "Oni, you need to learn how not to be so feisty all the time."

"And you need to learn how not to be so uptight."

"I'm not. I'm focused."

"Well, focus on these niggas I just called over here to swim with us."

Gia sat up and snatched her glasses from her face. "What nig-gas? You know I got a boyfriend."

Oni sucked her teeth. "And I have Isaac, but who cares about that? You wasn't thinking about that fine-ass Samoan when you was talking to me about Carrottop."

Gia smirked and turned her head. She couldn't even front. She hadn't been thinking about Kainoa. Kainoa was her on-again, off-again boyfriend. He was Samoan and one of the other reasons she missed Hawaii. Even though right now they were on one of their off stages, she still missed him.

They had been together since her freshman year in college and were still managing to hold on. If Kainoa could get over his crazy mood swings, then they would have a pretty decent relationship. Kainoa was born and raised in Hawaii. Coming from a full-blooded Samoan family, he was a lot larger in stature than Gia.

His skin was the color of a perfect jar of peanut butter, with hair longer than hers that he normally wore in a ponytail at the back of his neck. He was one of the sexiest men Gia had ever laid eyes on and was only getting better with time. He was just crazy. She'd learned by living in Hawaii that most of the people there were pretty mild-mannered and easygoing.

On more days than one she had questioned whether or not he was really from there. In the beginning Gia's father had liked him a lot, but after their third breakup, he was no longer a fan. He thought Kainoa played too many games to be as old as he was.

Oni snapped her fingers in Gia's face. "Snap out of it, girl, and get with it. Willie and his cousin will be here in a minute."

Gia turned her nose up. "Willie? What kind of old-ass-man name is that?"

"Old as hell, but that nigga got a big dick, though." Oni smiled. "You remember what the father from the movie *Friday* said? They called him Big Dick Willie." She fell over laughing, holding her stomach and all. "Well, that's that nigga too. Look." Oni pushed her cell phone in Gia's face.

The name on the screen read *Big Dick Willie*. Gia shook her head and pushed the phone away. "I can't take you right now."

"Sometimes I can't take myself, but I can tell you what I can take."

Gia waited for an answer as Oni fingered through her hair.

"That dick!" She screamed and so did Gia.

Both of them were so wrapped up in Oni's silliness that they hadn't heard the patio door open until her Auntie Ann's voice interrupted their banter.

"What y'all out here laughing at?"

"Nothing, Ma." Oni stood up. "I didn't know you were stopping by. I'm about to go brush my hair real quick."

"Well, your company was pulling up at the same time as I was," Gia's Auntie Ann told Oni as she rushed past her.

"Let them in," Oni yelled over her shoulder, already in the house.

Ann walked over to where Gia was sitting and touched the top of her head. "You enjoying yourself, Gianna?"

"Yes, ma'am. I'm good."

"Good. I just got off the phone with your mama. She wanted to check on you."

Gia smiled. "I bet she's been calling you every five minutes, hasn't she?"

"You know she has. That's my big sister and I love her, but her ass be getting on my nerves when it comes to you."

Thinking about her mother and her Auntie Ann's relationship had Gia laughing. Her mother and her aunt were only eighteen months apart, and sometimes one would never know. They argued about everything. It was funny, though. Their bickering was always more of a joke than anything.

Gia thought about her mother and smiled. "You know how she gets."

Ann dropped her hand from her hip and turned to walk back into the house. "And you know how I get. I guess I'll see y'all later since Oni has company."

Gia was still laughing as she watched her aunt disappear into the house. She was still lying back on the beach chair with her sunglasses on when she heard movement behind her. Then male voices. She sat up quickly and looked over her shoulder. There were two tall, brown-skinned men wearing swim trunks and tank tops. One had the popular haircut with his sides shaved low and a miniature fro in the middle. Gia didn't know what they called it in Georgia, but in Hawaii she and her friends called it the thot haircut. The other guy had a low cut with waves.

Both of them were very handsome, but that didn't move Gia, so she waved and turned back around and faced the pool. It was a few seconds before they were back in her line of vision, sitting in the chairs that were next to her.

"What's going on, shawty?" the one with the thot haircut asked her.

"Nothing. How are you?" Gia spoke properly.

"I'm good. What's your name?"

Gia turned to them both and pulled her shades from her face so that they could see her. With her hand extended to shake theirs, she introduced herself. "I'm Gianna, but everyone calls me Gia."

They both shook her hand before the one with the waves allowed his eyes to travel over her body. Gia watched him openly gawk at her.

"You straight?" She needed to make sure he was good because he most definitely didn't have any manners.

He chuckled. "Yeah . . . yeah, I'm good. My fault. You sexy as fuck. Oni told me you were cute and shit, but she ain't say you looked like this."

Gia gave a friendly smile. "Thank you. What's y'all's names?"

Thot haircut spoke first. "I'm Willie, and this my cousin Jarvis."

Ooh, Mr. Willie. No wonder he has that haircut. Gia gave them the once-over before nodding slowly.

"Where Oni?" Willie asked her.

"She ran in the house real quick. She'll be out here in a minute," Gia said. "Y'all ain't got to wait on her to get in the pool. Y'all can go ahead if y'all want to."

They both looked at the pool while Willie stood up and pulled his shirt over his head. "Bet." With no further comment, he walked to the edge of the pool and dove in. He swam around in the deeper end of the pool as Gia and Jarvis stayed where they were.

"Hey, y'all." Oni's voice came from behind them.

When Gia looked over her shoulder and saw that Oni had changed out of her orange swimsuit into a black and gold one, all she could do was shake her head. On top of that her once wild and curly hair was now pulled back into a neat ball. It was still wet, but it was brushed down sleekly so it looked nice.

"Took you long enough," Willie yelled from the pool.

"Whatever. How long y'all been here?" Oni asked.

"Not long. Why you ain't tell me your cousin was this fine?" Jarvis looked from Oni back to Gia. "Dark-skinned women ain't even my thing, but li'l Gia is fine as fuck."

"Nigga, what you mean why I ain't tell you?" Oni snapped back. "I did tell you my cousin was the shit. You just didn't listen."

Jarvis smiled at Gia and winked when she smiled back. "I'm glad I did." He stood up and pulled his shirt off, showing the few tattoos that he had on his chest. "You swimming, Gia?"

"Maybe in a minute, but not right now." Gia looked down at her pink bikini with the white lace around the edges.

Her hair was up in a messy ball on the top of her head with a few locs falling out of it. She had been swimming earlier and was really focused on letting her hair dry, so getting back in was somewhat out of the question.

Jarvis gave her another sly smirk before diving into the pool near where Willie was swimming. Oni quickly occupied the dark green beach chair next to Gia and lay back as well.

"They cute, ain't they?" Oni swept water from her eyes.

Gia nodded. "Big Dick Willie looking thick in them shorts."

Oni's eyes moved to where Willie had just stepped out of the pool and was standing near the diving board. As Gia had noted, the imprint of his dick was massive in the thin white swim shorts.

"Oh got damn." Oni fell limply in her chair, making Gia laugh.

"Get up and stop being stupid, Oni, before they see you."

"He needs to see me. Hell, he needs to come fuck me."

Gia frowned her face up. "You are so barbaric."

Oni shrugged and stood up. "I think I'm about to go hop on that."

"All right now, Auntie Ann double back and see your fast butt, you gon' be looking crazy."

Oni waved her off. "Girl please, she a hoe too."

Gia nearly choked as she laughed. She sat up in her seat and held her mouth and everything. She couldn't do anything but laugh at Oni as she watched her walk up to Willie and say something in his ear. His smile was large but got even bigger when Oni's small hand ran down the front of his shorts and rubbed the bulging meat that she and Gia had been fixated on moments prior.

Gia watched in awe at the boldness that Oni displayed. She'd always known that Oni was more experienced than she was, and was a lot more promiscuous, but she hadn't known it was like that. Well, not touching a man's dick out in the open like that. She had been caught completely off guard by that small gesture.

Ever since she and Oni had been younger, Oni had always been the more advanced one. Always sneaking off with her boyfriends, kissing, and letting boys feel on her, but this was something totally different. They'd stayed up on the phone late at night on many occasions talking about Oni's sexual encounters with boys, so Gia really couldn't understand why she was so shocked.

Even being thousands of miles apart, she and Oni remained close like sisters. It was easy with each of them being an only child. On top of that, their mothers had always made sure to raise them close; from spending summers at the other's house to going on spring and Christmas break trips together.

When Oni had first started telling Gia about her and boys, she had been all ears because it was always a lot more than she was doing. Oni always made sure to tell Gia everything because she didn't trust anyone else with her business like that, and neither did Gia. Between the two of them they had secrets galore.

Even though Gia told her father everything, some things were for Oni's ears only. From her first kiss to the first time she'd had sex with Kainoa, Gia had called Oni for everything she needed to know, and that had been years ago.

"You're wild, Oni." Willie's voice brought Gia back to their present situation.

Gia focused back on them just as Willie picked Oni up and jumped into the pool with her. They went beneath the water immediately and stayed for a minute before popping back up. Oni's hair was still in her ponytail, but there were a few strands sticking to her face now.

"Come get in, Gia." Jarvis's voice sounded closer.

When Gia looked up at him, he was pulling himself from the pool and headed toward her. He held his hand out for her to take when he got close to her.

"I don't feel like getting my hair wet no more," Gia said.

"Man, don't be like that. It's hot as hell. Come get in the water with us."

Gia looked past him at Oni and Willie playing in the water, then back at him. "Okay." She smiled and removed her shades. Gia figured she'd might as well jump in and enjoy herself. After all, she was on vacation, and the men were actually really cute.

When she stood up, Jarvis could barely contain the smile on his face. He rubbed his hands together, and before she could even fix the strings of her bikini, he'd thrown her over his shoulder and was running toward the pool. Knowing what was next, Gia didn't even try to fight it. Instead she held on to his neck and held her breath.

Moments later she was completely submerged beneath the water with Jarvis's arms around her waist. All of the unnecessary touching of her breasts and butt by Jarvis alarmed her temporarily, but she figured maybe that was just something men in the South did. When it began to be too much, Gia pushed him away and swam toward the wall of the pool.

"Damn, you swim like a fish," Jarvis told her after wiping water from his face. "You don't splash water or nothing."

"She's been in Hawaii all of her life, that's all they do over there." Oni was leaning against the wall of the pool, smiling at Gia.

"We sure do," Gia said.

"Oh damn, you from Hawaii?" Willie asked.

Gia shook her head. "No, I'm from here. I've just been living there since I was six."

"Oh okay, that's what's up. So you just here for the summer?" Willie leaned back so that his head rested against Oni's chest.

"Yep, until it's time for me to go back to school."

"Well, you should let me take you out while you're here." Jarvis swam closer to her.

"I'll think about it." Gia smiled at him and ducked beneath the water, swimming away.

For the rest of the day, they all sat outside swimming, laughing, and playing. For the first time since she'd been there, Gia had actually enjoyed herself. Being that the water was also her home away from home, the outdoor activity had been much needed. She'd even felt a little sad when the men left, but that feeling quickly went away once her Auntie Ann came back to Oni's house and bought them take-out plates of barbecue from a local spot called Chester's. It was so good and so different from what Gia had been eating since being in Hawaii. Maybe she really had been being a little too uptight, and it was time to really loosen up.

Chapter Three

"I've always had a thing for men. Young or old, it didn't matter to me. A man was a man; however, meeting Isaac changed all of that for me." —Oni

The lights were out and candles were already burning when Oni stepped through the front door and into the living room of Isaac's home. Immaculately decorated in an array of tan and dark green colors, it was spacious and always so clean whenever she came over.

The atmosphere was more relaxed and welcoming the farther she went in. Like always, Isaac had instructed her to use her key and to come right in once she got there. That was one thing she loved about him. From the moment she'd met him, he had always been so open and free with her.

Anytime she came over or they went somewhere, he did whatever he could to ensure her comfort. Initially she'd assumed it was because she was so much younger than him and he was trying to impress her, but the more time they spent together, the more familiar with his personality she became.

Isaac was a very open person. He never hid his phone, he never interrogated her about the younger men she entertained, nor did he make her do things that she wasn't comfortable with. But even though he was very fine and in awesome shape for his age, their age difference was still very noticeable. Had she not been almost positive that her father would kill him the moment he walked into their house, she would have made him her main thing a long time ago. Even with her being as grown as she was, her father still liked to interrogate the men she dated.

Oni kicked her shoes off and left them near the door before proceeding down the hall. When she reached the dining room she noticed the table was covered with various delectable-looking dishes.

Her mouth watered at the sight. She'd eaten dinner a few hours prior, and judging by the way her stomach was growling, one would think she was on the verge of starvation. With a quick movement of her hand to her abdomen, she tried to silence the noises before seeing Isaac.

The various smells wafted up her nose as she felt the coolness from the wooden floors beneath her feet soothe her every step. The warm, inviting feeling coming from the kitchen had her rounding the corner with urgency.

"I was wondering how long it was going to take you to get in here." Isaac's deep voice serenaded her ears.

Shirtless and sexy, he stood at the stove stirring something in a silver pot. His back was to her, but he was leaning to the side so she had a clear view of his stove. The large muscles poking from everywhere her eyes landed made Oni smile.

He was so ripped and toned to be so old. How could a man old enough to be her father have a body better than some of the men her age? The dark gray sweatpants hung loosely from his hips, displaying the deep cut lines that led to the old-man dick that he gave her on the regular.

The way his curly black hair lay down around his head and ears always made her imagine what their babies might look like if they were to ever have some together. His hair was so silky and smooth she used to think that he was mixed with something, but every time she asked, he assured her he was 100 percent black.

"I was coming." Oni walked to him and wrapped her arms around his waist.

He turned to the side and kissed the top of her head. "I couldn't wait."

Oni's heart fluttered as she smiled like the young bashful tenderoni that she was. When she felt his head turn again, she looked up to find him looking at her.

"I hope you're hungry. I made us some dinner."

"I know. I saw it, and I am." Oni released his waist and leaned on the counter opposite him. "What's the occasion?" she teased.

Isaac looked from the pan of white sauce he had been stirring and landed his gaze on her. His eyebrows were slightly frowned as his head cocked to the side.

"You forgot?"

"Forgot what, sexy?"

Oni knew today was their unofficial anniversary. They had been together for an entire year, and tonight they were supposed to celebrate it. She'd been excited about it all day and couldn't wait to show him the little red outfit she'd gotten from Victoria's Secret earlier.

Isaac was a man who liked to role-play, so she made sure to indulge whenever possible. At the moment, she was acting as if she had forgotten their anniversary because she already knew that it would anger him. Which was always a good thing when it came to their sex life.

He would ravish her unlike any other man had before. The forcefulness and control in which he delivered whenever he was angry made her wetter than the Pacific Ocean.

"Oni, tell me you're kidding."

Her eyes darted to the side momentarily as she bit on her bottom lip. "But I'm not. That's why it took me so long to come in here. I was staring at all of the food trying to figure out what it was for."

The vein in the side of Isaac's neck jumped a few times as he looked away from her and continued stirring the food. Oni could see the anger brewing, so she continued. Even though she was starving for some food at the moment, she was starving for him even more.

After playing around with Willie earlier in the pool, she had been on the edge. She'd already known that letting Willie finger her would start something inside her that only Isaac could finish. Now that the time was here and she was in front of him, she didn't think she could wait any longer.

"Just tell me, sexy, and I promise I'll do better next time."

"No. It's fine. Let's just eat." Isaac flipped the burner off and carried the saucepot into the dining room.

Oni felt like a starving dog as she watched him lean over the plates and pour the sauce onto their food. His body was perfect, and she, well, plainly putting it, she was a horny young hoe who was feigning for some grown-man loving.

The way he walked was an orgasm by itself. Then to sit and listen to him talk made her want to crawl around on all fours and allow him to order her around all day and night. She stood against the counter crossing and uncrossing her legs, trying her hardest to contain the beast, but it was about to burst out.

Oni chuckled to herself as she thought about how he never had any idea of her little games. He was much older and probably a lot more mature than she was, but she played him every time. Sure he was into the role playing, but only when he was in charge.

Clearly, that wasn't the case at the moment, and it was showing all through the quick rough breaths he was releasing, along with the tightness in his shoulders and uncomfortably tense posture. He was riled up and had no idea that it was all due to some hot sex that was soon to come.

"The food is ready." He spoke without even turning around to face her.

Oni, being who she was, walked right up to him, wrapped her arms around his waist, again and laid her head against his back.

When he didn't move to touch her or make her stop, she slid both hands down the front of his pants and rubbed her fingers through the silky hair along his shaft.

Having done this so many times before, she was familiar with what made him moan, so she did it again. With just the tips of her fingers of one hand, she rubbed the tip of his dick until she could feel the early secretion of his warm fluids while grabbing a handful of his balls with the other hand.

Just like he did every time, he released a deep groan and his head fell back. Oni continued her loving assault on his hardening tool as he rested the back of his head against hers. His breathing got a little throatier as she massaged him faster.

"Just tell me what I did, so I can do better." She pressed her lips onto his back. "I can do better. I know I can," she whispered again as she wrapped his entire dick in her hand.

"You like to be a bad girl, don't you?"

"Always."

Isaac didn't say anything else before setting the pot down and spinning around to grab her waist. His full pink lips were on hers immediately as his strong hands ran up the sides of her body. He kissed her hard just like she liked it. He moaned into her mouth before pulling away and breaking their kiss.

With one hand he pushed her away from him, pushing his sweatpants down with the other one. His dick sprang out with a vengeance, nearly poking her in the stomach. Oni's mouth watered immediately. Isaac's dick wasn't the biggest she'd ever had, but he knew how to work it, and that was all she desired.

"Get on your fucking knees." His eyes were low as he spoke to her in an irritated tone.

Happily, Oni dropped to her knees before him and waited for him to tell her what to do next. He was leaning against the table in front of her when he grabbed the back of her head and snatched her body roughly to him. Oni stumbled a little, losing her balance before steadying herself on her knees again.

"Suck my dick, and you better do that shit right." With no other words to her, Isaac pulled her head the rest of the way, forcing her mouth onto him.

As soon as she felt the weight of his dick on her tongue, Oni's eyes closed. She was licking and sucking on him like he'd taught her to when his eyes began to drift close. Oni sat on her knees looking up at the ripped abs and sexily distorted face as she did her best to please him. That wasn't hard because he'd already taught her everything that he liked.

Oni had caught a smooth rhythm that was working for her when all of a sudden he slammed his pelvic bone into her face, nearly shoving his dick down her throat. She immediately began to gag as water gathered in her eyes. She pushed at his thighs, but that didn't help because he pushed his hips right back toward her.

"Don't gag. Take it," he ordered from above her.

Even though she could barely breathe and tears were now falling down her face, she nodded anyway. The roughness he was exhibiting was something new and something that she was most definitely not expecting, but for him she'd do it. Ironic as it sounded, she never wanted to seem like she was a child when it was time for sex. She could and would do everything a woman his age would do.

"Yeah." He grunted. "That's what I like."

Oni nodded again as she tried to catch her breath.

"You gagging?" he asked like he couldn't see her on the floor nearly killing herself just to suck him off.

When she didn't say anything, he chuckled and pulled himself from her mouth. Oni wiped her mouth and eyes quickly before resting back on her knees. She watched quietly as Isaac held the base of his dick in his hand and reached for her with the other. Oni willingly rose to her feet.

He pulled her with him as he walked to the chair at the head of the table. It was the only free spot. No plates or food was there, so she wasn't surprised when he picked her up and sat her on the edge of it. Unsure of what was next, Oni sat patiently watching him.

When he took his seat in front of her and pushed the skirt that she was wearing up so that it was around her waist, she opened her legs. She smiled at him when he kissed the front of her legs before licking his lips.

"You're such a bad little girl." He winked at her before diving face first between her thighs.

Like every other time she came to see him, Oni wasn't wearing panties. The way he was eating her made her very happy that she wasn't. She would have hated to have anything stopping him from doing to her body what he was doing right then.

"Let me hear you moan, Oni." He grunted and bit the inside of her thigh.

A quick pained yelp came from her mouth as she grabbed the back of his head and pushed him back to where she needed him to be. Like the skilled man that he was, Isaac ate her like he was on death row and she was his last meal.

The moans coming from both of them could probably be the soundtrack for some sort of porno, they were so loud and sexy. Oni's eyes rolled and rolled as she rode the orgasm that was ripping through her body. She was holding on to the back of his head trying to maintain as much control as she could, which didn't last long.

Before she could even think of what was to happen next, he was pulling her to the edge of the table and entering her body. The moment he was all the way inside her, Oni closed her eyes and moaned. Being with Isaac was seriously the best feeling she'd ever had.

The way he worked her body and talked to her in the process always made her feel so wanted, so desired, and so loved. Even though she made jokes with Gia about him and his money being the reason she kept coming back, it was all a lie.

His passion for her was it. She'd given her body to a few men in the past, and none of them made her feel like they needed it. Only Isaac. Anytime he was near her he made her feel so wanted, and that feeling was too addicting to leave.

"I love you, li'l mama." Isaac grunted into her ear as he slammed into her continuously.

"I love you too, Isaac."

He leaned down to lick her stomach before standing back up and looking into her eyes. "You feel this?"

Oni nodded.

"It's right. You and me. I need it."

Oni nodded again because she agreed with him wholeheartedly. She needed him too. "I need you more."

The fire in his eyes made Oni's entire body hot as she began to tremble with satisfaction again. Soon after, he was doing the same thing and collapsed on top of her. Being that she was on birth control, there was no real rush for him to pull out, so she wrapped her arms and legs around him instead.

His breathing was still a little ragged as he lay on top of her. "Can you stay with me tonight?"

Oni closed her eyes because she hated when he would ask her that. He knew she worked like a madwoman and needed her rest, so staying out all night was something she did only rarely. She went for it sometimes, but with Gia in town, it would be a bit much for her to be spending the night off.

"I want to but I can't."

He raised up from her body and sat back in the chair. He stuffed his flaccid penis back into his pants and looked at her with pleading eyes. "Why not?"

Oni sat up and pulled her skirt down, trying to fix herself the best she could. "You remember when I told you my cousin was coming into town to visit me? Well, she's here. Got here the other day, and it would be pretty rude of me to leave her at my house alone while I go visit someone else."

Isaac was quiet as he nodded his understanding. "You could have brought her with you." He smiled, and so did she.

Oni shook her head. "Nah, I don't think that'll be a good idea."

"Why not? She doesn't know about me?"

"No, she knows. Gia just isn't your average girl. She's a little stuck up, so I don't really know how well that might go." Oni giggled as she thought about how many jokes Gia would have about Isaac if she was to spend the night with them.

"Just ask her for me and see." He rubbed his hands up and down her thighs.

"I'll see about it." Oni looked behind her at the table. "Can we get cleaned up and eat right now, though?"

Isaac's beautiful smile crossed his face as he nodded and picked her up from the table. Oni wrapped her legs around him as he carried her down the hall to the bathroom so they could clean themselves up. Dinner came right afterward. When it was time to go, Oni hated it.

"I hate leaving you." She rubbed his hand as he walked her to her truck.

"Don't. I tell you all the time I can take care of you over here. You ain't never got to go home if you don't want to."

"I wish." She stood on her tiptoes and kissed his lips. "I love you so much."

He pecked her forehead. "I know you do. I love you too. Drive careful and let me know when you get home."

"You have to work this weekend?"

"Yeah. I have a few out-of-town loads."

Oni nodded before getting into her car. Isaac was a truck driver, so he spent a lot of time on the road, which was why their time together was so special to her. He waited until she cranked up and pulled away before going back into his house. Oni thought about Isaac the entire drive home. Maybe one day she would get bold enough to let it all go and just be with Isaac, but sadly she didn't know when that would be.

Chapter Four

"I knew Gee was different from the first time I saw her, but it wasn't until I willingly risked my life for her that I knew just how different she really was. I think about that day a lot, and there was nothing I would have done differently. I would gladly give my life for Gee. Then and now. No questions asked."
—Milli

"Zazazzzzaah." The annoying sound of his mother's incoherent mumbling caught Jamil's attention as soon as he walked in the house.

She was slouched over on the sofa with her head lying back against the cushion. Her eyes were halfway open and her arm was facing up with a needle hanging out of it. There was one cream-colored stocking tied around her arm just above where the needle was and one still on her leg.

"Zzzzzzaazaah."

Jamil turned his nose up as he watched her ride the high she'd just given herself. From the look of what she had on, she'd apparently just come from work or something, because her clothes were somewhat decent and her high heels lay beneath the coffee table.

How could an insurance rep be a crackhead? Ask Zanetta, because she made that shit look easy. For a moment it angered Jamil to see that his parents were still finding drugs from somewhere, but he let it go. They were grown and could do what they wanted.

"Jamilllllll, is that you?" His father's doped up voice came from the end of the hallway.

"Yeah," Jamil answered.

"Where your mama?"

"In here." He heard his father clearing his throat.

"She got the rest of my medicine in there?"

Medicine?

Jamil looked around where his mother was sitting, trying to see if he could see the rest of the drugs that she'd just been shooting up. When he spotted the empty bag on the floor near her foot, he sucked his teeth. He already knew what was to come when he told his father that it was all gone.

"Nah, O, she took it all."

A few cuss words could be heard before his father did exactly what he knew he would.

"I know you got something for your old man, don't you?"

Jamil hated that whenever they ran out of drugs they would try and use the fact that they were his parents to score some off him, even when they knew it wasn't happening. It was funny that they forgot that one little detail when they were sober, but the moment they were out of drugs and money, they all of a sudden wanted to be Mama and Daddy. That shit was so dead.

"I ain't got it."

Jamil heard shuffling and something fall over before his father came staggering up the hallway. He had one hand on the buckle of his belt and the other sliding against the wall holding him up.

"Come on, Milli Rock, let your daddy hold something."

Milli Rock?

Yeah, that nigga was definitely on one. Just like stating that he was his father, calling him his street name was another way to try and scam drugs off him.

"I said I ain't got nothing."

Owen stopped in front of Jamil and stood to his full height. Owen was tall as hell and the reason why Jamil was four inches from being seven feet tall. Not the least bit intimidated by anything that might have had Owen feeling bad enough to confront him, Jamil stuck his hands in the pockets of his shorts and waited for what was next.

"So you gon' treat me like that? Like I ain't shit, huh?"

As badly as Jamil wanted to tell him that he wasn't shit and he hated the day he'd been shot out of his ball sac, he didn't. He could have, and probably was going to wish he had later, but for now he was in no real mood for theatrics. It was hot outside, and he'd had a long night and day. All he wanted to do was shower and fall into his bed.

"You all big and grown now, so you feel like you're better than me, huh?" Owen hit his chest dramatically. Looking just like the crackhead he was. "Mama and Daddy, the neighborhood crack addicts. Well, you know what?" Owen stepped closer, into Jamil's face, and leaned down so that they were eye to eye. "You ain't shit either. You ain't no better than me and her. You sell it and we smoke it. Because of punk-ass niggas like you, we have a way to continue to get what the fuck we want."

Owen's breath was atrocious, and it literally felt like it was burning the hair in Jamil's nose. The putrid smell and the degrading things that were coming out of it only made Jamil angry. So angry that he had to take a step back to keep from beating Owen's old ass. There had been many times in the past where he wanted to crack him across his old-ass head with a brick or something, but he'd respected the fact that they were his parents and let the shit slide. But today?

Today was not his fucking day. So instead of breaking him off with an ass-whupping that would have him aching for days, Jamil simply held his hands up in surrender.

"You got it, Owen. I'm out."

Owen pointed toward the door. "That's right! Take your ass on, and don't come back unless you have my shit."

The vulgar language and idle threats came and went as Jamil exited the apartment. It was a little after seven, which was normally right around the time he lay down for a nap before his long night of trapping. Jamil took a few deep breaths as he walked toward the store. It was getting harder and harder to live with his parents, but he wasn't quite ready to dip out on his own yet.

It wasn't like he didn't have the funds, because he did. He was actually pretty well-off when it came to money, he just wasn't really into living alone like that yet, or handling too many responsibilities with bills and such. Living with his parents was easy. Hand them the money and keep it moving. They may have been crackheads, but they knew how to handle their business. As long as Jamil had the money there, Zanetta paid the bills faithfully every month.

He was almost positive that living alone would probably be better than living in that small-ass apartment with the dope fiends, but he'd cross that bridge when he got to it. For now he would deal with their bullshit because, plainly putting it, he wasn't ready.

Once he was across the street, Jamil went into the gas station, got his chips and a pack of gum, and left. Being that he had no real place to go and the fair was in town, he decided to walk across the street and go. It wasn't like he had much else to do. Eating and walking around would give him and his parents the break they needed from each other.

Before going across the street he called Iverson to see where he was. Maybe he could slide through.

"Milli Rock, my nigga. What up?" Iverson's voice came through his line.

"Ain't shit. About to head to this fair. You trying to slide?"

Iverson yelled to somebody in his background. "Nah, I'm on the eastside right now. I ain't gon' be back down that way until later. Taking care of some business."

"A'ight. Bet. Just hit me when you get back this way."

"Bet."

Jamil hung up his phone, stuck it back into his pocket, and headed toward the crowd over at the fair. He wasn't pressed that

Iverson couldn't come. That nigga was always somewhere doing something. He was about his paper, and he made it his business to get it by any means necessary.

Since the sun had just gone down, the fair was packed. Girls with their babies, niggas with their girlfriends, and a buttload of young-ass children were walking around thinking they were grown.

Different color weave and loud talking floated throughout the parking lot as Jamil walked through it. The smells of cotton candy, vinegar fries, and funnel cakes filled his nose as the carousel and other kiddie rides played what sounded much like circus tunes. It was a warm summer evening with just enough of a breeze to keep the sweat from arising.

Jamil looked around at everybody, nodding and dapping people up along the way. Casually dressed in a pair of orange gym shorts and a black and orange shirt, with his all-black Jordan 12s, Jamil took a seat on the bench and stretched his arms and legs out. His hair was all down but tied back with two of his locs.

He hadn't thought to put on much of anything since he'd just been running to the barbershop to get an edge up earlier, but he was glad he at least looked decent. He hated to be out in the streets looking like he ain't have shit. He wasn't big on labels, but he had way too much money to be looking like a bum.

The women walking past making sure that he saw them was starting to get annoying. He was doing his best to ignore the blatant stares and even the loud talking, but these young hoes ain't have no chill. They were doing everything but taking their panties off and putting their pussies in his face.

Jamil chuckled to himself as the girl who had just been trying to get his attention tripped over one of the large wires in the middle of the walkway.

"So you do know how to smile?" a female voice said from beside him.

Jamil looked over, and just that fast his smile was gone. It was the brown-skinned girl from the gas station yesterday. She was a very pretty girl and even kept herself tight, but he wasn't into casual shit. That wasn't him. Plus she was a little too bold for his liking. He liked a woman who chilled, one who knew how to keep a low profile like him.

"You are so rude. You know that? You really should work on that shit."

Her attitude was so strong and annoying. First of all she was in his space, then she had the nerve to be telling him what he needed to do? Hell nah.

"I'm not rude, I just don't know you."

"And you never will with an attitude like that."

"Didn't say I wanted to."

Jamil rose to his feet, prepared to walk away until he thought about the sexy chocolate girl she'd had with her earlier. For a quick second he thought about asking where she was but changed his mind. Ask her for what? It wasn't like he was going to fuck with her for real anyway, so he walked away.

It had been a little over an hour that he'd been there, and the sun had gone completely down. It was dark outside, and illumination in the parking lot was the large streetlights and all of the lights from the rides and stands. It was definitely time for him to go home.

One thing he'd learned about the fair was that trouble could break out at any given moment, and he wanted no part of that. Even though he had his strap and would handle anything that popped off, he still wasn't up for no shit like that. Getting hurt in another nigga's fight had never been his style, so versus continuing around the rest of the fair, he made a left and headed for the exit.

Just as he was getting close, he noticed the police running toward him. For a minute he stood still until he realized they weren't running to him, but behind him. When Jamil turned around he noticed a large circle of commotion. There must have been a fight, and if there was one thing he would never do again in his life, it was run to a fight.

His stride became a little more eager as he headed out. He looked over his shoulder once more when he heard yelling. The moment he was about to turn around and see what it was, he heard gunshots. It was like déjà vu. People were running and screaming, knocking each other over, pulling each other down. It was all bad, and all he could do was watch.

It was pandemonium, and he was frozen in one spot. For some reason he couldn't make himself move. It was like he was living the day that had changed his life forever all over again. With his heart going into overdrive, his hands began to shake as his knees threatened to buckle. For a moment, one moment only, he felt helpless.

He probably would have still been standing there and never snapped out of it had he not noticed a familiar face crouched next to a metal trash can near the funnel cake stand with her hands over her head.

Gia.

Jamil watched her look from side to side as the commotion moved around her. How had she gotten caught directly in the middle of the fighting parties?

Shots were fired off again while people did their best to run to safety. From that second to the next he was running across the parking lot, not caring who he was bumping into or the fact that he was running into the firing zone. All he cared about was not allowing history to repeat itself. He wouldn't allow another beautiful life to be taken in his presence. Jamil sprinted as fast as he could, ducking and barely dodging the uproar of people in front of him.

He squatted down next to her as soon as he was on the other side of the trashcan. He held his hand out to her and she looked up into his eyes. Jamil swore on everything he loved that in that moment his night had become lighter.

The bright round eyes filled with fear locked with his, and it was like he could hear some soft-ass love song playing in the back of his mind. He knew there wasn't really a song playing, but she made him feel like there might have been.

She looked extremely scared as she placed her hand in his. Jamil pulled her from the ground and close to his body as he snatched his gun from the holster resting at the bottom of his back. Her eyes widened when they fell on the large piece of black steel.

"Just keep your head down, okay?"

Gia nodded. "I don't know where my cousin is," she yelled frantically.

Jamil didn't even bother to acknowledge that because there was nothing he could or would do about that at the moment. With his gun in his hand ready to shoot anything that looked sus-pect, Jamil pulled her from the lights toward the parking lot. Sur-prisingly, she was keeping up with him. She had a death grip on his hand, but he had one right back.

Scared to look away from her for too long, Jamil looked over his shoulder every so often, making sure she was still with him. Every time she was staring right back at him, her eyes laced with an intensified amount of fear.

"Aye, ain't that that nigga Milli Rock?" Jamil heard some-body say.

He looked to his left quickly to see two young niggas with guns and blue bandannas tied around the bottom half of their faces pointing at him. He didn't know who they were or why they would be singling him out at the moment, but he was ready for whatever. Jamil quickly pushed Gia behind him and pointed his gun toward the boys. In return they held theirs up and began walking toward him.

"Gia, run to the gas station. I'ma come get you in a minute."

He could feel her shaking behind him, but he heard her say okay before taking off like lightning. She shot off fast and made her way across the grass. He wished he had time to admire her run, but he didn't. He had begun firing shots at both of the boys the moment she took her first step.

Jamil didn't want one of them to shoot her because of him, so he made sure to give her a smoke screen. Much to his surprise, after he let off his first free shot into the air, the boys took off running in the other direction. Clearly they'd thought he was going to be an easy target, but that would never happen.

Jamil quickly put his gun down and meshed himself in with the throng of people running past him. Being that there was so much going on, he wasn't worried about the police seeing him. With the new surge of adrenaline pumping through him, Jamil took off across the street toward the gas station.

When he got there it was already packed with people, all trying to escape the gunplay that had just erupted. Jamil searched the crowd for his li'l chocolate baby. So many people were calling his name or pulling on his arms that it took him forever to make it through the crowd, but once he had, he still didn't see her.

After not finding her in the parking lot, he ran toward the entrance of the gas station. He caught hell trying to get inside, but once he did, he located her instantly. She was standing near the back by the coolers that held the beer. She was standing alone with her arms folded over her chest. When she saw him, it was as if they'd known each other forever, the way she ran to him.

He opened his arms and allowed her to slam into his chest as soon as she was close enough to him. She held him around his waist as he draped one arm around the top of her shoulders.

"Come on." Jamil was pulling her from the store, but she too was pulling, only in the opposite direction.

"My cousin is meeting me here. I talked to her."

"Bet." Jamil released her and got ready to walk away. "Stay in here, and when she gets here, y'all go home."

Alarm spread across her face. "Don't leave me," she yelped,

and then covered her mouth. "Please." Her voice was a little lower with that part of the request.

Jamil liked the need that she held in her voice for him, but he wasn't about to stay in that gas station when he'd just had some niggas trying to run up on him. He wasn't really feeling leaving her there either, but if she wanted to stay, he wasn't going to make her go.

"I don't want to leave you, but I'm not staying in here."

"Why?"

"Niggas gunning for me. I have to dip."

Gia's eyes watered as she looked down at the floor and let his hand drop from hers. She nodded and took a few steps back. Jamil watched her and momentarily debated whether or not he wanted to stay, but the more he thought about it, the more he knew he had to go. He couldn't risk his life for a girl he didn't even know.

Jamil looked at her long and hard before walking to the door. His hand was on the handle when he heard her talking.

"Hurry up. I'm scared."

Even though he knew she had to be talking to her cousin, he couldn't leave her like that, scared and alone. He remembered hearing her say something about going home the day before, so clearly she wasn't from there. Jamil battled with himself until he was turning around and reaching for her hand again. Reluctantly, she took it and allowed him to usher her toward the door.

"I'm not gon' let nothing happen to you, okay?"

She nodded.

"You ain't got to be scared. Tell your cousin you with me and she can come get you from my spot."

Gia looked skeptical as she held her phone to her ear. She relayed his message before asking where his *spot* was.

"Across the street. The first building facing the library. Apartment C."

Gia told her cousin what he'd just said as they pushed their way through the crowd and across the street to BTW. He held her hand, pulling her behind him. Along the way he thought about Lauren and pulled Gia up to where he was at. He tucked her securely beneath his arm and walked with her close to his body.

He felt better with her being close to him. Her constant shivering and shaking was slowly simmering away, so apparently being close to him relaxed her as well. Jamil felt safer once he was back in his hood, but he was still watching his back. When they finally got to his doorstep, he pulled his key out and sent up a quick prayer asking God to let his parents be asleep or at least in their room.

He didn't really want to take Gia inside, but the block was still too hot to be out, so he had no other choice. There was no noise or weird mumbling when he pushed the door open so that was a good sign. With Gia still tucked close to him, he pushed the door closed behind him and locked it.

No words were spoken as he led her down the hall to his room. Not that he could have said anything anyway, he was so busy holding his breath hoping neither Owen nor Zanetta would show their face. Once his door swung closed, he locked it and released Gia from his grasp. He flicked the light on, and she walked over to his bed and took a seat.

Like always, his room was clean. He didn't have much in there, but it was decent. Black bedroom set with matching dressers he'd purchased for himself last Christmas, a black and gray comforter, and a black bean bag chair and a dirty clothes hamper in the corner. No pictures, no posters, nothing personal, and most definitely nothing of value. He didn't trust his parents.

"You straight?" he asked Gia as she sat with her hands in her lap.

He leaned against the wall and watched her nod. Her locs were hanging down and around her shoulders, the red and purple parts grazing against her soft, dark skin.

Entertaining himself more with her beauty, his eyes roamed

down over her perfectly round breasts tucked away in the plain white shirt. The thick but sexily toned thighs spread across his bed as she sat with her hands tucked between them.

The loose strings from the ripped blue jean shorts she was wearing lay across her legs, teasing him.

"Where your cousin was at?" Jamil asked, breaking the silence.

"She said she was walking to her truck and she was coming."

"Cool." Jamil walked to his closet and kicked his shoes off before pulling his gun from his back and sticking it in the shoe box at the top of his closet.

"Did you shoot them?" She cleared her throat. "The boys from the fair?"

"Nah."

Jamil could tell she was uncomfortable. She was sitting on the edge of the bed and hadn't moved an inch since they'd come in.

"You fast as hell, you know that?"

A small smile tugged at her lips, letting him know that running was an open subject. "Yeah, I know. The second fastest in the nation, actually."

"You for real or you playing?"

Gia finally looked up at him. She was wearing the prettiest smile he'd ever had the privilege of seeing.

"I'm serious."

"I don't know if I believe you." Jamil pretended not to believe her so that she would keep talking.

Gia quickly pulled her phone from her pocket. She tapped it a few times before typing something.

"Come here real quick. Let me show you something."

Jamil walked over to her and sat down. He leaned over her shoulder and looked at the writing on the screen that she'd pulled up with her picture on it. Whatever it was, it was long as hell and the writing was too small. He couldn't really make sense of it, but he wouldn't tell her that.

"What's this?" he asked.

"It's an article *Sports Illustrated* did on me and the number one runner in the nation," she stated proudly.

"Damn. That's what's up. For real. That's some dope shit."

Gia nudged him with her shoulder. "Shut up."

"For real. That's dope, li'l baby."

Gia blushed and held her head down. Her locs fell over the side of her face so that he could no longer see her.

"I like your hair. That shit dope too."

"Thank you. I like yours too. I've never seen orange dreads before."

Jamil turned his nose up. "Orange?"

Gia nodded, still wearing her smile.

"It ain't orange like that. It's kind of burnt orange, almost brown." Jamil picked up one of his locs and looked at it.

"Whatever it is, I've never seen it before. What's your name?" Gia asked with an eagerness like she'd been waiting to ask.

"Jamil, but the streets call me Milli Rock."

"Like the dance?" Gia giggled.

"Man, you wild." He pushed some of her hair out of her face. "Kind of. It's short for Jamil Rock, but you know black people like you have to assume it's because of the dance."

"What you mean black people like me? Don't be trying to be funny because I'm dark with your extra-light-skinned ass."

Her tone was accusing, and he hated the fact that she'd taken his comment the wrong way. "I wasn't saying that because of your color, because I think that shit is sexy as fuck. I love dark-skinned women. I was saying black people as in African Americans as a whole. Chill."

Gia looked away as her phone began ringing. Instead of saying anything, she answered her phone. She said a few things before hanging up.

"My cousin is outside."

Jamil stood and walked toward the door with her behind him.

He opened the door and looked down the hallway before telling her to come on. The coast appeared to be clear as they made their way to the front door. His hand was on the doorknob when he heard Zanetta call his name. It sounded like she was in the kitchen, so he hurried to push Gia out of the door.

Once they were outside on the porch, he saw the little black truck that Gia and her cousin had been in the day before. Talkative brown skin was sitting in the front seat, hanging out the window. When she saw them walking toward her, she smiled.

"Look at this shit here."

Jamil was about to frown but stopped himself and just nodded.

"Thank you for helping her," Oni said.

"It was nothing." Jamil walked Gia to her door and opened it.

Before getting in she turned and wrapped her arms around his waist. "Thank you."

"No problem. Just get home safe."

"You want me to text you when I get there?" Gia's voice sounded a little unsure.

"Nah. Call me."

Jamil handed her his phone so that she could put her number in. When she handed it to him, he called her so that she could save his number. Once they finished exchanging numbers, he pulled her back before she got into the car.

"What you save your name as?"

"Gia."

Jamil squinted his eyes at her playfully. "Spell it."

Gia giggled at his silliness. "G . . . I . . . A."

Jamil smiled before shoving his phone toward her. "Show me."

Gia was still giggling as she scrolled through his phone and went to her name. "See, it's right there."

Jamil looked at it for a good minute before pulling her in for another hug and letting her get into the car. He closed the door behind her and waited to go into the house until they pulled off.

Zanetta was still in the kitchen, but he bypassed her and headed straight for his room. He grabbed him some boxers and a pair of pajama bottoms and went to the bathroom.

He flipped the water on, stripped down, and hopped in. He allowed the water to run down over him as he thought about Gia. She was so pretty and meek, not to mention how good she smelled. Her perfume had him wanting to push her back on his bed and lick every inch of her skin. Sexy as she was, she probably tasted like chocolate too.

He showered and got out quickly. He threw his pants on before returning to his room. He looked at the clock and made up his mind that he wasn't hitting the block. He was too tired. He'd handle that shit tomorrow. Before getting into his bed to finally get some rest, he made sure his money was still in the safe beneath his bed.

Finally comfortable, Jamil closed his eyes. He was damn near dreaming when he heard his phone ringing. At first he thought about letting it ring, thinking it might be a quick play, until he remembered he'd told Gia to call him. He snatched his phone from beside him on the bed and answered it.

"Yeah."

"You know it's not polite to answer the phone like that." Her soft voice relaxed him even more.

"Well, I'm a rude-ass nigga."

"You shouldn't be."

Jamil scooted lower in the bed and closed his eyes, picturing her face as she spoke. "That's just who I am."

"I'll change you."

"I doubt it."

"Why?"

"Ain't nobody did it yet."

Her soft titter made Jamil smile subconsciously. "I'm different."

Her statement was simple but held a lot of meaning. Even before she'd told him that, he'd already known. From the moment he'd seen her in the gas station, he could tell she wasn't like what he was used to.

To be honest, she didn't look like she was much like any girl. Gia was in a league of her own. There was something different and unique that set her apart from everyone else. He wasn't sure what it was yet. He didn't know whether he was going to keep her around long enough to find out, but for now she was good. He would take it one day at a time. After all, it had really only been one day anyway.

"You ain't fell asleep on me, have you?" She brought him back to her.

"Nah, I was just thinking about how different you really are."

"I'll show you soon. Get some rest, light skin. I'll talk to you later."

Jamil opened his eyes when he realized their conversation was about to be over. "Where you at?"

"In the bed at my cousin's house."

"She in there with you?"

"No. I'm in the guest room."

Jamil didn't know where his next statement came from, but it was the first thing that had popped into his head. "Well, don't hang up. Stay on the phone with me and go to sleep."

"'Kay. We can do that, but put your phone on speaker. It's not safe to go to sleep with your phone on your face."

"Different, huh?"

Her soft giggle serenaded him again. "Very. Good night, Milli."

Jamil liked the way she called him Milli without the Rock on the end. It sounded nicer, more endearing. It was hers. Dope shit he could rock with.

"Good night, Gee. Sweet dreams, beautiful."

Chapter Five

"How in the hell did I ever feel unsafe with Milli? I still have the hardest time trying to figure that out. He was then, and always has been the one person that's given me this inexplicable feeling of contentment. Giving me every reason to have butterflies, and have my heart beating faster than normal, but not because of fear. But Love . . . damn . . . I love me some Milli Rock." —Gee

Gia tossed and turned until she woke up. Lying still on her back, she looked up at the ceiling and yawned. She'd gotten some much-needed rest and was ready to start her day, but she had one thing she needed to do first. Gia moved the pillows and cover until she located her phone. When she picked it up, she noticed the call was still running with Jamil.

"Good morning, Jamil." She wasn't sure whether he was still sleeping or had awakened already.

"Morning, Gee. How'd you sleep?" His voice sounded lazy, but he most definitely sounded wide awake.

"Dang, you're up? I just knew you were about to still be sleep."

"To be honest, Gee, I don't sleep much at night."

Gia pulled her locs stocking from her head and tossed it on the dresser with a smile on her face. She was in love with the way he'd given her his very own nickname. *Gee.* She liked the sound of that, and it sounded even better coming from him.

"Well, when do you rest?"

"During the day, mostly."

"That's not good."

Jamil yawned. "I know, but what you getting into today?"

Sitting up on the side of the bed, Gia looked at herself in the mirror. "I don't know. Probably nothing too major, but then again I haven't talked to Oni yet. She always has something planned."

"That's your cousin, right?"

"Yep."

"Well, once you talk to her, if you find out you have some free time today you should let me come pick you up for a while."

Gia smiled at the thought of spending more time with Jamil. "How about we just do that anyway? I'm about to go for a run. I'm positive I'll be hungry afterward." Gia waited for him to respond. "I love Waffle House, by the way."

When she heard groggy chuckles coming from Jamil, she could already tell she was about to get her way.

"What time should I come?"

"Give me two hours. I need to run, shower, and change."

"FaceTime me when you get in the shower."

Gia's mouth fell open as she tried to muffle her laugh. "I'll think about it."

"Nah, I'm fucking with you. Just go do your thing and hit me up when you're ready."

Gia told him she would, and they ended their call. The first thing she did after setting her phone down was sprint to her cousin's room, which was right across the hall. Oni's hot pink and black room was still dark when Gia entered, so she flipped the light on.

"Get up, Oni."

Oni pulled the covers over her head and didn't move. "Get out, Gia."

"Let's go running."

"Hell no." Oni was so grumpy in the morning it was ridiculous.

It didn't matter what time she went to bed or how much rest she'd gotten, she was still grumpy and the worst person to ever come in contact with early in the morning.

"Well, what are we about to do today, then, because I have plans."

Oni lay still for a minute digesting what Gia had just said before shifting some and pushing the covers from her head. With her red satin scarf still tied around her head, she looked at Gia with squinted eyes.

"What kind of plans you think you got, Ms. Fast Behind?"

Gia smiled goofily and plopped on the bed beside her. She snuggled beneath the covers and faced her.

"Well, Jamil asked could he see me again today and I said yeah. We're going to Waffle House after I get done running."

Oni sucked her teeth. "See, you ain't shit. Why you ain't see if he had a homeboy for me?"

"Ain't you fresh off old-man dick?"

Oni pushed Gia's forehead until she fell back onto the bed. "Shut up, bitch. I can't hang out nowhere in public like that with Isaac."

That hadn't even crossed Gia's mind. "I guess so, honey, but my fault. Hold on, I'll text him." Gia hopped from the bed, ran back to the guest room, and grabbed her phone before joining Oni back in bed.

Gia: You should bring a friend for my cousin J

She and Oni both lay still with giddy smiles on their faces, waiting for him to text back. When her phone finally did start vibrating, it wasn't a text—he was calling. Gia hated when people did that. If she'd texted, more than likely that meant she didn't feel like talking. Luckily for Jamil she actually did want to talk to him.

"Hello," she answered.

"What up, Gee?"

Gee . . . It sounded so natural. Like it had always been somewhere in the atmosphere just waiting for him to come along and affectionately tag it to her.

"You got my message?" That was such a dumb question to ask. Why would he not have gotten it? That was the whole reason he'd called. *Come on, Gia, get it together*, she thought.

"Yeah, I got it, but I don't text, so anytime you have to say something to me, just hit my line, okay?"

That was almost a mood damper for Gia because she loved to text. She wasn't a big fan of talking on the phone, but Jamil didn't seem like the type of nigga who budged on how he felt.

"Okay. I just said that you should bring a friend for my cousin."

"I don't really fuck with niggas like that, but I'll see what I can do."

Gia gave Oni the thumbs-up. "You're the best, Milli. Thank you."

She could hear the smile in his voice when he told her he'd see her later before hanging up. The excitement and happiness that Gia felt was unlike anything she'd felt since being in Georgia. Hopefully Jamil would keep it that way, at least for the rest of the summer.

"You need to get up and run with me now since I got you a date."

Oni pulled the covers back over her head.

"You make me sick. Bye." Gia pushed her head playfully before jumping from the bed and heading back to her room.

It didn't take her long to change into a black-and-white Reebok sports bra and a pair of jogging shorts to match. She quickly pulled all of her hair up into a ponytail and went to the bathroom to brush her teeth and wash her face. It took a little over ten minutes for Gia to walk out of the house and embark on her morning run.

She had been running every morning for the past five years, and she didn't plan on stopping just because she was on vacation.

She'd worked hard to be where she was in life, and she wouldn't allow Oni's laziness to hinder her. Gia stuck her Beats earbuds in, looked both ways, and decided to head left.

Oni and her Auntie Ann had shown her around the neighborhood on her first day there, and she'd memorized an easy running route right then. From that night to this morning she had run in that same circle, sometimes two or three times before returning home. Gia breathed in through her nose and out of her mouth as she ran up the hill behind Oni's house.

The fresh air brushing against her skin had her feeling refreshed and open-minded as she enjoyed the scenery. No dogs were out, barely any people, and not too many cars. The perfect place. Gia's mind drifted to Hawaii and her morning runs on the beach behind her house. That was the most peaceful thing she'd ever encountered, and she was counting down the days until she could return.

Thinking of Hawaii made her think of Kainoa. Gia wondered what he might be doing right then. Though they weren't together as a couple at the moment, he was still a big piece of her heart. She hadn't talked to him since she'd been there due to him having an attitude about her leaving in the first place.

In his mind she was coming down here to hang out with Oni and meet some other man. Gia rolled her eyes as she thought about the horrible argument they'd had the night before she left. He had downright forbidden her to fly to Georgia for the summer. As if they were seriously committed enough for her to just do what he said.

She didn't know what kind of world he was living in, but it was most definitely not the same one she was in. Even with him being such a butthole at the moment, she missed him and had actually tried to call him yesterday before going to the fair only for him not to answer. She knew then that he was still in his feelings about her trip and would call when he was able to.

When Gia reached her cousin's house for the second time, she decided to stop. She didn't want to spend her whole day running and miss out on spending time with Jamil. Maybe spending time with him would help her to get over Kainoa and his craziness.

She was breathing hard with sweat dripping from her body as she rested her hands on the top of her head. Before walking into the house she paced up and down the driveway around the cars, trying to cool off. When she felt she was cool enough, she pulled her earbuds from her ears and entered the house.

She immediately smelled eggs, bacon, pancakes, and grits. Intoxicated by the smell, Gia almost fell to her knees. She was so hungry and wanted nothing more than to indulge, but she'd already set up a breakfast date, and plainly putting it, she'd rather eat with Jamil.

"Good morning, Uncle Rick." Gia sat her iPod on the counter and pulled a bottle of water from the refrigerator.

"Morning, sunshine." He smiled at her over his shoulder. "How was your run?" He pulled more bacon from the frying pan.

"Awesome. You should have come with me."

Gia's uncle Rick was in the Army, like her father. Though her father had retired, Uncle Rick had two more years before he could. She wasn't sure of his exact age, but he was at least forty-four, if not older, and still in very good shape.

"Catch me next time. I have to host the officer call this morning, and your lovely cousin offered me her house since her dining room is more spacious."

Gia explained her shock over Oni's generosity before moving on. "An officer call? What's that?"

"That's when all of the officers in my company get together and bullshit mostly. We're supposed to get to know each other and talk about what we can do to better our work environment, but that rarely happens."

Gia finished her water as she listened to him.

"Ooh, okay. The Colonel has had a few of those too."

"Still calling your old man the Colonel, huh?"

Gia smiled and held her head down. Her uncle Rick had been teasing her about that for years now. "Yes, sir. I can't help it. It started out as a joke, but it kind of just stuck."

"He loves it too, don't he?"

Thoughts of her father had Gia smiling even harder. "Yep."

Rick poured the grits from the pot over into a large clear bowl. "I have to give that man a call and see how he's holding up with you gone. I know he's barely making it."

"I'll tell you now, he's miserable." Gia and her uncle shared a laugh. "So how long is the officer call going to be?"

He turned around and smiled at her. "Probably no more than a couple of hours. I don't want to abuse Oni's generosity. You know that's few and far between."

Gia's smile spread across her face. "You mean to tell me she's allowing you that long?" She laughed briefly. "You saving us some?"

Uncle Rick looked at her with an amusing smirk. "It's a lot of officers coming." He smiled at her. "May not be enough left over."

Gia surveyed the large platters of food that she'd paid no attention to at first. "Oh, I probably could have squeezed a plate or two out."

He laughed. "I'm kidding, baby girl. You girls are more than welcome to grab a plate, but everyone is due here in the next ten minutes, so y'all will have to hurry."

Gia pushed her chair back in and shook her head. "No, it's okay, we'll grab something else. Entertain your officers."

"All right. Just be careful."

Gia told him that she would before heading upstairs to see if Oni was ready. As soon as she hit the top step she could hear the music from Oni's stereo system in her room flooding the entire upstairs. It was so funny to Gia how much alike she and Oni really were, both an only child who did whatever she wanted to.

Whenever she was home, at any given moment she too would have her music blasting without one single thought about it. The light in Oni's room as well as the hallway and bathroom light was on. Future's "Freak Hoe" sounded like it was coming from every corner of the house, it was so loud.

Gia, being who she was, couldn't stop herself from bending over in front of the door of Oni's room and bouncing her butt.

"Ayyyyye, bounce that ass!" Gia was full-out twerking in the middle of Oni's room now.

"Get it!" Oni stood on the top of her bed and started dancing too.

"Freak hoes." Gia turned around so that she could see Oni as she continued to shake her butt.

Future's voice had both of the girls neglecting everything they were supposed to be doing at the moment. Whereas Oni had been flat-ironing her hair, she was now head down, ass up on her bed with the clip still hanging, holding up the hair on the top of her head.

"Look, Gia, look. Twerking on the bed, twerking on the bed."

Gia held her hands up and started clapping. "Get it, bitch. Get it," she screamed as she made her way to the dresser and hopped on it.

"Twerking on the dresser, twerking on the dresser." Gia put her hands on her knees and began bouncing her booty to the beat.

The bass from the song had the girls feeling like they were somewhere in a club, smiling and dancing without a care in the world. Gia smiled at Oni as she danced around her bed in a sports bra and loose-fitting boxer shorts. They had been best friends since birth, and not even distance had changed that.

"Ayyyyye, get it, Oni!" Gia yelled as Oni hopped from her bed onto her nightstand and bent over dancing.

Every time they linked up, it was like they had never been apart. Lost in their own world dancing, they hadn't even paid attention to the fact that Ann was now standing at the door of Oni's room.

"If y'all don't get y'all grown asses off that damn furniture like y'all ain't got no sense. I don't know where the hell y'all two freak hoes think y'all at, but this ain't damn Magic City."

Gia and Oni looked at Ann standing at the door with her hands on her hips, and then the two fell out laughing.

"Look, Auntie." Gia bent over and grabbed her ankles, making her butt shake again.

"Make your knees touch your elbows, Gia," Oni yelled across the room as the song changed from Future's "Freak Hoe" to Speaker Knockerz's "Freak Hoe."

Gia bent a little lower and held her hands out in front of her, making her butt move. "Show her some real quick, Oni."

It was Oni's turn to start dancing. Gia was cracking up as Oni danced like a stripper in such a small spot. The top of her nightstand wasn't as big as the dresser Gia was on, but she was still getting it.

"Oh, y'all think I'm playing? I'm about to whup y'all ass." Ann walked into the room and popped Gia's butt with her flip-flop before going over to Oni and doing the same thing.

Both women hopped from the dresser and onto the bed laughing while Ann continued to hit them with her flip-flop.

"Okay, Ma, stop." Oni held her stomach as she laughed. "This my house. I can cut up if I want to."

"I don't give a damn about this being your house. Y'all up here acting like y'all crazy." Ann laughed as she popped them both again before dropping her shoe on the floor and sliding her foot back in it. "All your daddy's coworkers down there, and y'all got it jumping up here like y'all at some kind of club somewhere."

Oni and Gia both made faces of surprise and sat up on the bed. Both knew they were coming but had no idea that they'd gotten there already. Ann looked at them both, smiling.

"Let me go call my sister and tell her what kind of fast daughter she raising." Ann walked out of the room as Oni and Gia started laughing again.

Gia fixed her clothes and headed for the door. "Man, let me go get in the shower before we be late."

"And I need to finish my hair. In here playing with you." Oni got off the bed and went back to the dresser where she'd been standing before.

"You know how we get when music's on. Don't play."

Oni smiled at her through the mirror. "You ain't lying. What you putting on?"

Gia shrugged. "Probably a dress. Nothing major."

" 'Kay, well, I'ma put one on too."

Gia left Oni's room and headed for hers. She quickly rumbled through the drawers she'd placed all of her clothes in, snatched a light pink sundress, and tossed it on the bed. The gray towel and washcloth were in her hand as she rushed to the bathroom and showered.

When she got out she stood wrapped in her towel for a moment, washing her face and brushing her teeth again. When she was done she played with her locs for a minute before going to get dressed. She had just retwisted them after they'd gone swimming with Big Dick Willie and Jarvis, so they were still looking extremely neat and pretty.

The Aqua Kiss lotion she'd gotten from Victoria's Secret accented her clean body before she pulled her dress over her head and slid her feet into her all-white Huaraches. She thought about wearing sandals but she needed her toes done, so that was going to have to wait. She was not about to have Jamil looking at the cracked-up purple polish on her toes.

Gia was spraying her CK perfume on when Oni burst into the room. "Ooh, that's cute. Where you get that dress from?"

Gia shrugged because she really didn't know. Her mother had gotten it for her one day while she was out. It didn't matter how grown Gia got, her mother still shopped for her clothing.

"My mama got it for me. You can borrow it, though, while I'm here." She looked at the dark blue skater dress with white stripes going across it that Oni was wearing. "You cute too, girl. I wish I would have gotten my toes done so I could have worn sandals too."

The red flower sandals on Oni's feet only made Gia wish she'd gotten her toes done even more.

"Next time you'll listen to me. Your sneakers are cute, though." She stood in the mirror next to Gia and ran her fingers through her neck-length brown hair. "You ready?"

Gia clipped her large gold hoops on and grabbed her purse from the bed. "Yep."

Ready, the girls headed down the stairs. The dining room was packed with people as they waved and passed by. Everyone smiled and made jokes with them about the music they'd just been blasting in Oni's room. The banter continued for a few more seconds before the girls told Rick that they were heading out and would be back later.

Once they were in Oni's truck, they turned the music up again and pulled out of the driveway. Gia pulled her phone out and sent Jamil a text that they were on their way to his side of town. It didn't dawn on Gia what she had done until her phone was ringing. She slapped her thigh in remembrance and answered the phone. Oni turned the music down once she realized that Gia was on the phone.

"I see you don't follow instructions well." Jamil's bedroom-deep voice gave her chills.

"I know. I'm sorry. I forgot."

"You good. What's going on?"

"We're on the way."

"A'ight, bet. I got my nigga Iverson with me. Which one y'all want to go to?"

Gia moved her phone from her mouth and asked Oni which Waffle House they were going to.

"Let's try the new one on Veterans Parkway near the Civic Center," Oni suggested.

Once Gia relayed the message and Jamil told her they would be there waiting, they hung up.

Oni turned her music back up only to turn it right back down, asking about who Jamil had with him. Being that Jamil hadn't given any information other than his friend's name, that was all Gia could give her. The rest of the ride was full of music and small talk about their anticipation about seeing the men.

They pulled up a short while later. Oni parked her truck right in front of the door and they checked their faces before hopping out. Oni hit the locks and they went inside. Upon entry they didn't see the men, but once Jamil's voice carried around the crowd of people standing in front of them, they came into view.

"Oh my God," Oni whispered to Gia. "That nigga is fine as all hell, Gia."

"Ain't he, though?" Gia agreed with Oni at Iverson's appearance.

The total opposite of Jamil, Iverson was dark skinned, about the same shade as Gia, with a low haircut and full beard. From the way his legs stretched out into the aisle, he had to be as tall as Jamil, if not taller. He was decked out in shiny gold jewelry with a red shirt that looked expensive as hell. They couldn't see his bottoms, but the red and black Giuseppe Zanotti sneakers he was wearing told it all.

"Ain't them Giuseppes?" Oni whispered just as they got to the table.

"Yep." Gia smiled at Jamil as he stood to greet her. "Hey, Milli," she sang into his ear as he grabbed her up in a hug.

"What's going on, Gee?" He squeezed a little tighter before releasing her. He looked her up and down as she stood in front of him, smiling. "Damn, you look sexy every time I see you."

Gia held her head down and Jamil picked it right back up before stepping to the side so that she could sit down. He then pointed over at Iverson, who was also standing up.

"This my nigga Iverson. Iverson, this Gia, and this her cousin Oni."

Oni smiled and stuck her hand out for him to take. When he

did, he kissed the outside of it and flashed her a smile that would get even the gayest bitch's panties wet.

"Nice to meet you, Oni." Iverson took a step back so Oni could sit down. He spoke to Gia as he made himself comfortable in the booth. "Y'all got some pretty-ass names. It ain't shit like what we hear in the hood every day."

Both girls laughed at him.

"What kind of names y'all normally hear?" Oni looked at Iverson.

"Shaniqua, Artasia, Shaquanna. Ghetto shit like that." Iverson smiled at Oni again.

The two of them clearly liked what they saw in each other because they were all smiles and giggles as they sat in the booth nearly touching. Gia smiled at them both, happy that Jamil had looked out for Oni. Her hands were in her lap as she looked over at Jamil. He was sitting catercorner in the booth with his arms thrown over the back of it.

His eyes trailed over her body slowly until stopping at her face. When he finally met her gaze head-on, Gia winked at him and his face turned red.

"Did I just make you blush?" Gia asked Jamil.

Jamil wiped his hand over his face and shook his head. "Cut it out," he told her, but he was still smiling.

"I'm only checking because I think your face just turned red." Gia leaned closer to him, pretending to be taking a closer look at his face. "Yeah, I made you blush. That's so cute." She smiled at him before winking again.

This time he didn't turn red, but he did smile again. "Move back, man." He pushed her out of his face playfully.

"I like your freckles." The small brownish orange dots beneath his eyes and across his nose were the most adorable thing to Gia.

"I like your hair." He picked up one of Gia's locs and inspected the color on the ends.

"I like yours too."

"Look at y'all over there complimenting each other and shit." Iverson interrupted their flirty play.

Gia looked at him. "I know you ain't talking. All that smiling and giggling the two of you were just doing."

Oni was still smiling when she and Iverson began looking at their menus. Gia took their lead and grabbed hers as well. She was looking over it when she noticed that Jamil wasn't looking at his.

"You not hungry?"

"Yeah, I just already know what I want."

Gia pushed her menu away and looked at him. "Well, I'm getting what you're getting."

"How you know what I pick ain't gon' be nasty?"

Gia shrugged. "I trust your judgment." She stared at him bashfully and he stared back.

They looked at one another, taking in each other's beauty. Jamil had already told her how attracted to her he was, but she hadn't done the same. Though that didn't mean she wasn't.

Jamil was one of the finest men Gia had ever seen. His demeanor was calm and collected as he sat in his dark green shirt and black shorts.

In the back of her mind Gia wondered why his friend was dressed so impeccably yet Jamil's attire was average. For a brief moment she wondered if she had hooked up with the right one. She wasn't a sac chaser by far, but she did like for her man to have at least a little bit of money. Especially since she had her own. She was still silently observing him and trying to feel him out when their waitress came over to the table.

She stood there taking their order as Gia sat back with her arms folded. She'd decided to allow Jamil to order for her since she was getting the same thing as him. Her mouth watered as she watched him speak and listened to the food he was ordering. She didn't know which part had her the readiest—the food, or him.

Jamil was fucking breathtaking to say the least. So unique but so ordinary at the same time. He was definitely not something she saw on a daily basis, but she was more than welcoming of it now. The southern drawl that accompanied every word that slid off his tongue was so sexy. Gia wondered if he knew just how much.

"You're so sexy, Milli, and the way you talk is amazing." The words just fell off Gia's tongue.

He looked confused. "The way I talk?"

"Yeah. You're so country."

Jamil's facial expression changed as he smiled at her. He didn't laugh or respond, he just watched her. Gia tried her best to return the intensity behind his eyes but was unable to because it was so overwhelming it was starting to make her nervous.

"What y'all got planned for today?" Iverson asked loud enough to gain everyone's attention.

"Nothing for real. We may go to the nail shop, but that's about it." Oni answered for them both.

"Well, I was thinking about riding to Atlanta to hit the outlets. Y'all down?" Iverson asked Gia and Oni both but had turned his head toward Oni.

Of course Oni was smiling like a Cheshire cat. "I am. You want to go, Gia?"

Gia was a little skeptical because she didn't know much about Atlanta other than it was an hour or two away. Going to another city with two men she'd just met wasn't at the top of her to-do list, but she didn't want to seem like a party pooper. However, she also knew how spontaneous Oni could be when men were involved.

"Umm, I don't know. Exactly how far is that away?" Gia asked.

Jamil answered her. "It's only like an hour."

"Where's the outlet?"

"Atlanta has an ass of outlets, but the one I'm going to is only like thirty more minutes out once we get there. It's the North Georgia outlet," Iverson said.

Gia bit the inside of her cheek as she looked at Oni for some sort of common reasoning. Even though the men didn't know her that well, Oni knew her well enough to know that this was not something that she was comfortable doing. Jamil was cute and all, and had even saved her life, but that didn't mean she knew him well enough to be taking spur-of-the-moment out-of-town trips.

The table was quiet as everyone waited for Gia to make a decision. It sounded fun. Outside of running and softball, shopping was her next favorite thing to do, but she didn't know about going to an entirely different city with strangers.

Iverson touched her hand to get her attention. "If you don't want to, Gia, that's cool. I just figured shopping might be some shit y'all would be into, and Peachtree Mall ain't got shit."

Peachtree Mall was the local mall that everyone went to in Columbus, and he wasn't lying. Gia had been in there with Oni, and she had thought the same thing as they walked through.

"Let me think about it while we eat," Gia said.

"A'ight. Bet," Iverson told her as the waitress walked up with their food.

She sat the food down and they all began eating. Every so often Gia would catch Oni's eye and she would smile at her. Gia just shook her head. She could already tell this was about to be a rerun of all of Oni's other escapades. She would fall for Iverson, fuck him, and move on to the next. Gia could see it already, and they hadn't even been sitting there long.

The foursome made small talk as they ate. When they'd finished eating and were preparing to go, it was almost two hours later. After the waitress brought their ticket over, Jamil and Iverson both began to dig into their pockets. Gia wasn't surprised to see Oni's eyes glued to the knot Iverson pulled from his pocket like it belonged to her.

Gia, on the other hand, tried her best to be discreet as she eyed the twenty-dollar bill that Jamil sat on top of their ticket. Again, she wondered if she'd taken an interest in the wrong one. Though she had her own money, thanks to her parents, and wasn't hurting for cash, being with the broke friend was not what she wanted.

After getting up from the table, Gia looked it over once again to make sure she hadn't left anything when she noticed that Iverson had left a hundred-dollar bill on his and Oni's ticket. That was crazy, but she kept it to herself. It was obvious by the way he dapped out of the restaurant that he was paid.

His whole swag screamed hood rich. Gia had definitely put her cousin on this time. When she looked over at Jamil, his swag was the same as it had been when she met him: calm, cool, chill. Although he wasn't wearing expensive clothing like Iverson, he was still killing his attire as well.

The slim-fitting black cargo shorts with the fitted green shirt and all-black 12s were sexy as hell on him. His cute tanned yellow legs stood pigeon-toed in his shoes, and every time he moved it made Gia want to lick her lips. His sex appeal was off the map. His dreads were all down and he had them tied back with two from each side, a style Gia too wore occasionally.

Jamil held the door open for Gia and allowed her to walk out in front of him. She wasn't sure what she was about to do now since she still hadn't made up her mind about whether she was going to Atlanta. Her eyes wandered around the parking lot trying to see what car was theirs.

She wasn't even shocked when the lights to a dark gray G wagon blinked. When Iverson walked to the driver side door and opened it, Gia's heart nearly dropped. She had gotten the broke friend. Oni's excitement at his car ignited her initial excitement about their trip to Atlanta.

"Gia, what's it going to be, cousin?" Oni asked.

Gia gave her a look like she should have known better than to put her on the spot like that, but instead of saying it, she just rolled her eyes and stood near the front of the truck where Jamil was standing.

"I don't know." Gia shrugged.

"Come on, Gia," Oni whined.

"It's going to be straight, Gia, I swear. You're in good hands." Iverson cosigned with Oni.

When Gia remained quiet, Jamil grabbed her hand and pulled her around to the other side of the truck. He pushed her against it slightly so that her back was pressed against the window. He stuck both of his hands in his pockets. Gia wondered if that was to keep from touching her. She figured her body in that skintight pink dress had him wanting to feel all over her. She stood there while she ran her hands through her hair.

Gia looked at him with his dreads resting around the bottom of his chest. His wide and well-defined chest stuck out through the thin fabric of his shirt. The various tattoos covering his left arm had her attention as he stood tall in front of her. His head was bent slightly as he tried his best to look into her eyes.

"You know you don't have to go if you don't want to, right?" His voice was softer than normal. Comforting, even.

"Yeah, I know."

"Talk to me . . . What's wrong?" He pushed the lone dreadlock that had just fallen into her face back with the rest of them before holding her chin to make her look at him.

Talk to me . . . What's wrong?

That simple statement had Gia in her feelings bad. It was so subtle yet endearing. It was so personal and touching. Like he really wanted to know what was bothering her.

"Don't take this the wrong way, but I don't know y'all like that. I don't know if I need to be going out of town with a man that I just met. Oni may be into it, but I ain't really feeling it."

Jamil smirked at her, rested his hand on the side of her waist, and gripped it softly, but firm enough to keep her from moving if she tried. When he stepped closer to her, Gia inhaled deeply and looked at his face. His light brown eyes were staring her down as he wet his bottom lip with his tongue.

The cologne he was wearing wafted up her nose, making her feel closer to him than she really was. It surrounded her fully and eliminated any personal space she had.

"You think I would hurt you?"

Gia shrugged but maintained eye contact.

"I would, but not in the way that you're thinking." He let his hand fall from her waist to her hand and held it. "You're safe with me. I promise. I wouldn't do nothing to you. I can tell you're different. It's all over everything you do. I wouldn't want you in any situation you're not comfortable with, but I would like it if you came with us."

How was everything this man said and did a turn-on to her? He was standing in her face telling her things like he would never hurt her, and it had her feeling like she was already in love.

."If I don't go, then what? Will you be mad at me?"

He shook his head. "I'll just stay here with you."

Gia liked that response, and because of that she decided to go. There was something about him that made her feel safe. "Well, I guess we can go, then."

When he smiled at her, she felt relaxed. "Look at your pretty ass. Come on." He grabbed her hand and opened the back door for her to slide in. "Aye, we gon' slide with y'all," Jamil yelled to Iverson.

Oni looked at Gia quickly before giving Iverson back her attention. "Okay. Where should I leave my truck? I don't want to leave it down here."

"I'll follow you to drop it off somewhere," Iverson told her.

He and Oni discussed where she was going to leave her truck before she walked off. Gia looked over at Jamil with alarm on her face, and he burst into laughter.

"Yo, shawty, chill. We ain't about to do nothing to you."

"I don't know that."

Jamil was still laughing when he pulled his gun from behind his back. Gia shrieked and scooted across the seat as fast as she could while still staring at him. Iverson stood at the door watching in amusement.

"I'ma need you to calm down, Gee, for real. We ain't gon' do shit to your ass." Jamil cocked his gun and handed it over to her. "Take this. If either of us do anything that you don't like, shoot our ass."

Gia held the gun in her hand trying to get used to the weight of it. It wasn't her first time holding a gun, nor would it be her first time shooting one if they pissed her off. The Colonel had trained her well, and little did Jamil and Iverson know, she would blow their heads off with little to no effort. She was a perfect shot.

She was just a tad bit nervous since she didn't know them very well. The gun was cool, but she was still not too fond of riding out of town with strangers. The only reason she was going along with it was because of Jamil. She wanted to spend time with him. Hopefully she wouldn't regret it.

"No." Iverson stuck his head into the car. "You shoot that muthafucka. Don't shoot me."

Gia began to relax and even laughed at Iverson as she sat with the gun in her lap. "I'm shooting both of y'all. You better not make me mad either."

Iverson shook his head and got into the car. When Oni's truck passed his, he drove out behind her. Gia watched every turn she made, hoping she wasn't about to make them follow her back to her house to drop her truck off. That would be the dumbest shit in America, but she still didn't put it past Oni.

Though Oni was smart, she was too hyped off their trip at the moment to use common sense. Gia wasn't exactly sure how to get back to Oni's house, but she could tell by the way she was going that they weren't headed there. When Oni pulled into the parking lot of Walmart, Gia breathed a sigh of relief.

She watched Oni hit the locks to her truck and walk to Iverson's truck. Once she was in, Gia handed Jamil his gun back and made herself comfortable in the backseat. He winked at her once he'd put his gun away. Gia's stomach fluttered. Hopefully she could relax her mind enough to enjoy her time away with him.

Chapter Six

"Before meeting my Gee, I was nothing. I was an empty shell of pain and disaster, dying a slow death. All I've ever wanted in my entire life was to have someone who loves me. A person who showed it more than they said it. I was an empty person just going through the motions of life until the day God blessed me with my angel. She was my saving grace then, and she's my saving grace now. She saved me from myself and she didn't even know it. With everything in me, I'll love Gianna forever." —Milli

The sun was shining as people of all races and colors went in and out of stores loaded down with bags or pushing their babies in their strollers. The sidewalks were crowded with chatter and moving feet. The sweltering heat and crowded walkways didn't make for such a good getaway, but as long as Gia continued to sway her sexy ass hips in front of him, then Jamil would be all right.

Polo, Gap, Armani, Converse, and J. Crew were only a few of the stores that Jamil and Gia had gone into so far. Gia felt the need to gasp and announce the name every time they entered one. He and Gia had split up from Iverson and Oni the moment they'd gotten out of the truck, so it was just the two of them.

Neither of them had purchased anything yet, even though they'd both seen a lot that they'd liked. Had Gia not been so quiet about her every thought, he would have been buying her shit left and right already. The only problem was that he didn't know what to do or where to start. She perused the racks, picking up things and putting them down in every store.

He had been following behind her obediently, and she hadn't kept one thing she'd liked. It was starting to slightly annoy him. Here they were at a nice-ass mall with every store that she could think of, and she wasn't shopping. What girl didn't like to shop, especially when it was on another person's dime?

Jamil picked up the red shirt Gia had admired moments ago, only to put back down, and handed it back to her. "Here, get this."

Gia gave him a quizzical look. "I don't want it."

"Yes, you do. Just like you wanted the black dress, the pink skirt, and the blue purse. Get the shit, Gia."

She stood there stunned, clearly unaware of what to say next. "You've been watching me?"

"Like a fucking hawk. Now, will you please get something?"

Gia looked away. "I don't want to shop by myself. It's no fun."

"What you mean by yourself? I'm right here with you."

Gia fidgeted with the tag on the shirt. "But you're not picking up anything."

So that was her problem? All of this time she'd had him confused about what it was that she liked. Jamil held his head down and laughed quietly.

"That's because we haven't gone in any stores that I like yet."

"Well, come on, then." Gia grabbed his hand and pulled him from the store. "Where you want to go?"

"Anywhere you take me. What kind of man do you think I am?"

Gia looked him up and down before walking toward the Nike outlet. He was smiling when she pulled him in behind her and over to the men's side. She stood in the middle of the section and gave him attention.

"Shop," she ordered.

"I'll go with you, then we'll come back to me."

Gia didn't look like she believed him, but she turned and headed for the women's section anyway. He watched her ass every time it moved in her dress. He wanted to reach out and touch it so bad, but he didn't know what she would say. In the back of his mind he didn't really care, but he still had to control himself.

The way her eyes lit up at all of the different workout gear made him smile. He leaned on a rack as she picked up one thing after another. When he noticed her hands were getting full, he grabbed everything from her and encouraged her to continue. Sports bras, leggings, running shorts, Dri-Fit shirts, and even a few running jackets weighed down his arms.

He didn't know how much more he could carry when she began grabbing full jogging suits. Just when he thought he was going to buckle from holding everything, she told him she needed to try on the pair of shorts in her hand.

"Sir, do you need a bag?" a perky white girl with a short blond ponytail bounced over to him and asked.

"Hell yeah. Appreciate that."

She laughed at his response before helping him stuff everything into the complimentary shopping bag and walking away. Now able to see the full store freely again, he followed Gia to the dressing room. She went inside one of the stalls while Jamil took his place near the door, where he waited for her to finish. Before he knew it she was sticking her head out the door.

"Come in so you can tell me how it fits."

"Say what now?" Jamil needed to make sure he'd heard her right.

"Come on." She held the door to her dressing open so that he could walk in.

Jamil walked in and took a seat on the black stool in the corner. Gia locked the door and wasted no time pulling her dress up around her waist.

"Oh got damn." Jamil cleared his throat as she exposed her butt to him.

The black thong Gia was wearing could barely be seen. Nah, scratch that, it couldn't be seen. All he saw was the strings around her waist. He was damn near having an asthma attack in the corner from seeing all that ass. She was sliding the pants on like it was no big deal. She hadn't even given him a second thought.

To further take his breath away, the shorts were too small and pushed all of her ass out of the top as they stopped under the bottom of her cheeks. Gia moved and swished around the room, and even jumped once trying to stuff her ass into the tiny shorts.

"Oh my good got damn," he mumbled to himself again.

Yeah, she was trying to kill him.

"I'm glad I decided to try these on. They're a medium, but they looked bigger on the hanger."

"You knew you had too much ass for those shorts when you brought them in here." Jamil picked them up from the floor and looked at them when she took them off.

Gia turned to the side in the mirror and looked at her butt. "It ain't that big."

"Shid." Jamil begged to differ.

She smirked at him through the mirror before turning around. She stood against the mirror with her dress ruffled around her waist shaking her head. Jamil didn't even bother to hide the fact that he was looking at her with eyes of lust. Hell, she didn't care about giving him a show full of ass, so fuck it. He was going to look. He was going to touch too.

Jamil left the bag where it was and stood up. He walked to her and pulled her from the mirror. His hands trailed from her back down to her round butt cheeks and cupped them. He groped and squeezed as she stood with her face in his chest, breathing a lot harder than she had been before.

He was already on the verge of busting a nut just by watching her. Actually being allowed to touch her had his dick about to bust and get her pregnant right there on the spot. With his head down near her ear, his locs fell forward and were now resting on her shoulders, mixing and mingling with hers.

"Milli . . . no," she told him breathlessly.

Jamil released her and took a few steps back, but his eyes stayed where they were. His eyes were hungry and full of desire for her. How in the world had this girl gained control over his body and mind this fast? It was crazy because she didn't even know it, but she could have him any way that she wanted to right then.

Friend, boyfriend, fuck buddy—whatever she desired, he wanted to be the one to provide it. Her chest was rising and falling roughly as she stood with her dress still up. Gia held a hunger in her eyes just as intense as his. She may have said no, but her body was screaming yes, and he was about to show her who was in charge.

Jamil grabbed her quickly, turning her around so that Gia's back was to his chest. He moved to the side as his palm rested against her abs. When they were both looking in the mirror, he ran his free hand up her neck and leaned her head to the side. Using his tongue, he made circles around her neck, licking and sucking hard.

Her sexy chocolate skin tasted just like he'd thought it would. He sucked harder, making her hand grab the one that was resting on her stomach. The soft moan that escaped her lips killed every ounce of control he had left. Jamil moved the hand that hers had been resting on down the front of her body until it was dipping into her panties.

"Open your legs," he whispered into her ear.

Gia obliged and nearly drowned his fingers in the syrupy juices she'd created for him. Jamil closed his eyes as he moved his fingers around in the hot, wet essence that belonged to the new love of his young life. His middle finger slid over her clit until it slid farther down and dipped inside her.

"Damn, Gee." He moaned quietly.

Jamil was so lost in just fingering her pussy that he hadn't even realized that his eyes were closed until he opened them. He looked at the mirror and admired the way she looked sprawled against his chest. His light skin meshed perfectly with her dark skin. Gia's long dark locs intertwined with his light ones as they stood in each other's space. They were totally opposite, but for some reason he felt like she was made for him.

Every difference they had was a plus in his eyes. Her full breasts moved as she arched her back. Jamil took this opportunity to work his fingers a little deeper. Her toned bowlegs spread a little more, showing off the defined muscles she'd developed from years of running. Her flat stomach and rock-hard abs were getting sharper with every dip of his finger.

"Open your eyes, bae," Jamil whispered into her ear, his lips softly grazing it.

Gia's eyes opened slowly and locked with his. Instinctively, she shrank back some, closing her legs a little more.

"We look like fucking magic together."

She stared at him through hooded eyes.

"Fuck with me." He kissed her neck hard before sliding his tongue on the spot he'd kissed. "With your sexy ass."

The bashfulness returned in Gia's eyes, replacing the desire. She only looked at him for a little while longer before pulling away from him and pulling her dress down.

He could tell she was embarrassed about what she'd just allowed him to do by the way she was avoiding eye contact. Though she was too grown to be embarrassed by a little finger fucking, Jamil thought it was cute, so he didn't bother to point it out to her.

Gia was standing in the mirror making sure her dress was straight when she finally had the courage to look at him. It just so happened that he was sucking her juices from his fingers when she did. The way her chest visibly sank in and she bit her bottom lip had him wanting to bend her over and give her his dick right then and there.

Her eyes were still on him as he picked up her bag and walked over to her. He leaned down so that his lips were near her ear again.

"I'ma get me some more of that." He kissed her ear before pulling the door open and leaving the dressing room.

Jamil stood outside near the door waiting for Gia to emerge. When she came out she still looked a little flushed, but she was back to her beautiful vibrant self.

"You ready to go to your side?"

Jamil nodded and followed her. He made sure to stay behind her because the view was better than anything else he could possibly be looking at right then.

She leaned on one of the racks while he looked through the clothes. There was so much he wanted to buy, so instead of trying it on like she had, he just grabbed his sizes in the items he liked so that they could move on to the next store.

Jamil tried to suppress his smile as he observed the way Gia's head was tilted to the side as she watched him in awe. Not only was her head tilted, but he swore he could see stars in her eyes as they followed him around the store. It was cute how she thought she was in love already when all he'd done was play in the pussy. He couldn't wait to see what she was going to be like once he actually put the dick in her life.

"Gee, stop looking like you just got fucked, baby."

"What?" She laughed immediately, which let him know he had been right.

Her ass was in a daze all over some little finger action. She was most definitely going to be fucked up in the head off the dick. Versus answering her, Jamil finished grabbing the things he wanted and headed for the counter. The line was long, but they stood in it anyway.

To make time pass, Jamil turned to her with interest in his eyes and marveled at the beauty in her face. "Tell me about yourself, Gee."

"What do you want to know?"

"Anything."

"Well, I'm an only child. My father is in the Army, and my parents and Oni are my best friends. Running and softball is life. I'm a straight-A student, I love to read, and I like to dance."

"Boyfriends?"

Her eyes darted away quickly, but he hadn't missed it.

"Something like that. We have this whole on-again, off-again relationship."

Jamil could tell she felt some type of way about telling him about her man, but little did she know, he really didn't care. She was going to be his. Fuck any other nigga. Worrying about other niggas had never been his style. He'd fucked plenty of niggas' bitches. Gia wouldn't be the first.

"That's what's up." He nodded and looked toward the register.

"What about you? Tell me about yourself."

That was a question that Jamil gave no real thought to. There wasn't much to him. He wasn't shit, basically. He was the product of two crackheads, had no education, and had sold so much dope that he was practically a millionaire. But all that shit meant nothing.

"I'm Milli Rock. I'm a hood nigga from downtown. That's it." He shrugged.

Gia gave him a look like he couldn't be serious. "Come on, Milli. There's more to you than that."

"No, there ain't," he told her seriously.

"There has to be. Don't be like that. I told you about me."

Jamil stared at her long and hard so that she could see how serious he was. "Let me put it like this. You ever met somebody that just wasn't shit? Like really wasn't shit? Well, that's me."

Jamil hated to put it to her like that, but Gia was different. He could already tell that she wasn't going to let it go until he gave her some commendable rundown like she'd just given him, so he needed to set her straight before she kept going.

Gia looked at him for a long time before turning her back to him and stepping forward. She kept her back to him the rest of the time that they were in the line. When it was their turn at the register, she tried to grab her bag from him, but he pulled it away. She cut her eyes at him but knew to take her ass on to the register.

The two of them stood a few feet away from each other, watching the girl ring up Jamil's items.

"This stuff is separate," Gia told the girl when she prepared to ring up the things she'd picked up.

"No, it ain't," Jamil said to the cashier. "Go ahead."

Gia looked at him again, but as soon as she did, he shot her a look to let her know not to fight him. She sucked her teeth and turned away.

"Okay, your total today is two thousand two hundred ninety-seven dollars and fifty-six cents."

"Fuck me," Gia said out loud, making the cashier laugh.

"I will later, right now I need to pay for all of this stuff you came in here picking up." Jamil pulled a wad of neatly stacked cash from his pocket, counted off the money, and handed it to the cashier.

Gia's eyes were on him, watching his every move. Jamil chuckled a little as he grabbed the bags from the counter. When he turned, getting ready to leave, Gia was still standing there with her arms folded looking at him.

"Gee, bring your ass on." He walked past her and out of the store.

"How are you going to tell me you're not shit, but you pulled all that money out like that? You're something." Gia looked to him for an explanation.

"Money doesn't make the man, Gee. Remember that."

"I know that, but I'm saying there has to be more to you than you're letting on to have that kind of cake." She walked so that she was in front of him. She stopped so that he couldn't move. "Tell me."

"Tell you what?" Jamil was getting really frustrated with her. Why couldn't she just let it go?

"Tell me who you are. I told you about me."

"There ain't shit to tell. Believe me."

Jamil watched her stand in front of him, clearly frustrated. She ran her hand through her pretty hair and sucked her teeth before walking away from him. He stood there in the middle of the sidewalk with an arm full of bags watching her walk away. For a second he wanted to run after her and see why she felt like showing her ass, but he chose not to.

Instead, he found the nearest bench and took a seat. This right here was why he'd avoided relationships and stayed single for as long as he had. Women could be so fucking dramatic. Quite frankly, he ain't have the time for that shit. It was a nice day outside, she was getting free shit, and she still wanted to act an ass. He didn't understand.

Two hours later, she still hadn't come back. Oni and Iverson had even linked back up with him, and her ass was nowhere in sight. They had walked back and forth through the outlet and still hadn't located her. As much as he didn't want to, Jamil was starting to worry about her.

"Aye, y'all take this shit and put it in the truck for me while I go find this damn girl." Jamil handed Iverson and Oni his and Gia's bags.

They walked toward Iverson's truck, and he went the opposite direction in search of crybaby-ass Gia. He looked up and down the sidewalk, and in every girl store he saw, and still didn't see her. Frustrated and tired of calling her phone, Jamil walked out of the Coach store and headed back toward the parking lot.

He was moving through some cars about to come out near the crosswalk when he spotted Gia near the bus stop, sitting on a bench and talking on her phone. He was relieved that nothing was wrong with her, but it angered him that she'd obviously had her phone in her hand all that time and hadn't bothered to answer for him.

Jamil marched toward her. As he got closer, he could tell she was on FaceTime. When he was only a few feet away from her, he could hear a man's voice. For some crazy reason, instead of being angry, he felt hurt, or something in that area of emotions. Whatever the feeling was, it was foreign to him.

"Aye, Gia, we're about to dip. Your cousin them in the car." With that Jamil turned around and headed for the car.

He could hear her behind him telling whoever she was talking to that she loved them and would talk to them later. Being that it was already getting dark outside, he tried his best to walk slowly without making it obvious. He didn't want to walk with her, but he didn't want to leave her. Niggas in Atlanta were crazy. They would rob your ass just because the sky was blue.

Oni and Iverson were waiting in the car with it running when Jamil, followed by Gia, finally made it back. Jamil got in on one side while Gia hopped in on the other.

"Damn, girl. We been looking all over the place for you," Iverson told Gia as she looked out the window.

"Well, here I am." Sarcasm flooded her every word.

"A'ight bet." Iverson laughed. "Y'all want to grab something to eat? I'm starving like hell."

"I do. Where we going?" Oni asked him.

When none of them could decide where to eat, Iverson chose to take them to Sun Dial Restaurant. It was a nice little spot they could eat, drink, and chill. Traffic was hell as they sat in the car for another hour trying to reach their destination. Every one of them was more than ready to get out when Iverson finally stopped the car.

They all got out and headed toward the restaurant.

Jamil walked slowly behind Oni and Gia. The atmosphere was nice and causal once they got inside. Much better than they'd all expected. Too bad Gia was still acting like a baby. Oni and Iverson were having fun talking and taking shots while Jamil and Gia sat around like they were total strangers. Fed up with the bullshit, Jamil ordered alcohol and began to drink as well.

A couple hours passed before Iverson and Oni were com-

pletely wasted, not too far from Jamil. Gia's face showed her dis-
approval at all of their actions, but especially Oni's.

"I can't drive. Y'all want to get a room?" Iverson asked.

Being that the restaurant was on top of a hotel, it wasn't such a
far-fetched idea. Jamil just didn't feel like being bothered with Gia.

"Hell nah, let's go." Jamil shook his head as he pulled Iverson's
keys from his hand.

"Bruh, we can't drive like this." Iverson spoke for himself and
Oni, who was barely holding her head up.

"I can drive."

Iverson pulled his keys from Jamil's grasp. "Nigga, your ass is
drunk too." He looked at Gia and handed her the keys with a big
smile on his face. "Looks like it's on you."

Oni snickered loudly and covered her face. "Gia can't drive."
She laughed again like it was the funniest thing in the world. She
continued on making jokes that weren't the least bit funny to
Jamil or Gia as they all stood to leave. Jamil and Iverson tossed
money onto the table before helping the girls toward the door.

Jamil could tell that Gia was getting a little uncomfortable as
Oni continued to laugh and tell Iverson that Gia was afraid to
learn. It angered Jamil that they were talking about her like she
wasn't standing there, so he grabbed her hand and pulled her behind him.

"We'll get a room, and that nigga can drive his own shit in the
morning," Jamil said to Gia. "You ain't got to feel bad. Everybody
can't do everything." There was so much feeling in his words.

Gia momentarily wondered why he'd gotten so angry on her
behalf, but ignored it. She was just happy that he had. Jamil stopped
at the front desk and checked the availability. There were rooms
available. The lady offered him the key cards and a piece of paper
that he needed to read over and sign.

"Here, read these while I pay." Jamil slid the papers to Gia and
continued to move the process along with the desk clerk.

When he'd paid for two rooms, he went back to get Oni and

Iverson. They followed him and Gia in their drunken stupor. He watched Gia help them into the elevator like they hadn't been clownin' her a few minutes prior.

She was a good one, because he wasn't thinking about their ass. When they got to their floor, Iverson and Oni stumbled behind them until they reached their room. Jamil used the key and opened the door.

"Y'all go ahead, Gee."

Gia spun around and looked at him. "I want to go with you."

"You don't want to stay in the room with your cousin?" he asked for clarity.

Oni stepped in front of Gia and held her hands up in front of her. "No. I'm staying with Iverson." She gave Gia a sloppy hug. "I'm sorry, cousin, but I'm about to fuck this nigga." She had been trying to whisper, but she was so loud anybody on that hall would have heard her.

"Whatever, Oni, move." Gia walked past her so that Oni and Iverson could enter their room.

Iverson dapped Jamil up before closing the door. Gia looked at Jamil, waiting for him to lead her to their double-bed suite, which ended up being two doors down. He used their key card and allowed her to walk in first. Once the door was closed, he pushed the extra latch on it and walked to the bathroom.

The Patrón he'd been drinking had his bladder about to burst. He was still at the toilet when Gia walked in and flipped the shower on. She moved around so freely it was as if she didn't even see him standing there with his dick out. When she began to undress, he was the one who had to stop his movements. Unlike her, he couldn't ignore her body parts.

When she was down to her panties and bra, she stopped and looked at him. "You can leave."

"Well damn. I guess I'm gone." He flushed the toilet and left.

Gia closed the door behind her. Jamil went and sat in the room alone. Tipsy and tired, he undressed and fell backward on the bed. He fell asleep so fast that he didn't even remember blinking. The only reason he realized that he'd fallen asleep was because he could hear music playing. He rubbed his eyes before rolling over.

He rubbed his eyes again to make sure it wasn't a dream. Gia had the blinds pushed back so that the skyline could be seen. All of the city lights made the perfect background for her beauty. She was sitting on the floor in a towel stretching. Her legs were open, but because of the way the towel hung down, he couldn't see anything.

The music he'd heard was coming from her phone as she danced subtly in her stretch. "Why I Love You" by Major was playing, and she was singing to it. Her hair was all down and leaning to one side as she held her head tilted. Her shiny dark skin was flawless and perfect. The tiny diamond in her nose caught the light every time she leaned forward.

"Gianna." Jamil sat up on the bed, letting her know that he was now awake.

She looked up to him before leaning back over to stretch the other side.

"Come here." His buzz had worn off, so now he was ready to address the little attitude she had. "Talk to me, chocolate girl."

Gia looked up at him and shook her head. "It's okay."

"No, it ain't. You said you wanted to come with me, but now you don't want to talk? What's good?"

Gia sat up from her stretch and turned the music down on her phone a little before sitting near the windowsill and looking at him. She was quiet as he sat with his arms stretched out behind him on the bed holding him up.

"I'm simple, Jamil, I really am. All I want out of life is to be happy, to run, and to be loved. I like you, I really do, and it's crazy because I just met you. But I feel like I want to spend all of my time with you. Growing up my parents always told me to express myself freely, and I can't be with someone who can't offer me the same thing."

Jamil could feel where she was coming from because he felt the same way about her. She had him so open already, and it had only been a few days. He was so open that he was starting to feel safe enough to let her in, but what if she made him regret it? What if she didn't want him anymore after he really did tell her about himself?

"I'm a good person for real, and it hurt my feelings earlier when you said you weren't shit. You shouldn't think like that about yourself. I think you're amazing, and you should too. I turned away from you in the Nike store so that you wouldn't see what your words did to me." She wiped her eyes quickly. "I had to walk away and give myself time away from you at the outlet. I didn't want you to think I was weird for being sad about your situation." Gia pushed her hair from her face.

Quiet and deep in thought, Jamil sat on the bed watching this beautiful woman speak more highly of him than he thought of himself.

"Tell me why you think you're not shit, Jamil."

Jamil took a deep breath and looked away from her. How had this girl come into his life and begun to make him question everything about his existence? He had come to terms with who he was, and now here she was making him feel bad about it all over again.

"Milli, please . . ."

Damn.

There she was with that Milli shit, making him feel like she actually cared about him. Nobody cared about him. He was the fuckup who was barely making it out of the hood, and she wanted him to believe that he was more when he wasn't.

Jamil looked over at her to see if she was still looking at him, and she was. He sighed because as much as he liked her, he knew it was all about to go away. She was giving him no choice. She hadn't let up all day, and it was clear she wasn't about to then either. Maybe he could give her just enough to satisfy her and leave him alone.

Jamil ran his hand over his face and looked back at her. "I say I'm not shit, Gia, because I'm really not. I'm the only child of two crackheads who only talk to me long enough to ask for another hit of cocaine. They've walked around me every day for as far as I can remember without really doing anything for me. I remember sitting alone in the car, some nights for hours at a time, waiting for them to come out of the dope house. It's been like that forever. When I got old enough to leave the house, that's what I did. I would stay outside and play all day sometimes, because I hated to go home." Jamil looked past her and out at the lights. "I spent so much time at dope houses that I never really had time for school. I was either in class asleep or falling behind because I didn't know anything."

Jamil laughed to himself. Nothing was funny, but his life was so fucked up that he had to laugh through the pain.

"Eventually I got tired of being the dirty dumb kid in class, so I stopped going to school."

"You dropped out?" Gia's soft voice interrupted him.

"Yeah, in the seventh grade." He looked away from her when he said that. He was embarrassed and ashamed of not having an education. "So instead of being in school like all of the other twelve-year-olds, I was on the block running dope, making plays, just trying to come up."

"You sell drugs?"

Jamil nodded. "That's about all I know how to do, Gee. I don't know nothing else."

"You can do more, Milli. You really can."

"No, I can't, and I've come to terms with that." He looked at her again. "See, girls like you and your cousin are so privileged. Y'all don't know nothing about the streets, and I'm not knocking you for that because it ain't your fault. But we see things two different ways. You have opportunities, you can grow up and get a good respectable job, marry you a respectable nigga, and have that nigga's kids. But me . . ." Jamil felt his throat getting tight as tears glossed his eyeballs. He quickly washed them away.

"A nigga like me, I can't do that shit. I am who I am, and that's who I'll forever be. You're a good girl. You're too good for me, and that's the only reason I'm even telling you any of this.

"You and I could never be together anyway because I ain't got shit to offer you. You could never take a dope boy home to your people and expect them to respect him. One of these bottom-of-the-barrel bitches could, and that shit would be cool because her parents would be able to tolerate an illiterate hoodlum like me," Jamil told her with a straight face.

Tears threatened to fall from his eyes and roll down his face as he spoke, but he held them in. Jamil took a deep breath when he felt himself getting overwhelmed before continuing.

"Don't nobody want my dumb ass." He chuckled again at something that wasn't even the least bit funny. "My own fucking parents don't even want me, so I know a woman like you . . ." He held his head down and took another deep breath to avoid his tears.

Jamil had been holding his true feelings about himself in for so long that now that they were finally coming out, he couldn't handle them. He wiped tear after tear as he tried to catch his breath. When he felt Gia's arms wrap around him, he gave way to the emotions that he'd been holding in for so long. She kneeled down in front of him trying to hold his head up so that she could see his face.

"It's going to be okay. I promise it's going to be okay." Gia circled her arms around his neck and held on to him tightly.

Jamil tried to pull away only for her to stand and wiggle her way into his lap. With her arms still around his neck, Gia held him tighter in her embrace. Being wrapped up in Gia was the best feeling in the world.

It was the only time in his entire life that he'd ever felt loved, and it was coming from a girl who hadn't known him any longer than a few hours cumulatively. Even if it was only going to last for this moment, Jamil was grateful for it. To feel sincere compassion and love, he would sacrifice every day of his life.

"A woman like you, Gee . . ." He tried again only to have his tears take over just as they had done the last time.

For the current moment, Jamil would gladly give away every moment of happiness he'd thought he felt thus far, because it was fake. Nothing about him before this moment was real. He'd been living a lie just to make himself feel better.

"Milli, I'm here for you. Everything will be better from now on."

"Gee,"—he sniffed hard and held his head up from the comfort of her breasts—"I'm not the man for you."

"You don't know that. You've made me feel things in these last few days that I haven't felt with any other man. Crazy, right?" She smiled down at him.

"You're too good for me." He tried catching his breath. "I can't give you anything."

"I don't want anything but your heart."

Jamil looked into her pretty brown eyes and felt so deeply in love, but just as quickly as it came, it was gone. Realizing his reality was too much for her, he was bummed out once again and began to sniffle. He felt like such a punk crying in front of her, but he couldn't help it.

Gia held him and rocked him until he was able to get a hold of himself. When he felt he'd had enough comforting, he washed his hand over his face and took another deep breath.

"Thank you, Gia, but we can't do this."

Jamil stood up, sat her down on the bed, and walked to the window. He held his hands on the top of his head and looked out as he tried to wrap his mind around not having her anymore. She had made him feel optimistic for the past few days, but that was all over now.

"Jamil, don't leave me." Gia wrapped her arms around him

from behind and laid her head against his back. "Stay here with me. In this moment. Let's just stay together."

"How can you love a person like me? You'll never be able to. I really ain't worthy."

Gia squeezed him tighter. "Yes, you are."

Jamil held his head down and looked at her hands resting against his stomach. "If only you knew the half, Gianna," he whispered.

Jamil was so embarrassed about his life that he couldn't even make himself say any more of it out loud. So when Gia's arms released from his body, he felt like collapsing. Before he could even stop himself, Jamil fell to his knees and held his head in his hands. This time his tears were trying to come a lot harder than before, but he held them in. He could no longer feel Gia's presence, and as badly as he wanted to accept it, he couldn't. At least not right now.

Jamil stood back up and turned to look for her. He found her sitting on the bed looking out at the city lights around him.

Now it was him who was kneeling in front of her. "Please stay, Gia. At least for tonight. Isn't that what you just told me? Just stay. I need you to stay here with me." He touched her face.

Gia touched his chest and maintained eye contact. "I'm not leaving you, Jamil."

With raised brows he asked, "Tonight?"

"Ever." Gia stood up and pulled him with her. "Stand up. We'll figure it all out. I'll let you get to know me a little more. Maybe then you'll be more comfortable with telling me everything about yourself. I know there's more. I feel it. Until then, I'll wait. I won't pressure you." She kneeled in front of him on the bed and pulled him to her so that they were eye to eye. "You've made it through life this long. With me you're going to make it even further." Her pretty, dark face was bright with a smile. She was lightening the mood, and he was grateful for it.

He tried to hold his head down again, but Gia stopped him. "Stop it, Jamil. Hold your head up. It doesn't matter that you don't want to tell me any of your business. I'll pull it out of you eventually."

They shared a brief laugh as he kissed the dimples in her cheeks. Even with him still in a somber mood, she was trying to make it better. Just what he needed. In that moment, Jamil didn't care what anybody said. He loved her. He felt it. He knew he did.

Jamil pulled her from the bed and she wrapped her legs around him. With her straddling his lap, he sat on the bed and held on to her sides. His eyes were low and puffy from all of the crying he'd failed so miserably at avoiding. He stared at her. Her eyes were the mirror image of his, red and swollen as well. They weren't as puffy as his, but were on the verge. It didn't matter, though, because she was still the most beautiful woman he'd ever seen. Even more so because her eyes were red and swollen on his behalf. Jamil marveled at her beauty as she ran her hands through his hair. Unable to stop himself, Jamil blew Gia's mind.

"I love you."

A comical yet awed smile crossed her face as she took his mouth with hers. She kissed him with so much passion he could feel it circulating through his body. Her tongue slid in and out of his mouth at a slow pace, savoring the taste of him.

"I love you too, Milli."

Heaven on earth. That's what it felt like to hear those words directed toward him. Jamil's eyes misted as he stared at her. When the tears began to fall, Gia sat on his lap comfortably and wiped them off.

"Why you crying?" she asked him.

"That's the first time anybody's ever said that to me."

Gia's heart sank and a look of pain crossed her face. She was hurting. Hurting for him, and it was all in her body language.

"I love you, Jamil." She kissed the tip of his nose while pushing some of his orange locs from his face.

When his body shivered, he knew this was it. This was the

woman he wanted to hear that from forever. The woman he wanted to feel this way about forever.

"Can I make love to you?" He stared at her with weary eyes.

That was one of the only things he was good at, and since words were failing him, he wanted to show her in another way how he felt. He knew if he could do nothing else, he could make her feel him. Feel his love.

"Please," she whispered into his mouth.

Jamil kissed her, taking her tongue onto his as he stood from the bed. He turned around, walked to the side of it, and laid her down, denting the mattress beneath her weight. Gia pulled him down with her by a few of his locs and held him close to her, kissing and rubbing all over him until he pulled away.

Jamil stood over her on the side of the bed and pulled his shirt over his head.

"You have more tattoos?" She looked at him in awe.

Jamil's entire chest and back were covered in tattoos, but only in places that his shirt could hide. Gia's eyes trailed over them all lovingly as he continued to undress. The beautifully designed tribal prints were shaded and darkened in various places, making her swoon.

"You like them?"

She nodded quickly.

"I'll get more." He touched the bare spot on his rib. "Right here. It's going to say 'Gianna.'" He was now smiling at her too.

"You might as well, since you call yourself in love with me already."

When his head fell back as he laughed wholeheartedly, Jamil felt a tight twinge in his heart at the same time as he felt his dick jump between her thighs. She was the sexiest thing he'd ever laid eyes on. They shared a carefree laughter, enjoying being lost in their candid moment. He was still chuckling a little when he began fumbling with his shorts.

"Wait. Let me do it." She sat up and unbuckled his belt before sliding the shorts, along with his boxers, to the ground.

Jamil stepped out of his clothes with his dick pointing straight out into her face. It was much larger than Kianoa's and made Gia's mouth water. That was the strangest thing, since she'd never indulged in oral pleasure a day in her adult life.

A little nervous and hesitant, Gia lay back and waited for him to make the next move. Towering over her naked in all of his light-skinned, dreadheaded, tattooed, thick heavy dick glory, Jamil licked his bottom lip before pulling at the towel she was wearing.

He sucked air though his teeth when it fell open. A raging desire for her overpowered every rational thought he had. All he wanted to do was savagely kiss and lick every part of her perfect body, from her perfectly perky breasts, down her flat stomach, to the perfectly bald piece of juicy chocolate he couldn't wait to put his mouth on.

Her body was nothing like he'd ever seen before. It was so toned and sculpted in every aspect. He was accustomed to seeing girls with stretch marks, a little bit of fat here or there, maybe a scar from the past adorning their skin, but never anything so pure and blemish free as Gianna's. The fact that her skin was his favorite shade of color was even better. He licked his lips as he ran his hand from her neck down the center of her body.

With the tip of his index finger, Jamil parted her lower lips and spread her moisture all over her opening. His fingers were skilled and smooth as he rubbed her in a way he knew she'd like.

"I want you so fucking bad, Gee." Breathlessly, he stood over her with his dreads hanging freely now.

They'd fallen loose and hung all around his face and shoulders as he stared down at her with an intense gaze of satisfaction. Gia's body shivered with his every touch as he lowered himself so that he was face-to-face with her bulging treasure of womanly power.

Wasting no time, he placed his entire mouth on it and began flicking his tongue over her clit while sucking her lightly. He moved his head from side to side just a tad to give her a rhythmic sensation as he slowly rolled his tongue around.

He took deep breaths in an effort to inhale her scent as he partook ravenously of her. Her hands on his head pulling his locs urged him further. He dove deeper, making sure to get his face wet. Gia's body was sensitive to his every touch and tasted heavenly, but right then he needed to be inside her. He'd save the rest of his foreplay for another time.

Jamil rose to his feet and hovered over her body, face slick and wet from her offerings. He slid into the bed, grabbing and pushing her farther up toward the pillows before lowering himself onto her. Her arms and legs went around him immediately, pulling him to her. With their chests pressed together, Jamil rubbed the large head of his dick around in her delectably rich chocolate.

"You're going to be everything to me, Gee." He pushed all the way in with no more warning, and she screamed. "I can see it." He gritted his teeth as he tried to hold off from coming so prematurely. "I can feel it."

Her pussy was so tight and warm, not to mention juicy. It was making all kinds of sloshing noises as he moved inside her. With her was where he belonged. The way her pussy fit his dick let him know that this was indeed his soul mate. No other woman had ever made him feel like she did.

Even with her nails digging the skin off his back, he was in bliss. He enjoyed the pain she was bringing him as he delivered her just the same. Her body welcomed him as if it knew that Daddy was finally home.

He grunted as a look of agony and pleasure traversed his face. "Feel my love, Gee."

Gia's legs were wrapped so tightly around his waist that he could hardly move, but he was a pro. He was going to damage her guts with or without her permission. Even with thoughts of dragging her body through pleasurable bliss, he couldn't. He didn't want to. He wanted to be molded with her like that forever.

"I love you, Milli," she moaned beneath him. "I think I love you too."

Jamil smirked because he knew the dick was good then.

"No, I do. I do love you." She patted his shoulder as her legs squeezed him farther into her.

Jamil grunted hungrily into her ear. "Fuuuuuuuckkk."

Gia yelped when he went deeper and began grinding a little slower. Slowly, she released the grip of her nails on the skin of his back and began to rub him, letting him know that she was no longer in pain.

"I'm making you feel good, Gee?" he asked her. Not in a sexual way, but in a way that let her know that he really needed to know. "Huh? How I make you feel, Gee? Tell me."

When she didn't say anything he pulled away so that he could see her face. Even with her pussy dripping the water he needed to survive, he still wanted to see her face. He had to look at something beautiful while they were doing something beautiful. Her eyes were on him and looking like they were going to burst open with fear and compassion.

"Talk to me Gee, please. Tell me how I make you feel."

He needed to know that he was making her body feel how her words made his heart feel. This was his way. She had to feel it. He was showing her. Giving her all he had.

"Gianna!" he begged.

"Oh, baby." She moaned when he moaned her name. "I love you, Milli. I love you so much. You're making me feel good. The best I've ever felt." She released a series of moans. "I want to keep feeling it. Don't ever stop."

Jamil closed his eyes and pounded all of the love and pressure he had built up for Gia into her tunnel of hot, sticky love. Just for him. His new home. With his eyes rolling and her legs shaking, Jamil thrust harder and harder until Gia was moaning loudly in his ear. He watched her face as the pleasure he'd given her took over her body.

"I think that's it, Milli!" Her eyes closed then opened right back up. "Is that it? Am I doing it?" Her eyes were wide with questioning. "I've never had an orgasm during sex before."

The pressure from her orgasm had her walls squeezing the life from his dick. He was so focused on watching her, he pulled away some so he could look down as he disappeared inside her.

"Oh fuck," he grunted.

"Ahhhhhh!" Gia released into his ear and on his dick at the same time.

"That's it, Gee." He leaned back down near her face. "That's it, baby. You're doing it."

That was all he needed to complete him. He came at the tail end of her orgasm, bringing about another one for her before their first session of lovemaking was over. Instead of pulling out, Jamil lay on top of her with his dick still nestled tightly within the walls of his newfound home. He kissed her lips softly as she rode her orgasmic wave.

When he felt that she was good, he rolled out of her and lay on the bed beside her. Gia turned over quickly and he pulled her the rest of the way so that she was lying on his chest. He rubbed her back absentmindedly as he thought about what would be next.

He'd bared just about everything to her, and she'd accepted it. As beautiful as their night had just been, all he could think about was her changing her mind about everything she'd said. Especially if the rest of his problems ever came out.

Gia kissed his chest. "You're safe with me."

"You mean everything you said?" He hadn't wanted to ask, but he couldn't afford any surprises.

"Every word. I love you."

"I've waited for the moment to be with you."

She snickered. "You didn't know me until a few days ago."

"No, I mean I've prayed for the moment God would send me someone who would love me past my flaws, and even if you are just saying it, I feel like it's real."

"That's because it is. Even though I'm a hoe. I can't believe I just had sex with you." Gia covered her face.

Jamil immediately moved her hands. "I don't think you're a hoe. We were just enjoying the moment. Don't be embarrassed."

She looked at him with worry in her eyes. "I know how y'all men are. Y'all love to talk about women that give it up fast." She groaned. "You're going to tell Iverson too, aren't you? Then you're probably not going to call me any more after this." She looked so annoyed he almost laughed in her face, but he masked it.

"Hell nah. I'm not gon' stop calling you. I love you, remember? You just better not tell anybody I was up in here crying and shit like a li'l bitch."

Gia laughed and shook her head, rubbing her locs across the pillow. "I wouldn't do that. I just said your secrets are safe with me. Why would I lie?"

He shrugged. "People lie."

"Not me."

The room fell quiet as Jamil and Gia lay in bed for another few minutes before making themselves get up to shower. Being that Gia was still extremely sore from the dick he'd just given her, he had to carry her into the bathroom as well as bathe her. He made sure to be extra gentle due to the fact she jumped anytime his hand grazed between her thighs.

Jamil hadn't meant to hurt her like that, but he'd wanted her to feel every ounce of emotion she'd made him feel. When he was done bathing her, he turned the water up a little warmer and held her up to it. The warm drops of water spraying against her aching body relaxed her a little more and he was able to take her out and dry her off.

He rubbed the lotion that he'd gotten from the hotel bathroom all over her body as she lay limply on one of the beds watching him. When he was sure that she was taken care of, he laid her in the other, dry bed and climbed in behind her. If he was able to take care of her like that every day for the rest of his life, then he would die a happy man.

His Gee . . . the perfect stranger who was turning out to be the answer to his prayers. Before turning off the last lamp, Jamil leaned over her shoulder to look at her face. She was sleeping and looked like a goddess. Her hair was thrown all over her pillow-case and her radiant skin was lighting up his world. He pressed his lips to her temple before shutting off the light and silently thanking God for, if nothing more, their night together. That was enough.

Chapter Seven

"Giving myself to Jamil felt like the right thing to do just by talking to him, so once I finally went all the way and chose to ignore the caution signs, I was the happiest I'd been in a long time. Many people will probably never understand the connection he and I have, and that's fine with me. As long as he knows that he's mine and I'm his, then that's all that matters."
—Gee

The wind blew into the open windows of the truck as Iverson sped down the highway. It was a little after ten o'clock the next morning, and the entire truck was quiet. Everyone was looking out of their windows, probably reflecting on the previous night.

If no one else was, Gia was. She'd awakened that morning wrapped tightly in Jamil's arms. It had felt so right, she'd closed her eyes and attempted to fall back to sleep but couldn't. All she kept thinking about was what he was going to think of her.

Though he'd said he wouldn't judge her based upon their premature revelations of love followed by their night of passion, that's just how men were. They would tell you one thing and do another. To further complicate her life, she hadn't had very much experience with men due to her running. She spent so much time training that she didn't have very much time for other things, mainly men. Kainoa had been her first everything, and he'd never made her body react to sex the way Jamil had. She'd been quietly torturing herself all morning.

She lay still, enjoying the moment until his breathing changed and she could tell he'd woken up. Instead of torturing herself any further, she turned in his embrace and caught his gaze, but only for a second. He looked to be thinking of a few things himself as he lay staring at the wall behind her head.

"You okay?" she'd asked quietly, trying not to give him a whiff of her morning breath.

"Yeah. You?"

"Yeah."

Questions and a tiny bit of awkwardness circled them as neither of them said anything else. Gia tried her hardest not to give in to the negative things that kept coming to her mind, but when she could no longer tame them, she scooted away from him. Well, at least she tried.

Jamil's grip around her waist, pulling her back to him, stopped her. He finally looked down into her face. Concern was etched through his eyebrows.

"You running?"

Am I running? Gia looked to the side for a moment, trying to decide for her own self if she was, in fact, running.

"I guess our one night is over?"

"It doesn't have to be." She spoke meekly and a little too quietly. Had they been anywhere but the sanctity of their silent hotel room, he probably wouldn't have heard her.

He pecked her forehead. "I don't want it to be."

"Then it isn't."

His lips pressed against her forehead again. "Good. Let's live in this night for a while."

"I think I can do that."

After that, Jamil released Gia so that she could move out of the bed and go on about her business. She took her time in the bathroom freshening up as best she could before sliding on her new pair of running shorts and Nike shirt she'd brought out of the car last night.

Being that she hadn't brought any panties with her, she didn't bother to put any on. She gathered all of her locs up into her hands before wrapping a band around them twice to secure her ponytail.

When she emerged from the bathroom, she grabbed her iPod from her purse and looked over at Jamil. He was still lying in the bed but was now turned over onto his back.

"I'm going down to the gym to run a few miles," she informed him.

He sat up in the bed, allowing the sheet to fall around his waist. The drowsiness still covering his face was so cute. She smiled at him and leaned her head to the side a little as he watched her watch him.

"You was just gon' leave me?"

"I didn't know you wanted to go."

He rubbed his eyes. "Yeah. Let me throw something on real quick." He looked around the floor. "Damn, I didn't bring anything else."

Gia dug into her bag and pulled out the black Nike shorts and bright orange shirt he'd picked out from the outlet.

"I brought these out of the car for you to change into today."

Before smiling, his eyes trailed from the clothes in her hand to her face. "Look at you."

Gia blushed before tossing the clothes onto the bed.

"Appreciate that, bae. I hadn't even thought about it."

"I figured that."

Jamil sat in the same spot for a few more minutes before standing from the bed. Gia tried her best not to stare at his semierect penis as he stretched. She crossed her legs a little tighter as her stomach flipped. Replays from their sex had her feeling bubbly inside.

She looked over at him again quickly, trying to steal another glance of his perfectly sexy naked body. It was so much lighter than hers, and so much larger. His arms were ripped with muscles, as were his chest and legs. His thighs were so large and muscular that she would have almost thought he ran too.

"What you looking at, Gee?" His voice brought her eyes to his face.

"Your thighs. They're so big and toned like mine, but I'm sure you don't run." She giggled to herself.

"I do run . . . from the police."

He was quiet for a minute until they both burst out laughing. He grabbed the clothes and walked past her, rubbing his shirt over her face. She swatted his hand away before watching him go into the bathroom.

After another ten minutes they grabbed their things from the room, made sure they hadn't left anything, and left. Checkout was soon, so they figured after their workout, versus going back to the room, they could walk and grab a bite to eat.

With Jamil walking so tall and out of the ordinary next to her, Gia felt small and safe. Her eyes roamed the broad open windows of their hotel. The sidewalks of the streets were packed with pedestrians either shopping or casually strolling with their family and friends. She was so busy people watching that he decided it was best if he held her hand whenever they moved through large throngs of people and pulled her to him so that her back was resting against his chest as they rode the elevator.

"You want to just run to the Waffle House down the street?" Gia looked up from the Google website on her phone.

"How you know it's a Waffle House near us?"

"I just looked it up."

"And you want to run there?"

She smiled and nodded. "Yes. It's not that far. It says here it's only like two miles away."

Jamil frowned like he wanted to decline, but she urged him to say yes, so he gave in. Once they were outside, he instantly regretted his decision to run and tried to change his mind, but she wouldn't allow him. Not only was it hot, but there were too many people to try and jog through.

"Nope. Come on, Milli. It's not that far, baby."

He turned his nose up at her playfully and they began running, but only because she called him baby. The entire run there ended up being a little longer due to the fact she had to keep stopping to let him take a breath. She couldn't stop the laughter that escaped her lips when she looked behind her and he was bent over with his hands resting on his knees, breathing hard.

"Damn, Gee, hold on. I can't run no more."

She was still laughing as she jogged in place.

"I don't know why you fucking laughing. When I make you carry me the rest of the way you won't be laughing."

"Jamil, come on and stop cutting up. It's right there. You see it?" She pointed down the street and he followed her finger.

"Fuck me!" he yelled breathlessly when he saw how far they still had to run. "You giving me some more pussy for this shit here."

Gia jogged to him and pulled his arm as she laughed. "I got you."

He looked at her with a serious expression as he stood back up, preparing to run again. "Today." He used his pointer finger, pointing at nothing really, just needing to reiterate her timing for sex.

Her hair slid over in her ponytail a little as she leaned her head to the side laughing at him.

"Okay, Milli Rock. Bring your complaining butt on."

He slapped her butt hard before taking off in a light jog ahead of her. "Don't worry. I'ma make you feel my pain later. Bring your ass on," he yelled over his shoulder.

Gia caught up to him and they jogged the rest of the way together, bickering back and forth the entire way. When they finally got to the restaurant, Jamil nearly collapsed into one of the empty booths. Gia slid in gracefully across from him.

He used a napkin to dab the sweat from his face as he looked over at her. "Nah, you come sit over here by me. Don't be trying to run from me now, because you know I should beat your ass for the shit you just pulled."

Gia shook her head and stayed on her side. "Just order you some water and hush."

The waitress came over, took their orders, and had their food on the table in no time. Breakfast went extremely well, and before they knew it, they were back in the lobby of the hotel waiting for Oni and Iverson to come from whatever sex trap they'd built the night before.

Gia was more than positive that if she, Gia, the most reserved and goody-good female in the universe, had given up the goods to a practical stranger, then Oni had as well.

She was sitting in the large fluffy chair in the center of the lobby reading the newspaper when she saw Oni and Iverson headed their way. Both of them looked terrible, Oni a little more than Iverson. With the same clothing from the day before, they moved sluggishly, with a very visible hangover still lingering.

"The fuck y'all been doing all night?" Jamil asked as soon as Iverson held his hand out to dap him up.

A slick smile spread across Iverson's face as he shook his head subtly. "Shit, what haven't we been doing is the question."

Gia frowned as she looked up at Oni standing there looking crazy. Her clothing was stretched out, hair all over the place, and she looked tired as hell. Her hands were crossed in front of her as she looked down at the floor. She looked as if she was embarrassed, but Gia knew that couldn't be it.

Oni had never been the type of female to be embarrassed about anything that she'd done. Iverson must have had her doing some seriously off-the-wall mess for her to be standing there acting as if she was afraid to even make eye contact. Gia's gaze shot up toward Iverson as he whispered to Jamil before her frown deepened.

"Come with me to the bathroom." Gia stood from the chair and pulled Oni's arm in one swift movement.

Oni followed obediently as they made their way through the lobby and over to the restrooms in the corner. Once they were inside, Gia pulled her toward the sink and stared at her in the mirror. The two of them were quiet for a minute while Oni kept her eyes cast down to the floor.

"Oni, what is wrong with you? What did that nigga do?" Gia's voice held a little more authority than it had before.

"Nothing."

"Well, why he out there smiling and telling Jamil all your business while you standing in here looking like a fool?"

Oni looked up at Gia only to look away again. She shrugged. "Of course we had sex."

"You have sex all the time. What's different this time?"

"It wasn't the kind I always have." She looked a little sad as she looked away again. "It was different."

"How?" Gia probed. "Worse than granddaddy dick?" Gia tried to make a joke about Isaac to lighten the mood, but it didn't help.

"I really don't want to talk about it right now. Can we just wait until we get home? I'm so tired."

Gia genuinely felt sorry for her cousin, so she agreed to wait to finish their conversation. Though their talk was going to wait, Oni's appearance was not. Still dressed in the dark blue striped dress and red sandals, Oni stood still, obviously waiting for Gia to tell her what to do next.

Gia dug into her purse and pulled out the black brush she'd bought for her Auntie Ann the day before at the outlet and turned Oni so that she was facing the mirror. Once she flipped the water on and stood behind her, she began brushing her hair for her.

The moment the water hit Oni's hair, it began to curl up even more than before. Gia brushed over the loose curls in her head, smoothing them out so that her hair would go into a neat ball. Oni stood obediently still in front of Gia until she finished. Gia then wet some paper towels and handed them to Oni.

"Wash your face," Gia said to Oni, putting the brush back in her purse.

Oni did that, then added the lotion and lip gloss Gia had extended to her. Seeing herself starting to come back to life must have perked her up some, because once she handed Gia her things back, she smoothed her dress out over her small body.

"Feel better?" Gia smiled at her.

Oni nodded with a light smile.

"You look better. Here, chew this, because if you ain't even comb your hair this morning, I'm sure you ain't brush your teeth either." The small stick of gum disappeared from Gia's hand and into Oni's mouth. "Now come on. At least let the man know why he fucked you like a lunatic last night. Don't be around here looking like no damn prostitute no more."

Gia and Oni chuckled as they left the bathroom together. Oni looped her arm through Gia's and laid her head on her shoulder as they walked back to the men.

"Thanks, bestie," Oni whispered as they walked. "And it was definitely worse than granddaddy dick." She giggled and so did Gia.

"No problem. We all have our moments, but that's hard to believe." Gia was speaking to Oni but had just caught Jamil's eyes.

He was staring at her so intently it almost made her feel as if she was completely nude in the packed lobby. The way his eyes trekked up and down her body, pausing on her face, had her stuck. She'd almost stopped walking when she watched him bite his bottom lip before winking. She blushed and he turned his head.

"Gia, Jamil so fine, girl," Oni said.

"You just don't know the half."

"What took y'all so long? Y'all stomach must hurt or something," Iverson asked as the ladies approached them.

Like it had done earlier, Gia's nose turned up at him. "Boy, shut up. Y'all ready to go?" She looked between Jamil and Iverson.

Once they all agreed to leave, they walked out to Iverson's truck and got on the road back to Columbus. They hadn't been driving any longer than maybe thirty minutes, and in Gia's opinion, they were getting there too fast.

Being cuddled up on the backseat with Jamil was everything, and she wasn't ready for it to end. She wished she could stay with him all day and do absolutely nothing, but she already knew that wasn't happening. She and Oni had stayed out all night, and even though they had done their best to put themselves back together, they were still in need of showers and fresh clothes.

"What's on your mind?" Jamil's soft lips brushed against her ear as he whispered to her.

"You," she replied. His arm was wrapped around her shoulders with her head pulled close to his chest.

"What about me?"

"Spending time with you."

"What's up with it, then? You chilling with me when we get back or what?"

Gia shook her head. "Not right away. We have to go home."

Jamil nodded and sat back in the seat. With her head still resting in the crook of his arm, he gazed out the window.

Gia pushed some of his hair from his face, giving herself a better view of his profile. Jamil was so gorgeous. She didn't know where such a unique-looking man had ever come from, but she was thankful.

The dark orange stubble along his jawline, the strong features of such a rugged-looking man aligned with those perfectly plump lips, made Gia's heart flutter. Gia had it bad for this man, and she wasn't even ashamed. Though it had only been a few days, the feeling of him inside her body last night had pushed her into an entirely different element. He was hers, and she wanted so desperately to be his.

"I can come scoop you up later if you want me to," Jamil offered.

"From where?"

He shrugged. "Your spot. Wherever, it don't matter to me. Wherever you gon' be, I want to be there too."

Gia was smiling when he looked down at her. She nodded at him, letting him know that she would like that.

"Okay, just let me get home and fill some things out first, then I'll let you know."

"Cool."

For the rest of the ride home they sat cuddled up on the backseat and whispered to each other about anything and everything. When Iverson finally stopped the truck in the Walmart parking lot where Oni had left her truck, Gia was slightly disappointed.

But instead of wallowing in her disappointment, she grabbed her things and prepared to get out. Jamil opened his door and slid out before helping her the rest of the way. When she was standing upright, he moved to the back of the truck and began getting the bags they'd gotten from the outlet and putting them into Oni's trunk.

"Your friend is so lazy," Gia told him as they stood at the back of Oni's truck.

Not that Jamil needed any help, but Iverson hadn't moved from the front seat yet, not offering to help Jamil with the bags or even hugging Oni goodbye. Gia could tell it bothered Oni a little just by the way she lingered at his window begging him to get out.

When he'd told her no for the fifth time, Gia got disgusted and turned her attention back to Jamil. He was standing directly in front of her with his hands resting comfortably in his pockets, his long, bright locs resting around his bulging shoulders and chest muscles. His hazel eyes studied her face as she looked at Iverson with disdain.

"That's just how that nigga is. He too pretty to do anything hard," Jamil said, taking note of the look Gia had given Iverson.

"That's no excuse for having poor manners."

"As long as I don't have poor manners, then it doesn't matter." Jamil stepped closer to her and pecked the tip of her nose. "Am I going to see you later?"

"I told you I don't know yet. I have to see when we get back to Oni's house."

He nodded and released his hands from his pockets to pull her to him for a hug. He held on to her tightly, pulling her as close as he could get her to him. Her smaller frame tucked perfectly against his. With her arms circling his waist while his went around the top of her shoulders, he kissed the side of her face and whispered into her ear.

"We still living in last night?"

She nodded.

"Maybe that's why I can still feel your body gripping mine." He kissed the side of her face again when she shivered in his embrace. "The way you held me close when I was up in it had me feeling too good." He let one of his hands drift down the side of her body, gripping her thick, toned thigh before stopping and rubbing it lightly. "I feel safe with these around me."

"Jamil." She sighed into his chest.

Gia couldn't take it. The way he was talking to her had her body and mind on fire. Was this the way it was supposed to be when you were with a man? Because in the past when she'd been with Kainoa, it had been nothing of the sort. It was cool, and he got the job done, but Jamil felt new. He made her feel like she had been missing out on her entire life just by being in his arms.

It was crazy, because now she understood fully why Oni was always entertaining men. If any of them made Oni feel how Jamil made Gia feel, then she was about to be on the same path as her cousin, but with Jamil, of course.

"You remember how you was breathing in my ear and running your hands through my hair last night?"

Gia nodded.

"I loved that shit. I swear I did. Then when you finally bust, your pussy was squeezing my dick so tight like it didn't want to let it go or something." He kissed her ear, then the side of her neck before pulling back some so that he could look into her face. "I didn't want you to let me go."

Gia tried her hardest to match the intensity in his stare, but it was hard because he was so unnerving. The way he looked at her made her feel nervous on the inside. That's why when he leaned forward and pressed his lips onto hers, she had to hold on to his shirt for support. If she hadn't, she probably would have fainted right there in the parking lot.

A deep moan escaped her lips in the form of his name when he finally pulled away. "You make my heart beat fast."

"Good." He pecked her lips once more before pulling her fully back into his embrace. He hugged her for a long time before letting her go and pulling her hand so that he could lead her to the passenger side of Oni's truck. After helping her in, he winked at her once more before heading back to Iverson's truck.

Gia watched him until he was in the car and they were pulling away. "Jamil is too much," she told Oni as she buckled her seat belt.

"Girl, you're lucky." Oni looked over at her.

"I thought Iverson was cool? Tell me what happened."

Oni shook her head. "Nah, let me get me a shower and relax some first. I need to get my mind right."

Gia's face distorted some in confusion. "What that nigga do to you, Oni? It had to be something, because you're acting like you're scared to talk. It must have been serious."

"It was, girl. It was."

That was all of the talking that the girls did on the ride home.

Gia was still a little tired from her late night and early-morning run, so she hopped in the shower again before going to her room to take a nap. Oni had told her she was about to do the same thing and that they would talk once they got up. With no objections, Gia went to the guest room and climbed into the comfortable bed.

She was about to close her eyes when she had the strong urge to talk to Jamil. She leaned over the bed, quickly snatched her phone from her purse, and sent him a text.

Gia: Thinking about you

She lay there waiting for a reply, but it never came. However, when her phone rang, she remembered his no-texting policy. She slapped her forehead lightly before answering it hesitantly.

"What's up, Gee? With your hardheaded ass."

She giggled beneath the covers. "I'm sorry. I keep forgetting."

"I see. What's going on, li'l chocolate baby? Tell me what's on your mind."

Gia smiled at him calling her his li'l chocolate baby.

"Nothing for real. I was just about to take a nap and wanted to let you know I was thinking about you."

"Nah, nigga, give me my money. You know what you owe. Don't fuck around," Gia heard him say before he cleared his throat and came back onto the line.

"My fault, baby. These niggas out here trying to play games."

"It's cool."

"But you said you was thinking about me?"

"Uh-huh."

"Well, let me give you something else to think about real quick. You listening?"

"Yeah."

"When we chill later, I want you to sit on my lap and wrap your legs around my waist. You think you can do that for me?"

Gia could feel heat rising over her body, and she wasn't even near him.

"You think you can handle that, Gee?"

"Yeah, I can do that." She spoke quietly.

"A'ight. Get you some rest, baby. Daddy will holla at you later."

Gia's smile spread further across her face. "Who said you were my daddy?"

"Ask me that again later and I'll tell you. For right now just say I'll see you later, Daddy, and get off the phone."

A laugh rolled off of her lips effortlessly. "I am not about to call you Daddy, Jamil."

She could hear him laughing. "You will soon. Get some rest, Gee."

"Bye, Milli."

"Peace, bae."

Gia hung her phone up, completely enthralled in Jamil. She lay on her back thinking about him and their night together as she closed her eyes. If she was lucky, she would dream of him while she slept.

The block was jumping so hard from the one night he'd been away, and all day Jamil had been paying for it. Going from here to there picking up the money he'd missed out on was slowly becoming a headache. Niggas was trying to duck and dodge instead of just paying what they owed, and quite frankly he was growing tired of it.

He had been on the block pretty much his entire life. Truth be told, he was ready for something new. The game was getting to be too much of a struggle, and he was getting bored. He'd been stacking his paper and building since he was a kid. He was ready for something bigger. If the job in Miami didn't come into play soon, he was going to explode.

Now a grown man, he was ready to move past the normal street life. It just didn't feel like the block had much to offer him. His only issue was what he could do to change it. Hustling day in and day out, running dope for others until he was established enough to work for himself had been his main plan. Now that he'd done it, it didn't mean as much. He was ready to be the boss.

When he was a child looking up to the dealers who had put

him on, all he aspired to be was larger than them one day. He worked as hard as he could, doing whatever he could to make things happen. Though it didn't always come easy, it came. By his sixteenth birthday he was seeing more money than any young hustler his age.

Because of the way he moved and stayed to himself, Jamil ended up gaining the respect of many of the older cats, which in return garnered the respect of the ones his age as well. He had a good street team and more money than he knew what to do with. For most people from his hood that was the American dream, but not for Jamil.

He was different and always had been. From his social status to his personal life at home, he wasn't like everyone else. Always having been a private person, no one really knew anything about him other than what he told them, which was next to nothing. He never really saw the point of letting his left hand know what his right hand was doing.

That was the main reason he was struggling with the biggest decision of his life right then. Shock had called him that morning with a few updates on the Miami spot, and though that was what he had been wanting, Jamil was hesitant to take it. Had these same stipulations been mentioned a few weeks ago, Jamil probably wouldn't have given it a second thought. But today, today he wasn't feeling it.

Shock had asked Jamil and Iverson to meet with him later to discuss specifics, but just from the rundown he'd received on the phone, Jamil could already tell this wasn't an avenue he wanted to travel. He was tired of being looked at as the bad kid; the boy who would never grow up to be anything. For some reason he was ready to prove everyone wrong. His only issue was there was no way that he could. Not without messing things up with Gia.

"Where you been?" Zanetta asked as soon as Jamil walked in the front door.

"Out. Why?"

She continued washing the windows with the dusty rag and the bottle of cleaner. "You hungry?"

Jamil scrunched his eyes up at her. What in the hell had she been smoking that had her caring whether he was hungry or not? She never asked that. If she cooked, she made sure to feed herself and Owen. Anything left he was free to have, but to just ask was he hungry, now that was unheard of.

"I'm straight."

"I made you some steak and mashed potatoes. It's some carrots in the Crock-Pot too."

Anybody that knew Jamil personally knew how much he loved steak and potatoes. So for her to not only ask was he hungry but to have made his favorite meal, she was up to something.

Jamil walked farther into the living room and took a seat on the sofa. "What you need, Ma?"

She looked back at him with a smile. "Nothing. Just eat, baby. Your father is out of town for the weekend. He says he's going to the casino with your uncle George. So it's just the two of us this weekend."

And there it is.

For as long as he could remember, whenever his father wasn't around, his mother was on her best behavior. Treating him like a mother was supposed to treat her child. Too bad for her that was over for him. He had long ago grown out of her sympathy treatment. When he was younger he would soak it up and even pray to God to keep his father away, but he was grown now. He wanted no part of what Zanetta had to offer because as soon as Owen returned home, she was back to being his drug addict sidekick.

"You had company the other day?" She disrupted his thoughts.

"Yeah. For a minute."

"A woman?" Zanetta turned around with a bright smile on her face and took a seat on the edge of the sofa. "Who is she?"

As badly as Jamil wanted to stay angry with her and ignore her efforts at being a normal mother, the kid in him desired this: a normal conversation with his mother about the girl he liked. Her thoughts and advice on Gia would be a nice try at a normal relationship, so he obliged.

Jamil nodded and tried to hide the smile that spread across his face when he thought about Gia's sexy chocolate ass.

"She's got you smiling that hard? She must really be something." Zanetta's face was bright as she waited for Jamil to spill the beans.

"She's different, Ma. Nothing like the girls from around here. She's a runner, just graduated from college and is about to play softball in the upcoming Olympics. Smart, beautiful, classy . . . she's just really nice." He looked from his hands up to his mother's face.

For a moment Zanetta almost looked like a normal mother, the way she smiled and listened intently to him speak about Gia. He wasn't sure, but he thought he even saw a few tears in her eyes.

"That's wonderful, baby. What's her name?"

"Gianna. I call her Gee, though."

"What does she think of you? Does she smile like this when speaking of you?"

Jamil's cheeks were sure to be red as he pictured Gia actually sitting down telling her parents about him. He shrugged. "Probably. She smiles a lot when I'm around her. I'm sure she likes me a lot too." He pushed some of his hair out of his face as he leaned forward, resting his forearms on his knees. "She told me she loved me last night."

Zanetta yelped and covered her mouth with her hand. "Oh, Jamil. That's so sweet, baby. You think she was serious?"

This time, along with his shoulder shrug came a small laugh. "Maybe, maybe not. I was giving her some of this D. That might have had a lot to do with it."

Zanetta leaned over and slapped Jamil's shoulder. "Jamil. You should be ashamed of yourself."

The two of them shared a quick laugh as he sat back in his seat again. "For real, Ma. You know how when you're about to get in trouble or you're really nervous about something and your stomach starts feeling all crazy?"

Zanetta wiped her eyes and nodded.

"That's how I feel when she's around or when I talk to her on the phone."

"Jamil, that's so sweet, baby. I am so happy for you." She paused for a minute and looked away before looking back at him. "Do you think I could meet her? I mean, I've never seen you talk about a woman. Not that we talk much." She sounded a tad bit sad. "But I would love to meet her."

All signs of emotion left Jamil's face as he stared at his mother. He looked at her long and hard, trying to see if she was serious. He just knew she couldn't be. Why on earth would she think he was going to bring Gia to their house for her to embarrass him? Apparently she picked up on his skepticism, because she touched his arm before he could respond.

"Today's a good day. I've only been cleaning. Nothing else. I cooked and that was it. I promise."

Though she didn't want to say it, he could tell she was trying to let him know that she hadn't done any drugs yet.

"I don't know, Ma."

"Please, Jamil. Just for a little while. When you're ready for her to leave, then she can leave. Let's just enjoy our time."

Jamil wanted so badly to believe that Zanetta wasn't going to flip and show out in front of Gia, but he just didn't. His gut was telling him that it was a bad idea and to leave Gia out of it, but his heart loved his mother and wanted to make her happy. Even if it was only for the weekend.

"Let me call her and see what her plans are for today, and I'll let you know."

Zanetta smiled and clapped her hands. "Let me finish cleaning and I'll bake you guys some dessert. Do you know what her favorite dessert is?"

Jamil shook his head at his mother's excitement. "I'll ask her."

"Well, hurry up so I can go to the store and get it."

"I'll go with you."

Jamil didn't trust her outside alone. She could run into any one of the corner boys and ruin the whole day. Nor did he trust leaving her alone while he went to the store for her. There was no telling what she and Owen had stashed away in the house for a rainy day. He wouldn't tell her that, though.

She was having a good day, and he would allow it to sustain. He'd just let her think he wanted to spend time with her. No matter what she'd done to him in life, she was still his mother. Even though he tried to fight it as hard as he could, he loved her.

"That's even better. Call her." Zanetta touched his shoulder as she passed him and left the living room.

Jamil sat still for a minute just staring at his phone trying to decide if he really wanted to do this. He was still thinking when Zanetta walked past him again with a sheet of paper and a pencil.

"I need to make a quick grocery list," she yelled over her shoulder as she entered the kitchen. "Call her, Jamil. Check with her about dessert."

After a deep breath, Jamil scrolled through his phone until he saw the letters *GIA* and pressed Send. It rang a few times before she answered groggily.

"I know you ain't still asleep, Gee?"

She giggled a little. "You wore me out last night, Milli. I'm tired. I don't normally get a workout like that."

He stretched his legs out in front of him and rubbed his hand across his stomach. "That's good to know. How about you come over and let me give you a massage?"

"To your house?"

"Yeah. I can come scoop you when I leave the store with my mama."

"What time?"

"In about another hour." He paused before saying what was

next. "She wants you to come over for dinner." He held his breath waiting for Gia to respond.

He heard some moving around before her voice cleared up a little. It had even gone up an octave. "Who? Your mama?"

He chuckled at the alarm in her voice. "Yeah. She cooked my favorite food and told me to invite you over."

"Well, in that case, yeah, you can come get me. I'd love to meet her."

"For real?" Jamil asked in disbelief.

"Yeah. I'm good with mamas. She's going to love me."

Jamil and Gia both chuckled a little at that.

"Cool. Well, get dressed and I'll call you when I'm on my way."

"If you want, I can have Oni bring me over there."

He checked his watch and looked down at what he was wearing. He would like to shower and change, so he agreed with that. He told her to give him about an hour and a half. Once they finalized plans and were about to hang up, Jamil remembered what his mother had said.

"Oh, Gee, hold on. She asked what your favorite dessert is. She's going to make it, I guess."

"Key lime cake with cream cheese icing and pecans on top." The smile in her voice didn't go unnoticed.

"Bet. See you in a few."

"I can't wait, Milli."

"Me either, Gee."

The two of them ended their call and he walked into the kitchen. Zanetta was looking in the cabinet with all of her seasonings. When she heard Jamil enter she turned to face him.

"What'd she say?"

"Key lime cake with cream cheese icing and pecans on top," Jamil told her with a smile on his face that matched hers.

"Did you tell her that was your favorite too?"

He shook his head.

"Aww, Jamil." Zanetta walked over and touched his cheek. "You

like her, and I just love it. Let me get my shoes and I'll be ready."
She left the kitchen.

Jamil leaned against the counter, digging in his pockets to make sure he had money. When he was ready, he went to the door to wait on his mother. He wasn't sure why God chose this day of all days to make it a good one, but he was thankful. Hopefully it would continue.

Chapter Eight

"Talking about got a nigga head gone? My muthafucking Gee keeps ya boy head in the clouds. She's so fucking amazing that it's hard for a hood nigga like myself to even believe she's real. You ever wanted something so bad, then you finally get it? That's how I feel every time I'm around Gee. At this very moment, if it's one thing that I could have for the rest of my life, it would be Gianna's li'l sexy ass."—Milli

"You are? That is amazing, sweetheart." Zanetta sat at the head of the table rubbing the top of Gia's hand.

She and Gia had been talking about Gia's life with track for the past few minutes, and they both looked to be enjoying it. Jamil, on the other hand, stood quietly at the door of the kitchen watching the two of them interact so lovingly.

Like she'd said, Gia really was good with mothers. Zanetta hadn't stopped talking since Gia arrived. From the moment Gia entered their house, Zanetta had kidnapped her and held her hostage. Every ounce of conversation that had taken place with Gia was with Zanetta.

Had she not jumped in his arms as soon as he opened the door, Jamil would have wondered if she'd even noticed that he was there.

"Yes, ma'am. Just for now, though," Gia said. "As soon as the time comes, I'm going to race against her and beat her, then I'll be number one in the nation." Gia gushed, "I can't wait. I've been training nonstop for that race and the Olympics so I'll be ready when it all finally does happen."

"That is so wonderful, Gianna. Make sure when that race happens that I'm there. I want front-row seats. Right next to your parents. I most definitely want to be at the Olympics cheering you on!" Zanetta touched the side of Gia's face. "You hear me?"

Gia nodded with a large smile on her face, the tiny nose ring catching Jamil's eye every time her head moved.

"I sure will. Hopefully your son will bring you with him." Gia looked over at Jamil with a sly smirk.

Jamil held a straight face as both of the women looked at him for his response.

"He'll bring me. Either that or I'll beat his ass."

Zanetta and Gia laughed like that was the funniest thing she'd said all night. Jamil didn't really see the humor in it, but he smiled anyway. Anytime Zanetta referenced him and beating in the same sentence, it brought back bad memories. Because he was actually enjoying his evening, he decided to disregard that comment and grab more cake from the kitchen.

When he came back, Gia's eyes were on the spot he had been standing in. When she saw him with the plate of cake, she smiled and held her plate up toward him.

"Can you give me another piece, please?" Gia asked him.

Jamil hadn't eaten any of his piece yet, so he exchanged plates with her and took her empty one. Zanetta smiled at his thoughtfulness and blew him a kiss as he walked back into the kitchen.

"So, Gia, tell me, baby, how long are you going to be here before Olympic training starts?" Zanetta resumed taking over the conversation with Gia.

That question had Jamil pausing as he stood in the middle of the kitchen floor. He too wanted to know the answer to that. He had been meaning to ask her, but it slipped his mind every time they were together.

"I'm leaving at the end of the summer, so a little less than two months then I have to go," Gia answered.

Less than two months? Jamil thought to himself.

Jamil's heart sank. That wasn't enough time to do much of anything. Just when they got to know each other it would be time for her to go. He tried to feel indifferent about it because he had known since meeting her that she wasn't there to stay. He just hadn't known it would be that soon.

"I'm so proud of you, sweetheart," Zanetta said to Gia. "That is amazing."

"Thank you," Gia said just as Jamil walked back into the dining room empty-handed.

"I thought you were getting more cake." Gia looked at him.

He shook his head and walked into the living room, taking a seat on the sofa. "Changed my mind."

His tone sounded a little more bummed out than he'd thought it would. He hadn't meant for her to hear how her words had affected him, so he tried to change the subject quickly.

"Ma, you need me to help you clean the kitchen?"

"No, baby, I got it," Zanetta replied. "You spend time with Gia. I can handle it."

He nodded and flipped the TV on. A few moments later Gia took up the space next to him. Since his legs were already propped up on the coffee table, she kicked her sandals off and threw her legs over his. She then wrapped both of her arms around him and laid her head on his shoulder.

"What's wrong, Milli?"

"Nothing."

"You're lying. Tell me."

"It ain't nothing."

"Don't lie."

"I said it ain't nothing," he snapped.

Gia sat up and looked at him so that she could see his face.

"Who you talking to?" Her eyebrows were raised as she looked at him, waiting for him to tell her who he had been getting snappy with.

"Gee, sit your ass back. You ain't hard."

"Never said I was, but I still need to know who you think you're talking to."

Jamil looked at her mouth as she spoke and how her lips moved so seductively over her teeth, her big round eyes staring back at him, slightly slanted in each corner. The light smell of whatever lotion or perfume she was wearing wafted up his nose with every breath he took. Her overall presence was too much for him to ignore, and her being only inches away from his mouth didn't make it any better.

With one swift motion, Jamil grabbed the back of her head and pulled her to his mouth. His lips claimed hers as his. Urgently and full of aggression, Jamil assaulted her lips with a hunger so strong he was sure she could feel it through his tongue.

They were still kissing when he felt her hands on his stomach pushing him away. "Stop it. Your mama is in there."

He shrugged. "She doesn't care."

"That's disrespectful, Milli."

He stared at her lips as she spoke. "If you say so." He looked back toward the TV. "You want to go in my room?"

Gia looked around for a minute before nodding.

Jamil stood first and pulled her behind him. She followed him down the hallway and into his room. He closed and locked the door before grabbing her and pushing her against the wall. Without giving her time to do anything more than hold on to his shirt, Jamil pressed his body flat against hers.

His mouth was on hers again immediately, pulling and tugging at the softness of her lips. With rough, hungry hands, he grabbed at the back of her thighs, pulling the bottom half of her body to his. The feel of her in his hands made him feel animalistic, almost like he was losing control.

"Wrap your legs around me." He spoke into her mouth as he lifted her into his hands.

Like she'd been told, Gia wrapped both of her long legs around his waist as he held her up by her butt. Her arms circled his neck and pulled at his hair. The way her fingertips massaged his scalp had his dick growing stronger and stronger in his pants.

"Milli," she moaned into his ear as he kissed and sucked on her neck. "I love you."

"Shit, Gee," he grunted as he paused his movement and just held her. "I love you too, baby." He kissed her mouth sloppily before taking her bottom lip between his teeth and sucking on it. "I love you too."

Gia sighed inwardly, relaxing in his arms. Jamil still didn't know if the love they shared was real or if it was just something nice to say in the midst of heated moments, but he felt it. He wanted to believe it was true even if it wasn't. So versus allowing his mind to get the best of him, he walked over to his bed and sat down with Gia on his lap.

She was grinding all over his hard dick as she kissed him. He was more than positive that she didn't know what she was doing to him with each move she made. Her body shifted so gracefully with every roll of her hips. The way she held on to his neck and moved so passionately against him revealed her desire for his love.

"Lift up for a minute, Gee."

Gia lifted only enough for him to pull down the black gym shorts he was wearing. As soon as he did, his dick sprang to action, standing tall between the two of them. He looked at her as she looked at it. He waited to see whether she was going to do something or if he was going to have to make the first move.

After a few more seconds passed and she was still staring at it, Jamil grabbed her hand and placed it on his dick. He moved her hand up and down slowly, his hand atop hers. Her soft fingers curved around his shaft. Her fingers grazing over the head sent pleasure-filled currents through his body.

His head fell back and his eyes closed as he enjoyed the feel of her rubbing on him. He moved his hand once he felt she was comfortable enough to do it herself. He leaned back on his elbows to watch her. Seated on his lap with his dick in her hand, Gia looked like a fucking dream.

All of her locs were hanging down around her shoulders, framing her beautiful face. Her mouth was balled slightly as she focused on what she was doing. For a few minutes Jamil had to make himself stop looking at her because the sight of her alone was making his dick jump with excitement.

"Fuck me, Gee." He pleaded earnestly with her to make him feel good. "Please." His hands went out to her and pulled the dress she was wearing over her head. "Fuck." He grunted once her body came into full view.

He had noticed earlier that she wasn't wearing a bra. Now to see her perky breasts and round chocolate nipples up close had his dick growing a few more inches. He licked his lips and grabbed them both. He massaged them only for a second before sitting up to put them in his mouth.

Gia's back arched as her hand went to the back of his head. "Milli," she sang sweetly. "Touch it, Milli." She grabbed his hand and stuck it between her legs. "Touch it for me."

Her body was so warm against his skin he could tell she was on fire for him. Her skin was slick with a light sheen of sweat, and she shivered every time he touched her. Listening to her ask him to touch her made Jamil even hungrier. So hungry he could hardly think straight. With one hand he held her up, and with the other he snatched her thong off.

"Fuckkk," he moaned as he bit her neck.

The moment he touched her, the slickness between her thighs coated his fingers, dripping from her like a faucet. He rubbed back and forth over her clit and she moved with him, sliding her body over his fingers. She was desperate. She wanted to get there. She *needed* to get there. She worked her body feverishly, trying to feel the feeling that only he had given her.

At the sound of another moan escaping her lips, Jamil lost all control and grabbed his dick from her hands. Lifting her up with only one arm, he positioned his dick at her opening and pulled her down on top of him. Gia screamed upon contact but quickly muffled it by grabbing his mouth with hers.

She moaned painfully into their kiss as his dick ripped apart her insides. Jamil hadn't even began to move the way he wanted to because he was scared. Scared that if he did, he would bust prematurely and the feeling of Gee's pussy wrapped around his dick would be gone too soon.

He needed to hold on to that for a little while longer. Inside her he felt at home, and he wasn't ready to leave yet. He wanted to stay forever, wrapped in her love. With her legs and arms now wrapped tightly around his body, Gia shivered and shook with every plunge he took into her valley.

"Say my name, Gia." He breathed deeply into her ear. "Call me Daddy."

Jamil could hear the huskiness in his voice as he enjoyed the squishy fluids that were drowning his dick and soaking his thighs. Her breasts pressed flat against his hard chest as he held her in his arms. Still sitting on the edge of the bed, Jamil held a nearly naked Gia on his lap.

Her ass spread across his thighs while her juices leaked all over him. She'd long ago pulled his hair free of his band, so now they sat tangled in each other with an array of colorful locs falling around them. Their hair shielded their faces from anything other than each other.

"Let me hear you, baby." Jamil pushed farther into her.

Gia's entire body tensed up upon feeling every inch of him. "Milli, it hurts," she whined.

Jamil stood up while still holding her and laid her down on the bed. Being that his bed sat pretty high off the ground, he was able to stand on the side and still slide perfectly into her. He pulled her to the edge of the bed while her thighs rested in the crooks of his arms.

He stared down at her body as he slid in and out. "Say my name, Gee." He pushed into her over and over, each stroke deeper and deeper than the last one. "Call me Daddy."

Gia's eyes were on him as she pushed at his abs, trying to stop him from giving her a complete dose of him. Too bad for her, he was in the zone. Gia was his, and he was about to make sure she knew what that entailed.

"Stop running and give me my pussy, Gee."

He watched as her eyes rolled to the back of her head when he spoke to her. Her face took on a totally different look every time he said something, which led him to believe she liked it. He too was full of desire for her, and the only way he knew how to show her was with his body.

Jamil's face distorted in pleasure the harder he stroked her. It was like the harder he went, the wetter she got.

"Gee," he whined desperately. "Your pussy feels so good to me." He grunted. "Is it mine, Gee? Huh? Can I have it?" He heard the words coming from his mouth, but it didn't sound like him. Gia had transformed him into someone else.

He watched her nod as she pushed at his stomach. With a quick, hard thrust, Jamil pushed deep into her, and she screamed again.

"Say my fucking name, Gee." He sped up, hitting her with harder strokes. "Say it," he bellowed. "I'ma beat this pussy until you say it."

After that Jamil went full throttle. He worked his hips harder and harder, giving her one rough stroke after another. Gia was moaning so crazy and loud that she was making his knees weak. Jamil swore on everything he loved that Gia was the prettiest thing he'd ever seen in his life, with pussy to fucking die for.

The way she held on to him with her legs, pulling him deeper and deeper only to drown him with her sugary sweet walls, had him teetering on the brink of euphoria. Jamil was so focused on the way his dick was turning white with all of the cream she released that he could no longer hold out.

"Fuck, Gee! Call me Daddy, baby. Say it. Tell me I'm your daddy, bae." He leaned over and kissed her mouth roughly, sucking and pulling at her tongue until her body tensed. Her back arched and her arms circled his neck. With her eyes closed and her lips to his ear, Gia moaned and her body shook uncontrollably.

"Daddy," she moaned incoherently. "I love you. Damn, Daddy, I love you so much." Her body was shaking so much that Jamil had to practically pry himself from her grasp just so he could look down.

"Gee, I think you just squirted, baby."

"Huh?" She sat up and looked down to where they were connected. "I did?"

Jamil scooted back some so he could see. Sure enough, light trickles of creamy white fluids had shot from her body against his stomach and down his balls.

"Hell yeah, you did, bae," he said in amazement. "That's some hot shit, chocolate baby." He pulled out and dropped to his knees quickly. "I got to taste this." His mouth was on her, immediately sucking at whatever was still leaking out.

"No! No! No!" Gia pushed at his head. "It's too much. Please stop." She was bucking against his face and pushing his head away.

Jamil laughed at her as he stood and grabbed his dick. He held it at the base and tapped it on her throbbing love before sliding it back in until his climaxed encouraged another one from her. He snatched himself out quickly, allowing just the head to rest at her opening until her body stopped shaking. He held her gaze as he stepped away and leaned down once more. He placed a sloppy kiss right on the opening of her love box before standing back up.

"Gee, you got the best pussy I ever had." He winked at her. "Li'l sexy ass."

Gia covered her face with her hands, trying to hide her blushing, which she didn't even have to do because he already knew she was embarrassed.

"I think your mama heard us." Gia sat up and tried to cover her body with the blanket from his bed.

"She'll be all right."

"No, she won't, Jamil. What we just did was so disrespectful."

"Well, it's done now. Here." He tossed her a towel from his dresser. "You want to take a quick shower?"

Gia's eyes widened as she looked at him like he was crazy. "No. Your mama is going to think I'm a hoe for real then."

Jamil sucked his teeth. "Zanetta is the last person that can pass judgment on anybody. So believe me when I tell you she ain't thinking about us. Do you want to take a shower or not?"

Gia looked down at her sticky, sweaty body and nodded. Jamil grabbed his shorts from the floor and pulled them back on. He told Gia to wrap herself in his towel while he went to check on Zanetta. Gia did what he told her and followed him to the bathroom when he got back.

Once he told her that Zanetta was asleep, she looked a little more comfortable. They showered quickly before going back to Jamil's room and getting dressed. Gia put his lotion all over her body and slid her dress back on. Jamil, on the other hand, just threw on another pair of shorts and lay back on the bed watching her.

"Stop watching me like a puppy in heat, Jamil." Gia snickered at the look on his face when he realized he'd been busted.

"Man, get your ass out of here, Gia." He laughed at her. "I wasn't a puppy in heat when I had your grown ass calling me Daddy."

"It wasn't like you left me much of a choice. You was going to beg until I said it."

Jamil smiled and grabbed her hand, pulling her down onto the bed with him. "I like for you to know who's in charge of this li'l body."

"I knew that without calling you Daddy."

He looked down into her face as she lay in his arms. "How you know?"

"Because of the way you make me feel here." She pointed at her chest. "And here." She pointed at her head. "Oh, and most definitely the way you make me feel here." She placed her hand between her thighs momentarily.

Jamil's smile grew as she stared up at him. "We still living in last night?"

She shook her head. "No. Let's just live in the now. I like now better."

"You'll be leaving me soon." Jamil's tone dropped a little.

"That doesn't mean anything, Jamil. We can still be together."

"So we're together?"

Gia looked away and shrugged her shoulders. "I don't know . . . I mean, I kind of thought we were. If you don't want to be, then we don't have to be," she said in a hurry. "We can just be friends. It's no pressure."

Jamil could tell she was nervous about his response, so he decided to ease her mind some. "Chill, Gee. We can be together, bae. I'd like that."

"For real?"

"Yeah. I mean, I'm not a good person or no shit like what you're probably used to, but I'll try for you."

Gia was smiling extremely hard at him as she wrapped her arms around his stomach. "I think you're perfect."

Jamil listened to her talk. What she was saying sounded nice, but he knew better. He wasn't perfect and Gia was too good for him, but being that they didn't have much time left together, it wouldn't hurt to live in la-la land for a little while. Maybe they would work, maybe they wouldn't. Who knew?

Gia stood beside Oni's car holding on to Jamil's neck as he groped her ass and whispered all types of thug shit into her ear. Oni could tell just by the way Gia was laughing and the way Jamil's hands gripped here and squeezed there that they had just got done messing around.

It was obvious, and to be quite honest, Oni was a little jealous. Jamil looked so into her cousin, and it didn't even look like Gia was trying that hard to make him like her. It was just so natural between the two of them. For a second Oni wished she'd been the one to get Jamil and Gia had gotten Iverson.

After thinking about it a little more, she shook her head. She wouldn't dare wish Gia had gotten Iverson instead. That nigga didn't deserve her cousin, and Gia most definitely didn't deserve his black ass. She watched them interact a little more with her heart bursting in awe for Gia.

She could tell how happy Gia was by the stars in her eyes. It was all over the glow in her skin. The warmth exuded from her due to the love of the right man. Oni sat back watching as she tried to think of a time when she'd felt that way, when any man had ever made her feel that way.

Isaac. Sadly, he was the only one she could think of who had ever treated her in such a manner that made her feel special. She smiled as she thought of the first time she met him. Oddly enough, it was almost in the exact same spot where Gia had met Jamil.

"I'm on it now. Just chill." The voice of the man next to her caught Oni's attention.

She was at the detail shop that she frequented and had just taken her seat in the nearby gazebo to wait for her truck. Ever since the tenth grade when she first got her car, she'd been taking it to the same detail shop. Not even her parents understood why she loved it so much—she just did.

Today, like every other Saturday, she was there waiting for them to clean her baby up. Apparently so were the other three men in the gazebo with her.

"You know me. I'ma get it done. I just have to do it when the timing is right."

Oni looked in the man's direction again, trying her hardest not to stare at how handsome he was, but it was next to impossible. He was gorgeous and so clean-cut. The way the black hair lying around his head curled up near his temples and down his sideburns made Oni's eyes wander a little longer than they probably should have.

He was so handsome, she could feel her inner hoe wanting to leap out and flirt with him, but there was one thing preventing that. Despite the fact that she didn't know him from a can of paint and he was on the phone, he was old.

Oni chuckled. He wasn't super old, like ancient, but he was indeed old enough to be her father. Even with him being as handsome as he was, his age still displayed vibrantly. Not in a bad way but in a noticeable one.

"You keep looking at me like that and I'ma come over there and give you what you want."

After nearly choking on the strawberry milkshake she'd been drinking, Oni turned her attention to the handsome stranger and tried to cover her face with her hands. When she'd masked her bashfulness enough to look him in the eyes, she did.

"Excuse me?"

The man set his phone down on his lap and stared directly at Oni. "You heard me."

"Yeah." Oni cleared her throat. "Yeah, I did, but I just needed to make sure you were talking to me, being that the content of your last sentence was a bit too forward for two strangers."

He smiled and gave her a light chuckle. "I agree, but I don't have time to waste." He nodded toward the dark blue car they'd just pulled around the building. "My car is ready."

Oni looked toward the car, then back at him. "You should probably get going, then."

He shrugged. "Maybe I should. Maybe I shouldn't." He leaned forward, allowing his eyes to trail up her long, exposed legs. "Give me a reason to stay."

Oni held her breath for a moment, trying to figure out how their conversation had escalated that fast. One minute he was on the phone, the next he was practically molesting her with his eyes. After the quick wave of heat spread over her body and disappeared again, she crossed and uncrossed her legs.

"I don't have one," she said.

"Tell me a little more about yourself. You live in this area?"

Oni shook her head. "I'm just down here a lot."

He nodded in understanding but didn't say anything. He sat quietly staring at her. The way he looked was a tad bit intimidating, but Oni was a confident woman, so she didn't back down.

"I bet you have a lot of li'l boyfriends, don't you?"

Oni giggled like the young girl she was. "No. What makes you think that?"

"You're too pretty not to." He sat back in his seat again. "So you don't hang out at all?"

"Yeah. I mix and mingle here and there, but nothing too serious."

His eyes left her face and returned to her legs again.
"That's a shame. You could have been a real asset."
Oni's eyebrows raised. "Asset?"
He grinned. "Yes, asset. I like to party and hang out.
As pretty as you are, you would have been the perfect
person to tag along."
That caught Oni's interest because she too liked to
hang out. Especially with men, but she wouldn't tell him
that. Instead, she smiled and fidgeted in her seat some.
"Maybe I still can be."
He winked at her before standing up to his feet.
"Maybe you can. Can I have your number?"
Oni smiled brightly at him and he returned the ges-
ture. They joked around for a few more moments before
exchanging numbers. He promised to give her a call later
that night, and he did.

From that day to this one, Isaac was still the only man who had ever made her feel really loved. The only thing that made it all wrong was the fact that he was too old and they could never be. It just wouldn't feel right.

"Say my name, Gee, and I'll let you go." Jamil's deep voice brought Oni out of her trance and focused her attention back onto the seemingly perfect couple.

"No, Milli." She sang his name like it was her favorite song.

Jamil grabbed a handful of Gia's butt, pulled her body flush against his, and held her there as he said something in her ear. Moments later she squealed and pulled away from him with one of the biggest smiles Oni had ever seen on her face. It was so big and vibrant it had Oni smiling, and she didn't even know what he'd said.

"See, Daddy knows what it takes," he told her and kissed the side of her face.

Oni had to take a deep breath when she heard him refer to

himself as Daddy. That was a major turn-on for her. The fact that he sounded so sexy saying it made her center thump.

"Yeah." Gia smiled. "Daddy sure does. Give me a kiss so I can go."

Jamil's bright orange hair fell over Gia's shoulder as he leaned down to kiss her. His light arms circled Gia's body as they kissed each other out in the open. The public display of affection was so cute and intense, Oni couldn't tear her eyes away. She watched them in envy as Jamil held on to Gia like he was afraid to let her leave.

His grip on Gia's body was so tight it was almost needy, kind of like the way Isaac held Oni. What made it even better was the fact that his eyes were closed as they kissed. He looked to be enjoying it just as much as she knew Gia was. Hell, had it been her in Gia's place, she knew she would most definitely have been enjoying it, so Gia had to be on cloud nine.

"Damn, Gee," he whispered against her lips. "I really ain't trying to let your ass go right now. You know that, right?"

"Don't."

"Aww," Oni swooned from the driver side of the car.

"I wish I didn't have to." He looked over at Oni, then back to Gia. "Stay here with me. You can go home in the morning."

"I can't, but I'll call you when I get home."

He turned his nose up at her and frowned playfully while pushing her away from him. "Man, bye."

Gia was giggling like a schoolgirl as she tried to grab him again only for him to continue pushing her away. Oni thought it was the cutest thing when as soon as Gia pretended to pout and walk away from him, he grabbed her from behind and pulled her right back to his chest. All Oni could see was the top of his orange hair as he nibbled on the side of Gia's face.

"Oni, tell Gee not to be mad at me," he yelled through the window of her truck.

Oni smiled at them. "Gia, don't be mad at Jamil. He's sorry."

Gia stood with her arms crossed over her chest and rolled her eyes in Jamil's direction. "Nope. He shouldn't have acted like he ain't want me on him."

"But I do want you on me, Gee. All over me. Hell, you can get on me right now if you want to."

Gia tried to hide her smile.

"Did I make any complaints when you was squirting all over me?"

Oni could tell he had tried to say it low, but his voice was too deep and she'd heard him anyway.

"Oh my God, Gia! You can squirt? Why you ain't tell me?" Oni couldn't even hide her excitement.

Gia covered her face as Jamil held his head down laughing. "She ain't know she could until today. I bring out the beast in her."

Neither Gia nor Oni could hold in their laughter after that. They were both giggling and shaking their heads at him.

"Don't listen to him." Gia turned around and pecked his lips quickly. "Bye, Milli. I'll see you later, Daddy."

The way his face lit up when Gia called him Daddy was something for the books. It was so cute Oni grabbed her chest. He seriously looked like a kid on Christmas Day. To make matters worse, he grabbed Gia again and pretended to be walking away with her.

"Go on home, Oni. She staying with me," he yelled over his shoulder before releasing Gia and pinching her butt. "Nah, I'm just fucking with y'all. Hit my line later, sexy chocolate."

Gia was smiling from ear to ear as she walked to Oni's truck and got in. She waved at Jamil as he stood watching them leave. Once they pulled away, Oni cut the music playing in her truck down and looked at her with her eyes squinted.

"What?" Gia blushed.

"Don't what me, bitch. Tell all. Right now."

Gia shook her head. "Nope. We'll have a 'tell all' session when we get home, because if I'm not mistaken, you still have some stuff to get off your chest too, remember?"

Oni shrank inside just a tad because Gia was right. She still hadn't told her about her and Iverson's night. She hated that she was going to have to, but she and Gia were more than cousins. They were best friends who told each other everything. It would only be right to let her in on her turmoil.

"Ugh! I guess. Since you want to be difficult." Oni smiled at her. "And because I want to know how good Jamil's dick is."

Gia and Oni both serenaded the inside of Oni's truck with laughter. Oni looked at Gia as she laughed giddily. Hopefully what she had to tell wouldn't taint her thoughts of her. She had already done enough of that for herself. What if Gia never looked at her the same again? What if she became so disgusted that she stopped talking to her altogether?

The loud music poured from the speakers on Shock's dresser as he sat on his bed scrolling through his phone. He'd just woken up from a much needed nap when he realized it was almost time to meet with his supplier. Though it was a routine stop, he didn't really feel like taking that ride by himself, so he called Jamil.

"What's good, my nigga?" Jamil answered the phone.

Shock began to talk as soon as he answered. "Ain't shit. Headed to meet up with this supplier, as always. What your ass doing?"

"Thumbing through cash, as always."

Shock laughed lightly. "A'ight bet. I was just trying to see what y'all niggas had going on."

"What you doing when you leave there? I'm hungrier than a son of a bitch."

"We can hit Applebee's or something once I wrap this shit up. It shouldn't take long. I'm just dropping off some money and getting the dates of the next drop." Shock looked at the time to make sure they would have time for food.

"Cool. Well, swing through here and scoop me up," Jamil told him, and they hung up.

Jamil never really accompanied Shock when he spoke to their

dealer because he had no reason to, but Shock figured he could wait in the car. Things shouldn't take too long.

After getting dressed and storing all of his money in his safe, Shock grabbed his phone and headed for the door. Hopefully Jamil would be ready when he got there. He rode all the way to Jamil's spot listening to music until he pulled up. With a quick flip of his wrist he turned the music down and looked out the passenger side window at Jamil. He was seated on the steps of his porch looking through his phone.

"Get your ass up," Shock yelled from the window.

Jamil chuckled as he made his way to the passenger side. After he was in and situated, they pulled away. Music pounded throughout the car as Shock rode with his windows down. The blunt hanging loosely from his mouth polluted every breath Jamil took.

"Damn, nigga, have some manners and at least pass the shit."

Shock grinned before taking another pull from the blunt and passing it to Jamil. "My fault."

The car was quiet minus their small talk. Being that Jamil had never been to their supplier's house, Shock was almost certain he wasn't really sure where they were going or how long it would take to get there.

Before long they pulled up to a large house that really was more of a mansion. Jamil looked like he was in awe as they pulled farther into the yard. Shock chuckled at him because Jamil's reaction was similar to his when he'd first seen the house. There weren't a lot of houses like that in Columbus.

He was used to seeing project homes and family houses. Nothing more. Jamil too, which was probably why his mouth was still hanging open. Clearly the spacious yard and winding driveway really had him thrown for a loop, not to mention the thick green grass being watered by sprinklers connected to the large fountain in the middle of the yard.

Large rock sculptures stood on either side of the massive staircase that led to the large glass doors. Everything seemed to be so beautiful that it looked fake.

"Nigga, stop looking like you ain't never been out of the hood." Shock's voice brought Jamil back to reality.

"Bruh, this shit is too legit. Where the hell we at? Because I know like hell we ain't in no damn Columbus."

Shock laughed as he slapped Jamil on the shoulder playfully. "We out here on the north side of town. Ain't nothing but doctors, judges, and lawyers occupying these premises." Shock nodded toward the door. "And this nigga, of course."

Jamil pushed his dreads from his face and looked around the yard some more. "I wouldn't even know what to do with a house this size."

Shock looked around with him. "Fuck bitches and get money." He then opened his door to get out.

He grabbed the large black bag that had been on his backseat along with the manila folder next to it. He closed the door behind him.

"I should be in here about ten or twenty minutes at the most."

Inside the mini mansion, Shock had just been shown to the back office where he went every time he was at Little Monty's house. Little Monty was their supplier and had been for the last few years. When Shock had first begun getting work from the Monty family, it was from the father, Big Monty, but he'd died a few years back from throat cancer.

His son, Little Monty, had taken over. Everybody on the block was surprised by his presence because no one had known about him before, and out of the blue one day he just showed up. He was a middle-aged nigga with a pretty-ass wife and some expensive-ass taste. The way their home was decorated was so out of the ordinary that if Shock didn't have money of his own, he might have hit their ass up.

He chuckled to himself as he thought about it. That would

probably be the dumbest thing in the world for him to do, but it was fun to think about.

"Shock, sorry to keep you waiting, man. Had some things to take care of with Daisy real quick." Little Monty walked around his desk wiping his head with a towel.

Small droplets of water were still gracing his skin and leaking from his hair. Clearly the "things" he'd had to take care of with Daisy ended with him taking a shower. Shock simply nodded and waited for him to speak again.

Who could blame the man? With a wife as pretty as Daisy, he'd probably spend all day fucking her too. She was a sexy, dark-skinned lady whose body was stacked to the fucking nines. Hips and ass for days. Big, succulent breasts that were made for sucking. Shock had found himself fantasizing about her a few times before but always caught himself.

Daisy and Little Monty were happy and it showed, so he was more than positive she wasn't looking for a nigga from the hood to run her crazy, because that was exactly what he would do.

"Got the money?" Little Monty took a seat at his desk shirtless and dropped the wet towel to the floor beside him.

"Yep." Shock set the large bag on the desk in front of him and pushed it toward Little Monty.

Little Monty unzipped it and proceeded to thumb through the bills. His signature smile crossed his face as he leaned back in his chair.

"This is why I fuck with you. You always have everything organized and on time. That's the way you do business."

"It being on time, now that's on me, but I can't take the credit for it being all neat and shit like that. That's my nigga Milli Rock's doing. He's in charge of our money."

"Milli Rock? I've heard his name too many times not to have met him."

Shock hesitated for a minute, unsure whether to tell Little Monty that he'd brought Jamil with him today. Little Monty wasn't a huge fan of strangers being in his home, and Shock wasn't really in the mood to deal with no extra bullshit.

"Why haven't I met this nigga before? I've met Iverson's punk ass."

Shock chuckled at Little Monty. He and Iverson had never been the best of friends, and it didn't look like that would be changing anytime soon. Little Monty said Iverson was too cocky and flashy, which was bad for business. He'd made it clear on more than one occasion he only dealt with him because he was good with their paperwork and because he was good for Shock's team.

Any reason outside of that and Iverson probably would have been kicked to the curb a long time ago. After their first couple of meetings, Little Monty hadn't invited him back.

"Milli Rock is a different kind of nigga. He likes to stay to himself and shit. He doesn't do new people very well."

Little Monty raised his thick eyebrow. "I'm that nigga's boss and he still doesn't see a reason to meet me?"

This was the part about Little Monty that Shock didn't like. He wasn't street enough for him. You could tell a nigga from the hood who slung dope from a nigga who was just in the drug business. They had no heart. Much like Little Monty. He was weak and too soft, in Shock's opinion, but that wasn't his business.

Like right then. Why in the fuck did it matter that Jamil never wanted to meet him as long as he had his money on time? That shit was straight-up crazy, and Shock knew Jamil better than anyone. He would straight nut the fuck up on Little Monty and ruin everything they'd worked so hard to build.

So being that he was technically in charge, he would leave things as they were. The two didn't need to meet anytime soon.

"I'll talk to him about it and see what he says."

Little Monty nodded and pulled a black calendar from the drawer of his desk. "Next two drops will be on the twentieth and the thirty-first. Depending on how things go, after that it may be Miami."

Shock smiled and rubbed his hands together. "Now, that's what a nigga is trying to hear."

Little Monty stood up and held his hand out for a shake, signaling the meeting was now over. "Hard work pays off."

"Indeed." Shock stood, dapped Little Monty up, and turned to leave.

He was just about out of the door when he heard Little Monty calling his name. "I have to meet this Milli Rock before anything in Miami is set in stone. I have to know who I have on my team. My end-of-the-summer party, he better be there."

"Got you."

With that, Shock left. He walked down the same hallway he'd come in and went back out to his car. When he got in, Jamil was scrolling through his phone.

"So what's good?" Jamil asked as they were backing out of the driveway.

"Miami might be on the horizon, nigga." Shock was smiling, while Jamil only nodded.

"Listen, don't take this the wrong way but I'm not sure if that's something I really want to do anymore. I know it's major money, but I have some other shit going on right now too that's major on my heart, so I'm still trying to figure that Miami shit out."

"You serious? This is major money we're talking about."

"I think I am." Jamil scratched his head. "Man I don't know, I guess you're right. I can't let something from one summer mess up something I've been working for my entire life can I?"

Shock looked over at him with knitted brows. "I don't know, can you?" He looked over at Jamil as he fidgeted around nervously. He wasn't sure what it was that had him second guessing things, but whatever it was it had to be serious. Milli Rock didn't fold for anyone. Shock looked away from him, but definitely had to find out what this was about.

Chapter Nine

"To see a love like the one Gia and Milli Rock shares is so re-freshing. To know that there's still men out there who know how to love a woman and aren't afraid to show it gives me hope. Hope that maybe one day I'll find someone to love me like that, or at least someone I could be with wholeheartedly."
—Oni

Gia scooted all the way to the top of the bed before fluffing the large pink pillow beneath her head. Oni watched her as she moved around the bed, kicking the blanket out over her legs.

"Comfortable?" Oni raised her eyebrows at Gia.

Gia giggled a little before getting completely still and nodding. "Okay. Now I'm ready."

Oni nodded before tucking her pillow tighter beneath her arms. She was seated directly opposite Gia on the bed. Cross-legged, she rested all of her weight on the zebra print throw pillow from her bed.

For a little while Oni looked everywhere but at Gia because she needed to get herself together. She had been thinking about how to start their conversation since she'd been in the shower. She still hadn't come up with anything.

"Tonight, please," Gia urged.

"I'm just trying to see where I want to start."

"Start at the part where we left y'all in one room and went to the other. Start there."

Oni's eyes rolled to the top of her head as she allowed herself to go back.

"*You sure you're ready for me?*" Iverson stood at the door smiling at Oni.

Drunk and excited to be with such a handsome man, Oni nodded feverishly. She even reached her hand out to him and motioned for him to come to her, but he declined. Instead, he walked over to the large window and began to remove his clothes.

Oni watched in anticipation as he removed article after article of clothing from his body. Iverson was sexy as all hell in clothes, but to see him without them was even better. His body was nice, long, and ripped with muscles. The dark mocha skin on his back shined beneath the bright lights of the hotel room.

Each part of him was perfect, from his strong arms down to his extremely large feet. So of course when he finally turned around and gave her a glimpse of his dick, her mouth began to salivate. It was long and wide and had some of the thickest veins in it that she'd ever seen.

"*You sure you're ready for me?*" he asked.

Oni, never being one to back down from a challenge, quickly stood and undressed as well. When she was stark naked as was he, she walked to him and began kissing his lips. They were tangled in one another for a few minutes before he pulled away. Oni was about to ask why he stopped, but he spoke faster than she could.

"*Slow down, li'l mama. We got the whole night.*" He pecked her forehead before walking over to his clothes.

He kneeled down so that he could dig into his pocket. When he pulled out a clear bag of pills with his condoms, Oni frowned a little. She was all about safe sex and having fun, but she had no interest in taking drugs just to do so.

"*You ever tried ecstasy?*" Iverson asked her.

Oni shook her head.

"You want to?"

Again, she shook her head.

He smiled before tossing the condoms on the bed and removing two pills from the bag anyway. "Come on, it'll be fun. Just one." He kissed her nose, then her chin, down to her breasts.

He stayed there sucking on them until she was grabbing at his head. It was like the moment she touched him, he knew he had her because he stopped. He slid his tongue back up the length of her body before backing her against the bed.

Once they were in front of it, he pushed her down gently and lowered himself to the floor. Iverson's oral sex was hands down the best she'd ever experienced, and after her third orgasm, she was willing to do whatever he asked. Needless to say, the next time he offered her the pill, she opened her mouth and took it.

Everything after that became a blur. She remembered bits and pieces of what happened, but the only thing that really stuck out was the fact that they were no longer alone. The hands of the man above her were different than Iverson's. Much smaller and a lot greedier. The way he touched her felt too urgent, and she didn't like it.

"Iverson." She looked around the room.

"I'm right here, baby. What's up?" When she followed his voice, she noticed that he was in the corner of the room seated in a chair.

She squinted her eyes a little more and noticed that there was another woman there as well. She was kneeling before Iverson, apparently sucking his dick like a porn star, because his eyes were rolling to the back of his head as he spoke.

"Just enjoy it, babe. For me . . . enjoy it for me."

Oni looked away from him, feeling a little weird. It

was like her body was enjoying it but her mind was being tortured. For the rest of the night Iverson whispered sweet nothings to her as the strange man and his woman took turns doing an array of things to her body while Iverson watched.

The entire ordeal was too surreal to believe. Oni could feel herself climaxing continuously as the couple performed all types of sexual acts on her. But still, in the back of her mind, she just wanted to scream for them to stop. The only piece of comfort came when Iverson took the man's place and slid himself into her.

He worked her body over like she knew he could, and all was well again. She began enjoying sex like she normally did, and this time her mind was okay with it. The way Iverson kissed her passionately and delivered stroke after perfect stroke to her body had her screaming and on the verge of begging for more.

She could hear the man and the other lady in the background saying things to Iverson, encouraging him to do more, so that's what he did. One minute Oni was on her back, and the next she was on her stomach with Iverson's face in her ass. Though it tickled a little, she had to admit his tongue felt just as good on her butt as it had on her pussy earlier.

Just as she began to enjoy it, she felt him kneel behind her. She'd done doggy style numerous times before, but the moment he entered her anally she felt like dying. Oni kicked and screamed. She was grasping at the pillows in an effort to bring herself some type of comfort as she yelped in pain, but it never came. Sex with Isaac was never like this.

The only thing that did come was Iverson. His mouth was to her ear, licking and sucking it as he begged for her to just take the pain for him. The soothing way he spoke

*made her relax a little more, and before long, it was no
longer as painful. Not enjoyable as normal sex, but not
too bad.*

*"That's my girl. Take this dick." He slapped her ass
hard and Oni yelped again.*

*A mix between sexual pleasure and sexual torture
went on for hours between the four of them before it finally came to an end. When it was over, all Oni could
think was that Isaac, Willie, or anyone else would have
never done her like that.*

"Oh my God, Oni. What did you do after that? Like, once it finally stopped?" Gia asked, her face contorted as if she'd experienced the pain herself merely at Oni's words.

Oni looked at Gia as she bit on her nail. "Took a shower and
fell asleep in the tub. I felt so dirty that even after I took a bath I
still wanted to be in water. I ran me a hot bath and that's where I
stayed until checkout."

"Where was his nasty ass at all this time?"

"He was in the bed asleep. When he finally woke up, he acted
like nothing had happened, so I did too. I didn't even want to
think about it, let alone talk about it."

Gia sat up in bed. "He didn't apologize or nothing?"

"I mean, in a way. He was just like, 'If that's not something
you're into, my bad, but I love freaky shit.'" Oni tried her best to
mimic Iverson's voice.

"That bastard," Gia seethed. "You should have told his ass no,
Oni. You didn't have to do that shit if you didn't want to. You
and I could have shared a room while those two niggas slept together."

"I didn't want to ruin you and Jamil's night. Plus, I was so high
off that damn ecstasy pill, I didn't start thinking clearly until this
morning."

Gia sat on the bed shaking her head. She looked to be in deep thought before she made eye contact with Oni again. "How do you feel about all of that now?"

Oni shrugged. "I don't remember a lot of stuff, but I know for a fact we used condoms. I remember watching them put them on, and when I woke up the room was littered with empty wrappers. I know this sounds crazy, but as long I know I was protected from any diseases, I guess I'm all right. I'm just disgusted with it all. I didn't even know them damn people."

"Were they white or black?"

Oni giggled. "Black, girl."

The room was quiet again before Gia looked at Oni with a weird smile on her face.

"What, Gia?"

"You let that lady eat the twat. You nasty bitch."

Oni and Gia fell over in laughter as they thought about what Gia had said. After a few more jokes, they both went back to their earlier spots.

"Girl, I ain't gay. You know I love me some niggas." Oni cheesed. "I really just didn't know what was going on."

Gia nodded in understanding. "It's cool. I feel you. So what's up with you and Iverson now?"

"Nothing. I don't even think I'm feeling him like I thought I was. That sex was just too much for me."

"Well, I wish I could say the same, but I can't." Gia's smile grew big. "Jamil's sex is too much for me too, but in a good way."

Oni squealed and hit Gia's leg. "Oh, I can tell, girl. The way he be touching all on you and saying nasty shit. I bet his big, fine ass be putting it down."

"Baby, let me tell you. Carrottop be putting it down, up, side to side, crisscross, in the middle. Bitch, he just does it all."

Oni fell backward onto the bed with Gia falling right next to her. "You're so lucky, Gia. He looks like he really likes you. It's all over him whenever you come around. It's so crazy."

"If I tell you something, you can't tell Iverson's freak nasty ass. And you can't bring it back up again."

Oni nodded.

"He was crying in our hotel last night. He's had a hard life with his parents and stuff, and it has really affected him. Oni, girl, he dropped out of school in the seventh grade."

Oni gasped.

"He was telling me how he don't know shit and all he know is drugs, so that's what he does. Girl, he called me and you privileged. He said we're going to find privileged niggas and have little privileged kids."

Oni and Gia burst into laughter again. This time they laughed so hard tears formed in their eyes as they lay next to each other.

"Tell that nigga don't make fun of us or our privileged kids with his yellow ass."

"Girl, it's funny now, but it wasn't then. He was real live venting to me, so I didn't want to mess it up by saying no silly shit. I just listened to him and told him I didn't care about that stuff and that I would be there for him if he needed me to."

"That's so sweet, Gia, and I know you would too. That's the kind of person you are. He's lucky too."

"Is it crazy that I think I love him?"

Oni looked at Gia. "Hell yeah. You've only known him for a few days."

Gia looked off into space and shrugged her shoulders. "He loves me too. He told me then, and again today. Over and over. I'm not sure if it's the sex or he's feeling vulnerable because I know all of his business."

"I don't know. Y'all are both grown. Y'all know what y'all feel. If y'all think it's love, then who am I to say different?"

Gia sat up. "That's the same thing I was thinking. It feels so real and right, you know? If it wasn't so powerful, I probably wouldn't even be feeling him like this. It's just him, though.

There's nothing about him that sticks out other than his appearance, but I really feel it. Like really feel it. When we're together, the force is so strong it's like we've been together for years."

"And he feels the same way?"

"I think so. He told me he's not good with words, so he has to show me the best way he knows how, and that's with sex."

"Gia," Oni sighed.

"I know, right, and Oni, girl, if he feels anything close to the way he sexes me, then, bitch, that nigga is head over heels in love. He's always so passionate. Touching and kissing on me. Talking to me and stuff. Then the way he looks when he's in it is like he's about to die or something. I mean literally about to die. His face be looking so desperate, like if I even move a certain way or say a certain thing, he's going to explode. He makes me feel like I'm his air or something, and that's the same way I feel about him."

"Jesus, take me now!" Oni screamed, "Lord, send me a Jamil."

Gia sat on the bed looking down at Oni, smiling. "You're so stupid."

"I'm for real, Gia, man. I want somebody to want me like that. I'm tired of niggas always wanting the box, then after they get it, they dip. You're always laughing, but Isaac is the only one who doesn't treat me like I'm some kind of hoe."

"That's because he's got one foot in the grave. He doesn't have time to be picky." Gia and Oni laughed together when Oni rolled her eyes. "But for real, Oni, maybe you should stop giving your body to them."

Oni was quiet as she thought about it. Gia was right, and she'd thought about it herself a few times before, she just wasn't sure if she could. She was such a sexual person. All she knew was to have sex. Relationships weren't her thing.

"Oh, and I'm going to slap Jamil for introducing you to that whore Iverson."

"Please do. Just don't tell him what we did."

Gia sucked her teeth. "It may be a little late for that. If he's anything like I think he is, he's probably told Jamil everything himself already."

"You think so?" Oni asked nervously.

She was so ashamed that she didn't want anyone besides Gia to know about it. But Gia was right. The moment they'd come down the stairs that morning, he had been whispering to Jamil. There was no telling what he'd said. Embarrassed, she covered her face with her hands and shook her head.

"Don't feel bad, boo. He's just a nigga. Just be more careful next time."

Oni nodded and rolled over to grab her phone. She checked her messages from Isaac, Willie, and a few other people before lying back down on the bed. For the rest of the night she and Gia sat in her room talking and laughing about a little bit of everything until they both fell asleep around three o'clock in the morning, only to be woken right back up by Oni's ringing phone.

"Hey, baby, I'm in town for the night. Can I see you?" It was Isaac.

Oni pulled her phone from her ear with her eyes squinted trying to check the time, but the light was so bright she could hardly see the screen.

"It's so late. I'm not sure if I can even move right now. Can I see you tomorrow?"

He sighed. "Yeah. I just want you really bad right now. I've been thinking about you the entire drive here."

Oni's heart raced as she thought about how much he needed her. It didn't help that she'd just relived her horrible night with Iverson. In all reality, she wanted him right then too. Against her better judgment, she hopped up from her bed and began scrambling around her room.

"Okay. Give me about twenty minutes."

She could hear the smile in his voice. "Thank you, baby. I'll see you soon."

Oni hung up before flipping her lamp on. As soon as the light shined, Gia began to stir. A few seconds later her head raised from the pillow and turned toward Oni. Her face was scrunched up as she tried to focus her eyes.

"Why you got the light on?"

"I'm about to go see Isaac. You want to come with me?"

Gia's eyes finally straightened up as she looked at Oni like she'd lost her mind. "Um, no thank you. I'll be here when you get back."

"Come on, Gia, please. I'm not staying long. Only an hour, maybe two," she pleaded.

Oni knew the odds of her getting over there and Isaac begging her to stay until the morning were fairly high, and she didn't need that kind of pressure right then. If she took Gia, then he would have no other choice but to agree to let her go.

"Gia, come on. Please." Oni slid her feet into her flip-flops.

After sucking her teeth and throwing the covers from her body, Gia stood up and began getting herself together as well. It took them both a little longer than usual, being that they were trying their best not to stumble over one another.

When they finally got outside to Oni's truck, they hopped in the car and closed their doors. Neither of them said anything until they were halfway down the street.

"I can't believe I let you talk me into getting out of the bed in the middle of the night to go to the nursing home."

Oni giggled as she pushed Gia's arm. "Bitch, we're not going to no damn nursing home. Stop being like that."

Gia was smiling as she fingered through some of her locs. "Call it what you want. Isaac is old enough to be our daddy, but I'll let you have that."

"Please don't say nothing crazy when we get over there."

After Gia promised not to make any out-of-line jokes, they rode the rest of the way in silence. Oni was on pins and needles praying that neither Gia nor Isaac felt too out of place. The only reason she ended up calming down was because she'd just pulled up to Isaac's house.

She sent him a text letting him know she was outside, and as always, he told her to use her key. Gia walked slowly behind Oni as they entered the house. Unlike all of the other times, Oni stopped in the living room. She flipped the TV on for Gia before continuing down the hall.

Isaac was lying across the bed smiling at her when she entered. "You look nice."

"I look like I just got out of bed." Oni sat on the edge of the mattress.

"Well, you look beautiful to me." He sat up and sat behind her. "Why you cut the TV on downstairs?"

"I brought my cousin with me." He stopped moving for a minute and she got nervous. "I hope that's okay."

"It's cool. I was just hoping you could stay, but I know she probably isn't going to want to."

Oni breathed a sigh of relief because she'd been right to bring Gia. He'd done exactly what she knew he would.

"Probably not." Oni pretended to be sad.

"I guess we'll make the best of the little time we have." He began kissing down her neck and shoulders.

Oni's body immediately began to melt beneath his touch. He kissed and touched her everywhere before finally undressing her and himself. Naked and ready for each other, he entered her, causing them both to moan. His eyes were closed as he stroked her gently. Though she was still a little shaken up from the night before, Oni wouldn't allow that to ruin her time with Isaac. It was way too special for her to allow Iverson's foolishness to interfere, so Oni closed her eyes and enjoyed the moment.

The way his body tensed in certain places made her hot with need. Him telling her he really wanted her on the phone was obviously true because he hadn't stopped kissing and touching her yet. Even though he was working her body gently, he still held a tad bit of force behind it, rocking her body with every stroke he delivered.

Oni lay captivated in the movement of his body. The way he watched her while he made love to her was all that she desired. It was all that she needed. She would gladly crawl out of her bed at odd hours of the morning to get it.

"I love you." She fought to keep her eyes from watering.

He kissed the tip of her nose. "I love you too."

Oni watched him as she wondered what kind of luck she had. The only man who made her feel all of the things she so desired, she couldn't have. Out of all of the people in her life right then, he was the only one who made her even consider the notion of being in love. Unfortunately, this was all they could ever be. Though she hated it, she'd accepted it.

When they were finally finished, he followed her down the stairs so that he could walk her outside. When they reached his living room, Gia was on the phone.

"Jamil, don't play with me."

"Why is that nigga up this time of night?" Oni's voice made her jump.

Gia looked in her direction and paused before holding her hand up. "Talk to the hand."

"Can you and li'l Milli Rock talk all that sweet shit some other time? We're about to go."

Gia looked at Oni once more before turning her head again. "Babe, let me call you back. This hoe being rude."

Oni and Isaac watched her as she laughed a few more times before hanging up and rising to her feet.

"That's your boyfriend?" Isaac asked.

Gia and Oni both looked at him.

"Yeah. I needed somebody to keep me company while y'all were back there being nasty."

Isaac smiled and kissed Oni's face. "Sorry."

"It's cool. I'm Gia." She smiled.

He held his hand out for her to shake. "Isaac."

"Nice to meet you, but next time can we meet at a decent hour?"

He and Oni both laughed before he told Gia that they could. They all made small talk for a few more minutes before Isaac walked them to Oni's truck and watched them pull away.

"Girl, I see why you're into that senior citizen–ass nigga. He fine as hell."

"I told you he was the shit."

"I know, but I ain't believe you. He a cute old thing."

Oni was cheesing. "He puts it down too."

"I heard, with your nasty behind."

The girls laughed and talked all the way home. After getting back into the house, Gia went to her room while Oni stayed in hers. She'd just texted Isaac, letting him know she was home, when he called. For the rest of the night or morning, she stayed up talking to him. Maybe being with an older man wouldn't be too bad.

Though the girls had finally fallen asleep, across town Jamil's late night and early morning was just getting started. He had just pulled up to Shock's crib and was headed down the sidewalk when Iverson's truck whipped into the parking lot behind his car.

Jamil looked over his shoulder before continuing up the walkway. He wasn't really in the mood to talk to Iverson right then. In the pit of his stomach he felt Iverson was up to something. He'd called him after Gia had gone home to see if he wanted to get up together and head to Shock's house. Iverson had come up with some lie about having something else to do, so Jamil dismissed it. The same way he'd dismissed him showing up late to the meeting with their client the other night, and dipping out on reviewing the contracts the following morning.

To be honest, it was no big deal because Iverson had been on some old disappearing act a lot lately. Jamil knew the nigga was about his money, so there was no telling what he was up to. Whatever it was, Jamil wasn't feeling it. If there was a get-money scheme that had that nigga acting funny with his day one homies, then he wanted no part of it.

Jamil and loyalty went hand in hand, so the moment he felt a shift in the loyalty in any of his partners, he moved along. Not saying that he wouldn't chop it up with them, it just wouldn't be the same.

"Milli Rock, wait for me, my nigga," Iverson yelled from behind him.

Jamil wanted to keep walking, but he stopped anyway. He stood on the stairs and watched Iverson walk up. When they were close enough, they dapped each other up and continued down the sidewalk and through the breezeway to get to Shock's apartment.

"Hell you coming from?" Jamil looked at Iverson.

"Getting some pussy. You know me."

Jamil shook his head and knocked on the front door. "Nigga, you better slow your roll out here with these hoes. The streets ain't safe no more, my boy."

Iverson gave Jamil a serious look before bursting out into a smirk. "I already know."

The front door to Shock's crib opened and the girl standing there smiled at them both before moving to the side so that they could enter. Once they were inside, she closed the door and they walked to the back bedroom where Shock conducted his business.

Shock was in the corner of the room seated in his recliner with a cigar in his mouth. He nodded at them both before standing up to shake their hands.

"Young niggas. What's good?"

"Ain't shit, my nigga. What's good?" Iverson said.

"You got it." Jamil took a seat on the sofa across from where Shock had been sitting.

"Milli Rock, you're one unique-looking muthafucka, you know that, right?" Shock chuckled as he always did when he told Jamil that.

Jamil smirked. "Nigga, tell me what's good. Why you got me way out here on the white folks' side of town this time of morning when I just left your ass not too long ago?"

"You know I have to fuck with you." He puffed his cigar again before picking up the remote and muting the TV. "Thought any more about what I asked you?" He held eye contact with Jamil.

Jamil nodded but didn't say anything.

Shock then looked at Iverson. "You're already on what we spoke about, right?"

Iverson nodded with a huge smile on his face. "You know I don't play around."

Iverson's response was the type of shit Jamil had been thinking about earlier on his way into Shock's house. When they had been on the phone earlier, Jamil had asked that nigga if he had thought any more about what Shock had offered them. His bitch ass lied and said he hadn't. Clearly he hadn't thought about it. There was nothing to think about. He was already on it.

Jamil fought the scowl that was trying to surface on his face. Versus getting angry about shit that had nothing to do with him, he took a few deep breaths and sat back on the sofa.

"How's it looking?" Shock asked Iverson.

"Like money."

Shock smiled and dapped him up. It was no secret to Jamil that Shock had offered him more weight to push into more areas—two more trap houses to run, with a warehouse of corner boys to make sure shit went right—because he'd offered Jamil the same thing. There was an added bonus to Jamil's that Iverson was more than ready to take if he said no.

Shock already knew Jamil could push the weight he'd given Iverson; he'd been serving that amount since he was eighteen. The load of product he distributed now was three times that, but that was no one's business. Shock knew Jamil was a hard worker and as silent as they came. If anybody could handle seeing the amount of work and paper that he was holding, it was Milli Rock. Hence the name Milli Rock.

"Young soldier, I knew you could handle that shit." Jamil watched Shock hype Iverson up for no reason at all. Old as he was, his ass had better been able to handle that little-boy distribution.

"Well, once that runs out, hit me. I got some more waiting. Also, try to get me the paperwork on the Miami job."

"Bet." Iverson looked at his watch. "I got this li'l joint waiting on me, though, so I'ma check with y'all later." He stood and dapped both Shock and Jamil up before leaving the room.

They both waited until they heard the front door close before saying anything. Jamil went first.

"Why you make that nigga feel like he a kingpin or some shit?"

Shock smirked and licked his lips after removing his cigar. "It's the game. If he's happy, then he'll do what he's supposed to do." He puffed on the cigar again. "Everyone ain't like you, Milli Rock."

"What you mean like me?"

"Self-made millionaire. Young fly nigga that's on the grind relentlessly. A hustler that's smarter than niggas twice your age." Shock nodded toward Jamil. "You're probably one of the richest niggas in the city, and nobody will ever know the shit because you're cooped up in the projects with your junkie parents, running around here dressing like a corner boy."

Jamil tried to keep a straight face but couldn't and started laughing. "Nigga, your ass is always trying to shade a nigga on the sly."

Shock grinned. "It ain't on the sly, young nigga. The shit I say about you is true. You don't buy yourself shit. I don't know why the fuck you're still at home with Owen and Zanetta's crackhead asses. And I don't even want to speak on the way you be curving these bitches."

Jamil pushed all of his hair over his shoulder and tied it back with a thick brown rubber band he'd been wearing around his wrists.

"These hoes ain't shit, that's why."

"Got damn right, but that don't mean you can't get your dick wet at least once a week, nigga, damn. You're twenty-four. You should be going to sleep and waking up in pussy. Blowing bags on these hoes just for fun." Shock took a sip from the cup of brown liquor in front of him. "Shit, it ain't like you don't have the money."

Jamil rubbed the hair on his chin as he listened to Shock talk about his life. He was right; Jamil had more money stacked than probably every nigga in the city outside of Shock. And he could have any woman he wanted, he just didn't want them.

He wanted more. He wanted a female who challenged him. Someone who wanted more out of life than a sack of weed, free VIP booths, and the latest pair of Jordans. He wanted Gee.

"These bitches don't want me, Shock. That's why I ain't giving they ass nothing."

"Oh, they want you. You just don't want them."

Jamil chuckled again. "Right." He kicked his legs out in front of him, debating on whether or not he wanted to tell Shock about Gia. "I don't know, though." He sighed. "I might have found me a li'l joint that can get it."

Shock had his cup in front of his mouth when he moved it and looked at Jamil. "A joint that can get what?"

Jamil shrugged nonchalantly. "Anything. Hell, whatever she wants for real. My money, my dick, my last name. Whatever Gee wants, Gee can get."

Shock looked at Jamil with a proud smirk on his face. "Gee? That's her name?"

"Gianna, I just call her Gee."

"Why is this the first time I'm hearing about her?"

Shock was the oldest of them all, so he was more like the older brother of the crew. He was always looking out for Jamil and Iverson, shooting them advice, and making sure they were good. They talked at least twice a day about anything from business to their personal lives. Jamil told him pretty much everything and had even considered telling him about Gee earlier, but she was there when Shock had called, so he didn't.

The two of them had long ago surpassed the business relationship. In Jamil's eyes they were family now. He had been there for Shock during his federal bid and when his baby mama left him for his younger brother and everything. They were as tight as two niggas from two different mothers could be.

"I just met her," Jamil said.

Shock didn't look like he believed him. "A girl you just met can get anything you have?"

Jamil smiled because it did sound crazy coming from someone else's mouth. "Nigga, hell yeah. When you meet her, you'll see why."

Shock downed the rest of his liquor and laughed. "Word? I get to meet her?"

Jamil nodded.

"Bet. Well, I'm happy for you, my nigga." He paused before looking back at him. "What you think about what I asked you?"

Jamil leaned his head to the side as he tried to think of what he wanted to say. He hadn't really come to a decision yet.

"I was game for it at first, but shit is different now. I mean, I just told you about Gee. I know we're not that serious or no shit like that yet, but that'll be a bad look, and I really don't know if I want to mess us up just yet."

Shock sat back in his chair and rubbed his chin. His mouth was twisted to the side as he bit the inside of his cheek. Jamil could tell he was thinking about what he'd just said.

"You know how much money this shit is?"

Jamil nodded.

"And you're willing to give it up?"

"For Gee? Yeah."

"You can't just explain to her what's going on? She does know that you move weight, right?"

"Yeah. Just not how much."

Shock nodded. "You need to hurry up and bring her to the house. I have got to meet Miss Gee."

Jamil was smiling when he told him that he was going to bring her with him to Shock's cookout the following weekend. After a few more tries at convincing Jamil to take the job, Shock agreed to give him a little while to think about it before they moved on from that conversation. By the time Jamil was preparing to leave, he remembered something he'd been meaning to tell him about.

"Aye, did I tell you some li'l niggas was shooting at me at the fair the other night?"

Shock's whole face frowned as he stared at Jamil. "Hell nah, you ain't tell me. You ain't know who they were?"

Jamil shook his head. "Nope. I just heard one of them say some shit about me being that nigga Milli Rock and then they started busting."

"You ain't wet them niggas up?"

"Nah. For one, we were in public, kids and shit was out there. Then I had Gee with me. I ain't want to do no shit like that with her there."

"You see their faces?"

"Nah. They were wearing bandannas."

Jamil rose to his feet and Shock followed suit. They walked to the front door and Shock opened the door for Jamil to exit.

"You know you're going to have to handle that, right? Shit like that doesn't go unpunished."

Jamil held his fist out for Shock to pound. "Most definitely. I'ma holla at you next weekend, though."

"Bet. Think about that job too, Milli Rock. That shit would be legit as fuck."

"I will." Jamil left Shock's spot and headed back to the hood.

While he drove, he thought about the offer Shock had extended to him. He had indeed been looked at for the Miami spot, but in order to obtain it he had to go live in Miami for a few months and help one of Little Monty's suppliers set up shop. That didn't seem too hard, and Jamil probably would have done it if he didn't have to pretend to be her husband in order to make it work.

Alira was one of Little Monty's main female dealers. She had pull in almost every state and was helping him expand more and more each day. This area wasn't a fan of female dope girls, so she would need some help.

Though Jamil had never seen her before, he'd heard a lot about her. From what he'd been told, she was the truth. Shock had told him that he would be the perfect person for the job because not only was he good with money, he was street smart. However, Gia had thrown a wrench into those plans.

Though they weren't together, he couldn't see himself living and playing house with another woman and expecting Gia to be okay with it. That just didn't make sense. He knew for a fact that if the shoe was on the other foot, he wouldn't go for the shit, so he wouldn't even bring it to her. It wasn't like he needed the money anyway.

He rode in silence lost in his thoughts until he pulled up at home. Like many nights before, it was light outside by the time he finally climbed in bed and closed his eyes. He wanted to call Gia before he fell asleep and let her know that he loved her, but chose not to.

Chapter Ten

"Should I always do the shit I do? Nah, probably not, but oh well. When it comes down to my money, anything goes."
—Iverson

"What do you mean you have a plan? How the hell do you have a plan when you haven't even done what I've asked you to do yet?" Little Monty barked.

His voice echoed off of the walls, making him sound a lot louder than he really was. Anyone other than Iverson probably would have been intimidated by it, but he wasn't. He knew Little Monty was a bitch and was only exercising all of the power he'd inherited because he had goons to back him up.

Without that, Iverson would have bet all of the money in his pocket that he would never raise his voice like that to him. He would know better than to do such a thing because he wouldn't hesitate to send Little Monty right back to his dead daddy's ball sac.

Iverson took a deep breath and sat up in his seat. "Like I said, I have a plan. That nigga Jamil's head is so far up that girl's ass, he won't even see it coming."

Little Monty took a drink from the brown liquor in his cup before slamming it back down roughly onto his desk.

"How can I believe that when your ass couldn't even follow through with getting his ass knocked at the fair? How the fuck does one nigga chase off two niggas with guns? That shit was weak and your credibility is shot. I'm starting not to believe anything you say."

Iverson ran his hand over his head. True enough, the two niggas he'd paid to kill Jamil at the fair had indeed failed. That didn't mean he was useless. All that meant was he'd picked a pair of amateurs to handle professional work.

"It was packed and they got spooked. That shit didn't have nothing to do with me. I paid their asses outright. I did my part, and when they didn't deliver, I handled them." Iverson scooted to the edge of his seat and looked at Little Monty. "That's why I'm telling you to let me handle this. All you need is someone who can distribute in Miami the right way. I can do that shit."

Little Monty gave Iverson the side-eye as he continued pacing around his desk. From the look on his face, anyone could tell he wasn't trying to hear shit Iverson was saying, but what other real choice did he have? He most certainly couldn't go head up with Jamil and expect a good outcome. He wasn't built like that.

"What's your plan?" Little Monty asked.

Iverson smiled and rubbed his hands together. "I think you should let me set that nigga up. Take him to a drug deal and have him get mixed up in some type of paperwork shit he doesn't normally handle. Shit will go south and you can have him killed for fucking up the product. Everybody in the game knows how it goes when money is involved. Nobody will ever expect it."

Little Monty took another sip of his drink before taking a seat behind his desk. He said nothing at first, trying to determine whether or not what Iverson was saying would work. It sounded good, but once again it would put him on the spot to do all of the dirty work.

Yeah, he wanted Jamil dead, but that didn't mean he wanted to be the one to do it. "Let me think on it. I'll give you a call tomorrow."

"Bet." Iverson stood up and left his office.

As soon as Little Monty heard his front door close, he flicked on his security cameras and watched him walk to his car. Once he was sure he was gone, Little Monty sat back in his chair and pulled the blunt from his drawer. After lighting it, he laid his head back against his chair and closed his eyes.

A few deep breaths in and out had him feeling a little better already. Taking Jamil out was proving to be a lot harder than he'd expected, the main reason being he simply wasn't into that kind of thing. The only reason he was even involved in the drug business right then was because of Big Monty's untimely demise.

For years Big Monty had been grooming him to take over if it were to ever come to that, but he still didn't have the heart for it. The only reason he'd survived this long was because he was smart. Sometimes being book smart outweighed being street smart. In his case, that was all he had on his side.

Movement at the door opened his eyes. When Little Monty saw Daisy standing there in her light pink gown, he could feel himself hardening beneath his desk. Daisy was so beautiful and perfect. He couldn't imagine living this life without her.

They had been through so much together, and she had held him down every step of the way, bending over backward to do whatever she could to make it all easier for him. She was a real winner. He turned to watch her as she walked into his office. Her full breasts bounced with every step she took. The wide set of hips spilling from beneath the gown led down to the thickest pair of thighs he'd ever had the pleasure of seeing.

Even at forty-four, Daisy was putting women to shame. There weren't too many women her age, or even half her age, who had a body like that, which was why he loved her. Not only did she take care of him, she took care of herself. She was a healthy eater and a regular at the gym near their house.

"I heard your company leave," Daisy said.

Little Monty sighed. "He's worthless."

Daisy walked behind his desk and made herself comfortable on his lap. "What happened? I thought he was the key to everything."

Little Monty shook his head. "I thought so too, but that nigga is too greedy. He wants Jamil's spot so bad he can't think straight, and that's bad for business."

Daisy's soft hands rubbed the top of his head. "So what are you going to do now?"

"Honestly? I don't know. I told Shock to bring him to the party, but now I'm not so sure. I was going to have someone put a bullet in his head the moment he got here, but I want that nigga to see me first. If I just let him walk around chilling, he might peep who I am and leave before I can handle his ass."

"Maybe we should just leave it alone and move on. It's been long enough, babe. Maybe it's time to just make peace with the situation. If you can't figure out an easy way to do it, then maybe it shouldn't be done."

Little Monty opened his eyes quickly and frowned at her. "How could you say that?"

"I just think it's too much. All of these years have passed and you're still after this same kid." Daisy shrugged. "I think maybe it's time we just start fresh. We can move away from here, find us a nice house somewhere else, and leave it all behind." Daisy kissed down the side of his face and he pulled away.

"Fuck no!" He grumbled, pushing her from his lap. "Get out, Daisy."

She looked at him like she wanted to say something but changed her mind. "I didn't mean to make you angry. I just think it's time."

"Get out!" he bellowed, causing her to scurry from the room.

Little Monty turned around toward his desk, pulled the picture frame from it, and just stared. He missed her so much. She had been his everything, and in the blink of an eye she'd been taken away from him. Something so sweet and so precious. How could he just let that go?

With a deep sigh, he held the tenth-grade picture of his daughter up close to his face and kissed it. "Even if everyone else gives up, Daddy won't." He kissed the picture again before placing it back into his drawer. "Daddy loves you, Lauren." He was looking up to the sky and thinking of her, as he had almost every night since she'd left.

He wanted the pain to get better, but no matter how hard he tried, it just wouldn't. Maybe it never would, or maybe it just felt like that because he hadn't killed Jamil yet.

Chapter Eleven

"I love you now, I loved you then, I'll love you forever. Your energy, your passion, your love. Everything about you is perfect, and not just plainly perfect, but perfect for me. The beauty in the love that you share with me is all I desire, and I wish to bask in it forever. My Milli Rock, my beautifully compassionate Milli. You deserve it all, baby, and I'm here to give it to you." —Gee

"Of course I miss you, Colonel." Gia smiled brightly as she swung back and forth on the swing.

She was on the phone with her father, and he was going in on her about them not speaking in days. Normally they spoke at least once a day, but ever since she'd been hanging out with Jamil, she had been neglecting him.

"What? What would make you think that?" She looked at Oni, who was swinging next to her. "I have not met a man."

Oni's eyes widened as she listened to Gia.

"Uncle Rick told you what?" Gia hit Oni's arm. *I'm going to kill your daddy,* she mouthed to her. "He's not my boyfriend, Colonel. We just talk sometimes . . . yeah . . . I mean, but why would you want to talk to him?"

Gia stopped swinging and held her head in her hand. "Yes, sir. Yes, sir. I will. Yes, sir. Later today. We're going to a cookout at his friend's house. No, he's not a thug, Colonel. He's nice. Okay. I love you too. Okay, bye." Gia hung up her phone and screamed. "I'm going to kill your talking-ass daddy, Oni."

Oni was too busy laughing to talk. "What he do, girl?" she was finally able to say.

"Told my daddy me and you been running around here with some men. Now the Colonel wants me to FaceTime him when I get with Jamil."

"Are you going to?"

Gia looked at Oni like she should have known better. "Of course I am. Colonel Ellis will kill me if I don't."

"You kill me calling your daddy Colonel."

Gia shrugged. "I can't help it."

"What time is the cookout?"

"Jamil said to come through around three. He sent me the address already. I think it's a pool party too, because he told me to make sure we bring our bikinis."

Oni danced around in her seat on the swing. "I hope some fine niggas be there."

"Don't get caught up. You know Iverson might be there too. Not to mention your little old-school love affair."

Oni rolled her eyes. "I ain't worried about Iverson. And Isaac isn't a threat. He knows I'm young and we can't be together like that."

Gia nodded. "Good. I'm glad you got all of that together."

They sat outside on the swings in the backyard of Oni's house for a little while longer before going inside to get ready to leave. It was already a little after two, so they didn't have much time.

"I think I'm wearing this one." Gia held up her red and gold bikini.

"That's so cute. I'ma wear my blue one." Oni tossed the thin piece of fabric toward Gia so that she could see it.

"All the little dope boys about to be choosing on us." Gia smiled as she ran her hand through her locs. She'd braided them the night before, so they were nice and wavy.

"You need to be worried about Milli Rock and that's it."

"You better believe that's the only one I care about." Gia tied the red satin band around the front of her locs and fluffed them up around her earrings, a large pair of gold ones to match with her swimsuit. The colored tips of her locs lay against her skin as she put on eyeliner and lip gloss. She continued getting dressed while Oni went into her room to do the same. With a pair of ripped black shorts over her bikini bottoms and a loose-fitting red cropped shirt over the top, she was ready.

On her wrists was a gold watch and a few bangles the Colonel had gotten her from Dubai. When she went into Oni's room, Oni had her wrap combed down and was sliding her feet into her sandals.

"You better be glad you washed that hair last night. It looks so bouncy today," Gia said.

"That's why I did it. How do I look?"

Oni was also wearing shorts, except hers were blue jeans, and her pink crop top looked more like a bra than a shirt. Since her stomach was so flat, it looked cute on her.

"You cute, girl." Gia grabbed Oni's arm and pulled her down the stairs.

They hopped into Oni's truck and programmed her GPS for Jamil's friend's house.

"What's this friend's name?" Oni asked.

"I think Milli said his name was Shock or something like that."

Oni nodded and kept driving. They listened to music and talked about the party on the way. It took a little over twenty minutes for them to get there, but they could tell by all of the parked cars that they were in the right spot.

Oni frowned. "Damn, it's packed."

"It probably isn't. This is an apartment complex. There could be cars from other residents too."

"If you say so. I just hope it ain't a bunch of bitches. You know I don't do bitches."

Gia giggled. "You must have forgot about that bitch you did at the hotel with Iverson."

Oni looked at Gia and pinched her arm. "Gia, don't do that."

"Okay, my bad. I'm just playing, but I couldn't let that slide by."

"Whatever. Let's go." Oni was smiling as she slid her sunglasses on her face.

Gia did the same thing as she exited Oni's truck. Before walking away, she leaned down and looked at her face in the mirror to make sure she was good. When the both of them were finally ready, Gia sent a text to Jamil letting him know that they were outside. When he didn't respond right away, they decided to go ahead and go in anyway.

They could hear the music as they got closer to the back of the building. As soon as they rounded the corner, there were people everywhere. Male and females crowded the pool and the walkway leading to the only balcony on that side. The sliding door to that balcony was open, so Gia figured that must be where Shock lived.

The pool was surrounded by a stone wall that looked like it was made out of pebbles. The tall waterfall that cascaded down the side of it was lit up at the bottom, making the water look a bright green color. White beach chairs surrounded the pool, as well as umbrellas and tables.

In the corner of the pool area near the gate was a large speaker system that had music blasting from it. Along with the speakers was a large table with drinks, chips, and food lined around it. Everything from alcohol to bottled water and soda flooded the table.

Gia and Oni stayed close to one another, observing the outside setup before moving through the crowd until they were inside the apartment. Gia was looking all over the place for Jamil but hadn't spotted him yet. Niggas were damn near drooling as Gia and Oni passed. Some even had the nerve to try their luck at talking to them.

With a smile and quick shake of their heads, both women turned them all down. Well, almost all of them. One dark-skinned dude with muscles like a bodybuilder and the smile of a model caught Oni's hand and wouldn't let go.

"What's your name, beautiful?" he asked her.

Oni blushed and tried to pull her hand away. He grabbed his chest as if she'd broken his heart as she and Gia moved past him.

"Don't do me like that, li'l bit," he called after them, only getting a smile in return. "I'll see you again." He winked and walked away.

"Girl, he was cute," Gia told Oni as they circled the house fully and headed back out the door.

"I'm trying to feel things out first. I don't want to be talking to random niggas until I scope out the scene."

"I got you, but what I'm trying to figure out is where the hell Jamil is."

"Right here. Waiting on you." A pair of arms that had become her favorite resting place snaked around Gia's stomach and held her from behind. Jamil's embrace was followed by a soft kiss to the back of her neck. "I've been looking for you all day," Jamil whispered in her ear.

Gia turned around to face him and wrapped her arms around his neck. His hair was pulled up into a large bun on the top of his head. Gia had never seen it like that before. She'd seen plenty of other niggas wearing it, and she'd liked it, but she loved Jamil's. It was so messy and cute on him. His eyes were red and low as he stared down into her face. The orange hair that made up his eyebrows and the small beard on his chin was neatly trimmed.

"You been smoking?" she asked him.

He nodded.

"And you've been to the barbershop?"

He smiled and nodded again.

"You look so sexy." She kissed his chin while he kissed her forehead.

As she pulled away, she felt his hands wandering down to the bottom of her back. He pulled her closer before dipping his head and kissing her lips softly. His kiss was so soft Gia wasn't sure whether she should deepen it or leave it as it was, but she couldn't help herself. Her mouth parted just enough to suggest she wanted more, and he obliged.

Sliding his tongue into her mouth and pulling at her top lip with his teeth, Jamil gripped her back a tad bit tighter as he got lost in their kiss. It was clear he had been missing her just as she'd been missing him all day. Even with the faint taste of whatever weed he'd been smoking, Gia desired more, but it was time to let go.

When she pulled away, Jamil held her bottom lip with his teeth until she began to giggle. He pecked her mouth once more before letting her go.

"Got damn, girl. That chocolate be having a nigga feigning."

Still being held tightly in his arms, Gia smiled and observed his handsome features. "I've been missing you all day."

"Shit, you? I was two seconds from calling your ass to see where you was at."

"Hey to you too, Jamil." Oni made her presence known.

Jamil and Gia both looked at her with a smirk on their faces. "My fault, cousin. What's good?" He held his hand up for her to high-five it. When she did, he wrapped his arm right back around Gia.

"Nothing, but y'all are killing me acting like y'all in this house all alone."

"We are not." Gia grinned.

"The hell you say?" Oni rolled her eyes playfully. "Anybody watching y'all would probably agree with me."

Jamil let Gia's body go only to wrap his arm around her shoulder and pull her right back to him.

"That's Gee. Coming up in here while I'm high taking advantage of me and shit."

"Oh, whatever, Milli." She pushed his chest playfully. "Show us around."

Jamil looked around the living room like he'd forgotten where they were. Gia surveyed the navy blue and yellow Corona swim trunks he had on before realizing he was shirtless.

"Why you ain't got no shirt on up in here with all these women?" She raised her eyebrow above her shades.

He looked down at himself the same way he'd looked around the house. Gia shook her head, because that weed had him zoned all the way out.

"Because I knew you were coming." He winked and she smiled. "Come on. Let's go outside by the pool."

"Wait. We need to take our clothes off first," Gia told him as she stood next to Oni.

"Cool. Y'all can do that in my nigga Shock's room. I can guarantee you ain't nobody up in there."

Gia and Oni followed Jamil through the house full of people. Once they reached the last door on the hall, almost the entire environment changed. It was as if they'd entered a dead zone. Not only were there no people near the door, but even the air seemed cooler back there. Jamil twisted the knob and pushed the door open.

Once he stepped inside and the girls walked in, he closed the door behind them. Gia and Oni both began to remove their shirts first, but Gia was stopped when he pulled her into the bathroom with him. As soon as the door was closed, he reached for her shorts, unbuckling them for her and sliding them down over her bottom.

He quickly became so distracted by her curves that he stopped pushing her shorts down and just held on to her butt. With a cheek in each hand, he squeezed and pulled her forward so that his erection was positioned just between her thighs.

"What do you think you're doing?" Gia rested her arms around his neck.

"You've been on my mind all day. Then you show up looking all sexy and shit. What you expect me to do?"

Jamil looked at her as if she really had left him no other choice than to casually molest her in the bathroom. Her smile returned his hands to her body, both of them aggressively touching and groping her thighs and breasts.

"I want to be inside you so bad." He growled into her ear as he assaulted her neck relentlessly.

Gia moaned and grabbed his dick through his shorts, sending him over the edge. She looked into his eyes as she massaged the length of it in the palm of her hand. With one of his hands still on the bottom of her back and the other holding the side of her neck, Jamil closed his eyes and allowed her free range to his body.

Gia reveled in how sexy he looked as she touched him the way he touched her. When she wanted to do a little more, she pulled down his trunks as quickly as she could before he could stop her or before she could change her mind. At the same speed that his pants came down, so did her body.

Gia was on her knees in front of him with her hands circling the girth of his manhood. Totally forgetting where she was or what was going on around her, Gia wrapped her mouth around just the head first.

"Oh fuckkkk," he groaned as her mouth slid farther down. "Fuckkkk, Gee." He grabbed the back of her head and held his hand there.

He didn't move or try to force more in than she was ready for, which she appreciated. He simply leaned against the wall and enjoyed it. The pleasured look on his face urged her to go further, so she did. Gia moved forward until her entire mouth had nearly swallowed him whole. She did this a few times until she found a rhythm that worked for her.

"Sssss." Jamil sucked air through his teeth as he watched her. "Ah yeah, Gianna," he moaned.

Gia kept her eyes on him as she watched him fall apart above her. His eyes closed as his head fell back. The muscles in his arms jumped every time she sucked harder or made a slurping sound.

The pleasure he looked to be receiving had Gia wanting to suck his dick forever and ever.

If he was going to look and feel like this every time she touched him with her mouth, she had plans to do it more often. Gia reached up and grabbed his hand, holding it in one hand while using the other to slide back and forth in her saliva, making rotating circles around his shaft.

"Damn, Gee." He finally opened his eyes and looked down at her.

Gia could only imagine how she must have looked kneeling before him on the bathroom floor of his homeboy's apartment with his dick hanging from her mouth, but at that moment she didn't care. All she cared about was making him feel the way he made her feel just by looking at her.

"Aye, li'l shawty, ain't nobody supposed to be in here."

A deep voice on the other side of the door interrupted Gia's flow.

With no warning, she hopped up off the floor and wiped her mouth while Jamil leaned closer to the door so that he could hear who was talking. It was Oni.

"I'm just waiting on my cousin. She's using the bathroom."

"I feel you, but my bedroom is off-limits. There's another bathroom in the hallway."

Gia heard the voice again and looked at Jamil for an inkling of what to do next. The way he pulled his shorts up and pecked Gee on the lips like it was nothing wrong relaxed her some.

"That's just Shock's ass." He unlocked the door. "Come on."

"You go first." Gia stepped behind him and waited for the door to open.

Jamil stepped out first and Gia decided to wait a second. She needed to check her face in the mirror to make sure she was still good. When she was sure she was fine, she went ahead and pulled off the rest of her clothes.

"Nigga, leave my homegirl alone. I brought her in here to change," Gia heard Jamil say to the man.

There was some laughter between the two of them before Gia heard the man talking again.

"I should have known your ass was the only one that would be up in here after I clearly stated my bedroom was off-limits . . . my fault, li'l mama. You should have told me you were with this nigga."

"I told you my cousin was in the bathroom," Oni said.

"Milli Rock your cousin?"

Gia stepped out of the bathroom in her sandals and bikini. "No, I'm her cousin."

Shock and Jamil turned their attention to Gia. She stood near the door with a nervous look on her face. She was surprised to see Shock was the same dude Oni had turned down earlier. His eyes trailed up her body before stopping at her face. He looked from her to Jamil before smiling.

"I know this ain't Gee? I mean, it better be since you got her all up in my shit." He laughed and looked at Gia. "Your name Gee?"

A gorgeous smile crossed Jamil's face as he nodded and answered for Gia. "Yeah." He winked at her. "That's my Gee."

"Well, ain't this some shit? I peeped her and her cousin over here when they first came in. I tried to push up on this one back here"—he nodded toward Oni—"but she shot my ass down quick."

Gia and Oni both laughed.

"Oni, I know you ain't doing my man like that," Jamil said playfully.

"Oni?" Shock repeated.

"Yeah. That's me. I wasn't doing you like anything. I was just chilling." She smiled at him.

Gia watched the way Shock made Oni blush and only hoped he wouldn't do her dirty and she wouldn't play herself short by falling all over him too fast. He was indeed a sexy-ass nigga, which meant he was Oni's type. But Gia hoped she practiced some self-control.

"So, Miss Gee, tell me how you got my little brother ready to give you everything he's got so fast," Shock said.

Gia smiled at Jamil because Shock kept calling her Gee, which meant Jamil had been talking about her. He was the only person who called her that.

"Everything you've got, Milli?" Gia looked at Jamil with a smile tugging at her lips.

When his face began to turn red, Jamil held his head down, trying to hide the fact that Gia was making him blush.

"Nigga, I know your grown ass ain't blushing?" Shock leaned over dramatically in front of Jamil, trying to see his face.

"Man, go 'head." Jamil pushed him away and held his head back up.

Gia smiled brightly as she walked over to Jamil. She wrapped her arms around his waist and held on to him. Like it was the most natural thing in the world, Jamil's arm circled around her, holding her body against his. He then placed a quick peck on her forehead before looking back at Shock and Oni. The two of them were staring at Jamil and Gia in awe.

"Bruh, I like this shit right here." Shock pointed between Gia and Jamil. "It's real fucking cute."

All four of them laughed before Shock touched Gia's cheek. "With a smile like this, I see why my little brother's head in the clouds."

"Thank you," Gia told him as he turned around to face Oni.

"Y'all ready to hit the pool or what?"

"I am." Oni tossed her clothes into the small bag she'd brought with her and sat it on the floor near Shock's bed.

He watched her with a smirk on his face. "I see you like to be hardheaded. If I just said my room was off-limits, why you trying to leave your stuff in here like you're coming back?"

Oni walked directly to him and looked into his eyes. "Because I am."

A smile spread across Shock's handsome face as he looked her up and down. "Well, all right then, baby. Tell me what to do," he said in a hyper tone. "Show me who's in charge."

Oni and Jamil both laughed at Shock as Gia watched in silence. She really hoped Oni didn't dig herself too deep into this one.

"Man, y'all wilding. Let's hit this pool," Jamil told them all.

"Y'all can go ahead. We're coming. I need to put my clothes down," Gia told them while walking to Oni's bag.

Jamil and Shock left the room, leaving the girls alone. As soon as the door closed, Oni was in Gia's face.

"I heard slurping noises. You nasty."

Gia showed all of her teeth as she smiled. "I sure am, and I'll suck him up again if it makes him moan like he was doing."

"Bitch, yes! That nigga was so loud. I was like what the hell Gia in there doing to him."

"I told you, Oni. That nigga is addicting."

Gia rose from the floor and headed for the door with Oni behind her. With them in their swimsuits and back in the mix of people, every man they passed was either trying to touch them or yelling slick stuff. Gia was a professional at ignoring thirsty dudes. The way Oni handled it, apparently so was she.

The sun blazed against Gia's and Oni's skin as they exited the house and headed for the beach chairs where Jamil and Shock were standing. Just like in the house, all eyes were on the two of them. Although their swimsuits were a bit revealing and they both had bodies to die for, they didn't expect as much attention as they were getting.

"You an athlete?" a guy standing next to Jamil asked Gia as soon as they walked up.

"Yeah. Why you ask?" Gia asked.

"Your legs. They're big as hell and muscular. Tight like a runner or something."

One of Jamil's long arms was around her before she even had the chance to answer the man. Once her back was to his front, he kissed the side of her face.

"My baby is a runner. The second fastest in the nation. Even though she's going to be the first after she beats that white girl's ass." He kissed her again. "And she in the Olympics this year."

"Damn, *Sports Illustrated*." Oni joked with Jamil for knowing all Gia's stats.

"That's what up, baby girl. Congratulations." The guy winked. "Keep that body tight."

Gia frowned slightly because that last comment seemed a bit disrespectful when Jamil had just made it more than clear that she was with him.

"Marco, you must want your ass beat out here?" Jamil tried to step around Gia to get to the man, but she sidestepped and turned around to face him.

"Let's go swim, Milli." She held on to him, kissing his chin and then his chest.

Jamil was breathing so hard that his chest nearly touched her face every time he exhaled, not to mention the way his breath blew against her forehead as it released from his nose rapidly. She could feel the veins in his arms moving as she tried her best to hold him still without causing too much of a scene.

Her kisses continued until she could feel his body relaxing.

"Yeah. Let's do that." He grabbed her hand and pulled her toward the pool with Oni right behind them. Being that everyone was basically trying to be seen, no one was really swimming and the pool was fairly empty.

"You want to jump first or me?" Gia looked at Jamil.

"You go ahead. I'll come in after you."

Gia looked at him suspiciously before shaking her head. "Nah, I don't believe you. Jump with me."

Jamil smiled and shook his head. "To be for real, I really ain't trying to get my hair wet. That shit be making my head feel like it weighs a thousand pounds."

Gia burst out laughing at him as soon as he said it, because he was right. Hers did the same thing. Water and dreadlocks did not mix.

"I feel you. We don't have to swim."

"Thank you," Jamil said dramatically.

Oni, on the other hand, wasn't feeling their decision. She loved to swim. "So y'all not getting in?"

Jamil shook his head at the same time as Gia shook hers.

"Y'all make me sick." She pouted behind them as they walked back over to where Shock and a few more of their friends were standing.

"What happened? I thought y'all was getting in the pool?" Shock asked.

Oni stepped in front of them. "No. Neither of them want to get their hair wet."

Shock looked from Oni to Gia and Jamil. He raised his eyebrows at them. When Gia and Jamil looked away like they didn't care if he knew the truth, Shock just shook his head.

"Ain't nobody told them to grow those damn locks if they knew they weren't going to be able to do everything with them," Oni sassed with attitude.

Jamil laughed at her. "You mad, ain't you?"

Oni folded her arms across her chest. "Hell yeah, I'm mad. I want to get in the pool."

Shock pulled his shirt over his head. "Come on, li'l bit. I'll swim with you."

Oni perked up. "For real?"

Shock grabbed her hand and pulled her toward the pool. With no warning, he picked her up and jumped directly into the deep end. Oni's scream was drowned out as soon as they were submerged.

Gia stood wrapped in Jamil's arms smiling at them. When they came up, Oni was wiping water from her face when Shock pulled her right back under with him. Gia laughed because she could only imagine the type of cursing out Oni was going to give him when he finally gave her the chance to catch her breath.

"What kind of person is he?" Gia hadn't wanted to ask, but she needed to look out for Oni.

"Shock's cool people. If he fuck with her, then she's good. That's if he fucks with her, though. That nigga worse than females when it comes to dating."

"He ain't cool people like Iverson, is he?"

Jamil frowned and shook his head. "Hell, nah. Two totally different breeds of niggas. Iverson shouldn't even be associated with a nigga as real as Shock."

The disdain in his voice could be heard loud and clear, but Gia didn't bother to speak on it right then. It wasn't the time or the place. Especially with the way Jamil sounded. That was definitely a conversation that was going to need to be held in private.

"Just checking, because Oni can be a little gullible when it comes to men. I don't want her to get run over."

"She's good with him, just like you're good with me."

Gia looked up at him over her shoulder. "You told him about me." It was more of a statement than a question.

Jamil nodded.

"You said I could have anything you have?"

Again, Jamil nodded.

"What all does that entail?"

"Anything, Gee. Whatever I have or don't have, and you want it, it's yours."

In that moment Gia's heart melted, and if she hadn't known before, she knew then. The love she felt for Jamil was real, just as the love he so effortlessly proclaimed for her was real. All she hoped was that they could have it forever, long after that moment, and long after she'd left for the summer and they were back to their everyday lives. Outside their summer bubble and outside their imagination of real love.

Chapter Twelve

"How am I supposed to help Gia deal with her problems when I don't even know how to deal with mine? She's my best friend, and to see her hurting behind something I can't change only makes me feel even worse. Hopefully we'll get through this the same as we always do, but only time will tell." —Oni

It had been almost three hours and the party was starting to wind down. It had been a nice relaxing day full of fun, food, and laughter until some of the men started getting too drunk. Just like any other social gathering with too many people, trouble broke out.

There was a fight between two niggas who had apparently been sharing the same girl for a while. She showed up with one not knowing the other one was going to be there, and all hell broke loose.

It took damn near three people to hold each one of them back as the stupid female stood there screaming. After that, everything pretty much went downhill. Shock had been throwing people out left and right since then.

Oni and Gia were among the only people still there, and the only women. While Jamil helped Shock clear the stragglers out of his apartment and from around the pool area, Oni and Gia took it upon themselves to begin cleaning up.

They grabbed two large black trash bags and got to work. With the music still playing, it was easy for them to get everything done.

"Aye best friend, work it, bitch," Oni yelled to Gia with her arms in the air.

The beat to Future's "Real Sisters" had just dropped and blasted through the speakers. Like the rest of the songs on that album, they loved that song.

Not even giving it a second thought, Gia dropped the liquor bottle she'd just picked up from the ground into the trash bag and bent over. With her hands on her knees, she started dancing and popping her butt. Head down with her ass up, Gia was twerking like a stripper in her bikini.

"Aye. Get it, Gee. Get it. Work it, best friend. Work it." Oni stood across the way on the other side of the pool hyping her up.

"Go, Oni. Get it. Aye. Aye." Gia stood up and started bouncing her butt while pointing at Oni. "That's my sister. That's my sister," she yelled, encouraging Oni to keep dancing as well.

"I don't care if they was real sisters." Oni sang along with Future as she stood on the stone entrance to the diving board.

"Get on the table, Gia." Oni's face was bright with a smile as she watched Gia hop onto the table that was next to her.

Just as they'd done at home on many occasions before, the girls danced without a care in the world. From the way they danced it could easily be assumed that they danced professionally in videos or one of the top strip clubs in the world, but they were just two young, carefree girls living life and loving it.

"Shake that shit, Gee." Oni had her hands behind her head while moving her butt in a circle.

Gia had just bent over and placed her hands on the ground in front of her while her butt moved to its own beat when she heard Jamil's voice behind her.

"The *fuck* y'all think y'all out here doing?"

Gia and Oni both jumped up like they'd been caught by their father.

"Nah, don't stop all that shit now. Keep on shaking your ass like you're at King of Diamonds some damn where. The hell y'all think y'all at?" Shock followed Jamil up with his own attempt at fussing.

Gia and Oni both stood with their mouths balled up trying their hardest not to burst out laughing. Jamil, Shock, and two other guys that they didn't know but had seen at the party were all standing there watching them.

"Gee, I should beat your ass out here shaking in that little-ass bathing suit for all these fucking niggas to see," Jamil told her in a stern yet playful tone.

Gia looked across the pool at Oni and smiled. When Oni rolled her eyes at the men, Gia couldn't hold it any longer and burst out laughing. Oni was right behind her. The girls were cracking up as the men continued to fire off one threat after the other.

"Out here looking like the girls in that damn 'Tip Drill' video," Shock mumbled as he turned his attention to Oni.

"Y'all niggas ain't our damn daddies. We can dance if we want to. Hell, we're grown," Oni sassed as she hopped down off the diving board.

"Yeah, your li'l ass had better get off that diving board talking all that shit."

Oni looked at Shock and rolled her neck. "Why? You weren't going to do anything."

Shock looked at her and turned his nose up. "If I had run over there and body-slammed your ass into that water, you wouldn't be doing all that talking."

Oni frowned her whole face up at Shock before she burst out laughing. She didn't even bother to argue with him anymore. She simply walked back to where she'd left her trash bag and began throwing the rest of the empty cups and plates into it.

She looked over her shoulder when she heard Jamil talking to Gee. He had walked to where she was standing and was directly in front of her with one of his hands in his pocket while the other was holding on to the side of her neck.

It was more than obvious by the way she was looking that he was fussing at her. Oni was about to say something on her behalf but stopped when she saw Gia smiling. A few seconds later Jamil's head was nuzzled into her neck as she held on to his waist.

Oni smiled at the couple as she watched Jamil's hand slide down the side of Gia's leg until he was gripping the back of her thigh. A few giggles escaped Gia's mouth as her head fell to the side of Jamil's arm.

"Now, don't do that shit no more," Jamil yelled dramatically, causing Gia to fall over in laughter.

"Why you looking at them like that?"

Oni turned around to find Shock standing there watching her. "They're cute. He makes her happy." Oni looked back at Gia and Jamil for a few more seconds before she went back to cleaning the table she was next to.

"That's how it's supposed to be. Your man should always make you happy."

"Well, it's too bad that it's not always like that."

"Why it ain't? Your nigga don't make you happy?"

Oni looked at him and shook her head. "I don't have a man. Well, not one like that, anyway."

Shock took the empty chair at the table so that he could see her face. "Why not?"

Oni shrugged but didn't say anything. Not because she didn't want to, but because she really didn't know why she didn't have a man. Sure she had Isaac, but she couldn't really count him. She needed someone younger or at least in her age bracket. She was probably one of the most social women in her graduating class, but she was always the only one who had never had a boyfriend.

She'd been on plenty of dates and hung out with plenty of men, but she'd never really been in a real relationship. Sure she had guys who had tried to be with her, but after the sex, they would go right back to doing the friend thing.

Oni had tried not to assume it was because she was too sexual, but she couldn't think of anything else. Though she was a bit promiscuous, she wasn't a hoe. She could count on one hand how many men she'd ever had sex with. The thing about that was, they did it all the time.

Her sexual partners might have been limited, but the amount of sex she had was off the charts. In her mind she figured that wasn't too much of a problem being that it was with the same men every time. Clearly the word had gotten around and she'd quickly become a household name.

"Oni, tell me why you ain't got no man. Or at least a good one." Shock brought her attention back to him.

"I honestly don't know." She shrugged.

"How about you let me spend some time with you and see if I can figure out why you don't have one."

Oni looked at him for a long time before shaking her head. "I think I'm going to have to pass on that."

"Damn. Turned down two times in a row. That's a record for me. I think I feel bad."

"Don't feel bad. I just have a lot of personal issues going on right now." Oni looked off toward the men who had been out there with them. They were headed into the apartment. "Plus, I kicked it with somebody in your circle once."

Shock's eyebrows raised as he waited for her to tell him which of his friends she was referring to, but she never did. Truthfully, Oni didn't even know why she'd volunteered that information from the beginning. She could have just as easily said no and left it at that.

That was another one of her problems. She talked too much. No longer really paying Shock any attention, Oni scrubbed the table and gathered all of the trash along the ground until she was finished. He'd only sat there for a few more minutes before getting up to leave anyway. By the time she was done, Gia was walking toward her with the other black trash bag.

"Jamil said we can leave them right here and they'll get them."

"Oh, I was about to do that anyway. We've already cleaned all this mess up. The least they can do is take it to the dumpster."

"I know that's right." Gia pushed some of her hair out of her face. "You okay?"

Oni nodded. "Yeah. I'm cool. I'm just kind of tired. How much longer you want to stay?"

"Milli said something about them having a few drinks and playing cards. You want to do that or just go home?"

"We can do that. It's not like we have anything else to do once we get home anyway."

Gia agreed, and together, the two of them walked into the house. Just like they'd done before, they walked straight to Shock's room to get dressed, totally disregarding his rule about being in his room. They quickly removed their swimsuits and put on the change of clothes they'd brought along.

"Girl, why Shock keep trying to talk to me?"

"For real?" Gia pulled her shirt over her head.

"Yeah, but I don't think I should. I turned him down twice already and told the nigga I kicked it with one of his friends already."

Gia stopped pulling her shorts up and looked at Oni. "You did what?"

Oni plopped down on the bed. "I don't know why I said that."

"Me either. You need to just hush sometimes. He ain't need to know that. As far as you know, he and Iverson might not even be friends. You see that nigga wasn't at the party."

"You know something, I didn't even think about that."

"You was too busy flirting with Shock to notice. That's why you didn't think about it."

Oni smiled at Gia as she rubbed lotion all over her body. "You right. We have been hanging pretty tough today."

"I think you should hang out with him. Jamil vouched for him, so he must be good people."

"That nigga older than us, though."

"I know you ain't acting like his age is a problem when Isaac is probably his daddy age."

"I'm so tired of you."

Gia shrugged. "And . . . what's your point?"

Oni thought about it and realized she didn't have one, especially since she was, in fact, dealing with a nigga that was way older than her. At least Shock was only older by a few years.

"I guess you're right. I'ma tell him I changed my mind."

Gia pulled Oni from the bed. "Thank you."

Since they were completely dressed, they headed back out front to help the men clean up. When they got into the living room, Jamil, Shock, and the other two men were all seated around the table with cards in their hands and liquor bottles and shot glasses on the table.

"I know I told y'all to stay out my room," Shock said with a blunt hanging from between his lips.

"We're finished now. We won't go back," Oni told him.

"Nah, Gee might not go back, but you will. As soon as I can get you to kick it with me for a little while."

Oni looked at Gia for reassurance. When she nodded, Oni smiled. "We'll see about that."

Just as Shock turned around to respond, a knock came on his door. Oni and Gia both looked at the door, neither of them moving to answer it. It wasn't their house.

"I'll grab it." Jamil stood and headed for the door while the girls busied themselves in the kitchen.

Oni and Gia had been raised to clean up, so no matter where they were, if there was stuff to be done, they had no problem doing it. Especially since they had no plans on drinking or playing cards.

"I know the party ain't over already."

Oni stilled when she heard his voice. Instinctively she looked up at Gia, who was looking at her as well.

"What should I do?" Oni whispered.

"Nothing. Iverson ain't your man. Chill like you've been doing.

Just don't let that nigga be all up on you like y'all go together. You know how niggas like to act."

Oni nodded and continued wiping off the counter.

When Iverson and Jamil came into view, Jamil was looking at Gia. He raised an eyebrow and she nodded. Gia really had herself something with him. It was very nice of him to even consider her feelings when it came to Iverson.

"Man, how y'all close the party down before I get here?" Iverson slapped hands with Shock first before following up with the other two men.

"Nigga, it took your ass all day to get here." Jamil sat down and picked his cards back up.

"Had business to handle, my boy." Iverson set his phone and keys down on the table. "Y'all ain't got no more food left up in here?" He was walking toward the kitchen when he noticed Gia and Oni.

A smile crossed his face as he headed for Oni. She could already tell by the way that he was looking that he was about to try something slick, so she moved and pretended to be putting the sodas in the refrigerator.

"Damn, y'all must be special. Y'all get to stay and kick it with the homies." Iverson was leaning against the counter staring at both girls.

"Something like that," Gia offered.

"What's up, Oni? You ain't speaking today?"

Oni smiled and waved. "You were talking."

Iverson's eyes trailed up her body, stopping at her exposed stomach. "Who you trying to look all sexy for? I ain't got to beat nobody's ass, do I?"

Oni gave an awkward smile and shook her head. "Nah, I'm just chilling. It was a pool party, so I wanted to make sure I dressed the part."

"Well, you definitely did that." He eyed her with lust. "Make a nigga want to do some things to you."

"Iverson, damn. Snatch her clothes off and fuck her already, why don't you? You're being way too disrespectful." Gia shot him an evil look.

Iverson held his hands up in mock surrender before showing all of his teeth to Gia, who found nothing amusing about his behavior.

"My fault. I ain't mean no harm. Just expressing my appreciation for something nice."

"It's easier ways to do that," Gia sassed.

"Understood." He winked at Gia and tapped Oni on her butt. "My fault, Oni. Just had me reminiscing for a minute."

"Nigga, what the fuck I just say?" Gia got a little louder.

Oni could tell Gia was starting to get pissed off because that was pretty much the only time she yelled. Though she was grateful to Gia standing up for her, Oni didn't want to cause any problems with Jamil and Iverson. She could already tell by the looks Jamil was giving Iverson that he was going to be up and ready to fight if he said one more thing to Gia.

"It's cool, Gia. I ain't worried about it, boo." Oni tried to deescalate the situation because clearly Iverson felt like playing games.

"I feel you, but you still don't let no nigga disrespect you like that." Gia threw the towel on the counter and walked out into the living room.

"Aye, Milli Rock, you need to check your girl's attitude. That shit is ridiculous." Iverson tried to laugh it off, but neither Jamil nor Gia thought it was funny.

"He don't have to check nothing over here," Gia said.

"Chill, Gee." Jamil stood. "Iverson, don't say nothing else to Gee, and leave Oni's ass alone too. Come sit your ass down and play cards and get out of there with them fucking females."

Iverson walked toward the table and took a seat on one of the barstools. "Everybody in this bitch in their feelings today?"

"Nah, we chilling. That's your loud mouth coming in here trying to start shit," Jamil told him.

"I ain't trying to start a damn thing. I was just making conversation, but I see y'all niggas ain't trying to fuck around." Iverson pulled some folded-up papers from his back pocket and tossed them across the table to Jamil. "Here. I brought you the identity information, and the money contracts and shit we agreed to with Alira's people. They faxed it to me this morning."

"Bet," Jamil said without even looking up from the table. "I'll look over it later."

"Nah, nigga. Look at that shit now so I can send that shit back to her on my way home."

"Boy, hell nah, ain't no stopping. This nigga got to play his hand first." Shock spoke up.

"Y'all can do that shit anytime. Business first." Iverson sat on the seat looking at them.

Jamil looked at Iverson. "What's the rush? Why you can't just send it in the morning?"

"Because I got some shit I need to handle in the morning. Plus I told her I was about to meet up with y'all boys and I would send it back to her tonight."

Jamil and Shock both ignored Iverson and went back to playing their hand of cards. They were talking junk to the other men at the table with them when Iverson hopped up and walked over. He snatched the paperwork from the table and opened it dramatically.

"Nigga, look at this shit and make sure everything is right. I'm about to dip."

Oni and Gia sat on the sofa next to each other trying to figure out what the big deal was with Iverson and why he was being so extra. The last couple of times they'd seen him he seemed a lot more laid back, but today he was being a tad bit too aggressive for their liking.

Versus speaking their opinion on something that had nothing to do with them, they both sat back and talked until Gia got up to stand next to Jamil.

Jamil laughed in disbelief. "Bruh, if you don't back the fuck up off me." He playfully elbowed Iverson.

Iverson took a step back but tossed the papers back down at Jamil. "See, y'all niggas in here playing and shit instead of taking care of business," he fumed as he walked back to where he'd just set his keys and phone. "Y'all niggas just call me when y'all ready to handle business, because clearly right now ain't it." When he turned around to face the table again, seeing Gia leaning on Jamil's shoulder must have pissed him off, because he really went off then. "If your ass wasn't so busy trying to show off for these hoes, you could get shit handled," he bellowed.

"Whoa," Gia yelled as she stumbled backward.

Jamil had jumped up from the table so fast, he'd knocked her over. With one hand around Iverson's neck, he used the other one to punch him in the face. After the first hit, the two men were involved in a full-out brawl, blow after blow being passed.

"Y'all break this shit up," Shock yelled as the other two men pried Jamil and Iverson apart. "Y'all stop that shit. Y'all boys. Come on, man." He tried to reason with them.

"Fuck that nigga," Jamil huffed as he sat back in his seat.

"Nigga, fuck your illiterate ass." Iverson wiped the blood from his mouth. "The only reason your ass ain't trying to read that shit right now is because your dumb ass can't." Iverson picked his keys up from the floor. "Dumb muthafucka. You so wrapped up in this black-ass bitch, make that hoe teach your retarded ass how to fucking read. Hell, make the bitch teach your stupid ass cursive. Maybe you can sign your own shit from now on."

The entire living room fell quiet for a minute as everybody looked at Jamil. Well, everybody except for Gia. She had just slapped the taste from Iverson's mouth and was well on her way to doing it again until the side of her face met the back of Iverson's hand. All hell broke loose after that.

Jamil didn't even pass go or collect two hundred dollars before he was on Iverson, practically beating his brains out with the empty Hennessy bottle. Oni and Gia both screamed for the other men to break it up, but they didn't.

Blood splattered everywhere as the heavy glass bottle connected with the bones in Iverson's face over and over. You could hear the low grumbling between the two men as they fought against one another. Sadly, Iverson wasn't putting up much of a fight with the anger from Jamil and the thick glass of the empty liquor bottle.

When Oni noticed Iverson was barely moving, she grabbed Gia's arm and screamed. "He has to stop, Gia."

"Nah. Let him get some. That nigga was out of line for that shit," one of the men told Oni.

"No. He's going to kill him," Gia pleaded.

"He's not going to kill him," Shock said solemnly.

"Yes, he is. You have to make him stop." Oni grabbed Shock's arm and pushed him toward the fighting men. "Please, Shock. Make them stop."

He looked at Oni and Gia once more before nodding toward the other two men. Like obedient little guard dogs, they put an end to the brawl. Apparently Shock had known what he was talking about when he said that Jamil wasn't going to kill Iverson, because Jamil put up no fight as they pulled them apart.

Jamil's chest rose and fell rapidly as he tried to calm his breathing. Iverson, on the other hand, was barely able to pull himself up from the floor. His entire face was swollen as he wiped blood from his face with the bottom of his shirt.

"Y'all help this nigga to his car," Shock told the two flunkies.

Each of them grabbed one of Iverson's arms and threw it over their shoulder as they exited Shock's apartment. When they were gone, Gia went to Jamil to check on him, only for him to snatch away from her and walk to the back of the house.

Gia went to follow him but was met with a locked door. Oni and Shock stood in the living room listening to her bang on the door, begging for him to open it for her. After five minutes of knocking, she slid to the floor and sat with her back against the door telling him that she wasn't leaving.

Oni's heart broke for them both because that was a tough situation. On one hand, Jamil's friend had just told some of the most embarrassing information in front of a room full of people. Though Gia didn't care and would be there for him anyway, he didn't know that.

"Iverson is so fucking lame," Oni said to no one in particular. Being that she and Shock were the only two in the room, of course he'd heard her.

"Yeah. That was fucked up. I remember when Milli first told us that shit. I told him he shouldn't have told Iverson, but he kept saying that nigga was like his brother." Shock sat next to Oni on the sofa and shook his head. "Iverson is the jealous type. He likes attention. If he thinks anyone is getting more than him, he'll do whatever he can to destroy them. Jamil always refused to believe that nigga would do him the same way, but not me. I saw the envy in his eyes for Milli. I knew it was only a matter of time before this shit blew up."

Oni sat quietly just listening to Shock, trying her hardest to figure out how someone could feel so much hate and animosity toward a person they considered to be their friend. That didn't make any sense to her. It didn't matter what her and Gia went through, she would never tell something Gia had told her in confidence.

"So he really can't read? Or was Iverson just being messy?"

Shock shrugged and scooted farther down on the sofa. "If he could, do you think your girl would be out there begging him to talk to her?"

Oni could tell Shock didn't want to tell Jamil's business and had answered her question the best he could without being disloyal. So instead of pushing any further, she simply nodded and lay back on the sofa with him.

She didn't know how long it had been before Gia finally walked to the living room telling her she was ready to go. Shock could tell she was bummed out and begged her not to worry about Jamil, but he and Oni both knew that wasn't happening. It was written all over her face.

On the entire ride home Oni watched Gia call Jamil again and again to no avail. She could hear the subtle sniffles every so often as she wiped her eyes continuously.

"It's going to be okay, Gia. He just needs some time."

Gia nodded and wiped her eyes again. "I just feel so bad for him because I know he's embarrassed. Iverson shouldn't have done him like that." Her eyes began to water again.

"Yeah. That was low down."

"It's crazy, too, because it all makes sense now. He doesn't like to text. Anytime I text him, he calls instead of texting me back. He's always making me spell stuff. Anytime we go out to eat, he never looks at menus. When I try to show him stuff on my phone, he always makes me read it to him because he's too tired." Gia cried. "Oh my God, Oni. He really can't read. I don't know how I didn't see it before." Gia put her head down on her knees and began to cry a little harder.

After listening to Gia explain everything, Oni felt extra bad. How could someone live their entire adult life without knowing how to read? Life had to be hard for him. Now with all of it making so much sense to her, she sympathized with Gia and Jamil even more.

Just being there for Gia and listening to her cry was all Oni could do. Offering her sympathy didn't even seem like enough anymore. It wasn't like she was in a very good position to be offering advice anyway.

What if she told Gia something wrong? What if she told her he would be back and he never came? Would Gia blame her for it? Oni didn't know, but she didn't want to take that chance. So with her hand on Gia's back, she comforted her as best she could without words. Hopefully everything would be all right in the morning.

They were still driving when Oni's phone rang. When she saw that it was Isaac, she answered. "Hey."

"Hey. Can I see you today? Maybe have a late dinner or something?"

Oni looked at Gia and made up her mind. "Not tonight. My cousin is going through some things with her boyfriend, so I think I'm going to stay with her until she feels better."

"Damn. She okay? Did that nigga do something to her?"

Oni smiled at his protectiveness of Gia when he didn't even know her. "No, just had some personal issues brought out, and it's kind of put a strain between them."

He sighed. "Damn. Well, I hope everything works out for her. Hit me up if you change your mind."

"I will. Love you."

"Love you too."

Oni loved Isaac for real. At first it had just been something nice to say, but the more time she spent with him, the more her feelings grew. Maybe one day they could make something serious happen between them. If not, there was always Shock. She smiled as she thought about the brewing possibilities between them.

Chapter Thirteen

"I never knew how hard it would be to live without Gee until she showed my ass. Our love had bloomed so quick that even I had to question whether it was real or fake sometimes. But then the days came where I no longer had her, and every negative thing that ever came to mind about our love not being real faded into the darkness of my mind. Never to be considered again." —Milli

Three weeks later

Jamil sat on the steps of his parents' apartment eating a bag of chips and drinking some soda. It was a little after eight o'clock at night, so the block was quiet other than the chatter of small children or other neighbors lounging on their porch.

The sun had set. It was still summer in Georgia, so minus the small breeze that came every so often, it was still scorching outside. Relaxing in a pair of gym shorts and a tank top, Jamil watched the cars as they sped up the street past his house.

He had been inside sleeping all day and had just woken up. Zanetta and Owen were in the middle of one of their drug-induced fights, and he honestly had no desire to watch any of their foolishness right then.

When he'd heard Zanetta call his name asking for his help, he'd thought for a moment that she really needed something. After hopping out of his bed and running to her rescue only to find out Owen had taken all of their extra drugs and she wanted him to give her more, he sucked his teeth and exited the apartment altogether.

The last couple of weeks of his life had been rough. He had enough on his mind and on his plate without dealing with the same old issues that had followed him his entire life. For just one minute, all he wanted was to relax and not think about anything. Not Zanetta, Owen, the block, or Gia.

Gia.

He missed the hell out of her. Outside of occasional updates from Shock, he hadn't heard anything from her since the night of Shock's pool party. The only reason he knew that she was still in Georgia and missing him like crazy was because Shock had been hanging out with Oni a lot lately.

The first time Shock had told Jamil that he'd seen Gia crying, Jamil felt like shit. He had wanted to run to her wherever she was and hold her until she felt better, but he couldn't. He'd already known it but had just recently come to terms with him not being good enough for her.

As much as he wanted to believe he could be with a woman like Gia, he knew better. Had he stuck to his first thoughts and not even taken it there with her, they wouldn't even be in this situation.

She wouldn't be sad behind a nigga who couldn't even write his own name, and he wouldn't be sick behind a woman who he'd known from the beginning was too good for him. Something in him put up a caution sign at every corner, yet he'd blatantly ignored them.

Had someone told him at the beginning of the summer that by the end of it he would meet a woman, fall in love, and end up heartbroken, he wouldn't have believed them. After all, he wasn't even on the prowl for a woman, let alone a serious relationship or the feelings that came with it.

"Boy, you still out here picking up the pieces to your heart?"

Jamil looked up when he heard Shock's voice. He was so busy

doing exactly what he'd said he wouldn't do, which was thinking about Gia, that he hadn't even noticed him drive up to the curb.

"Nigga, fuck you. Where you coming from?" Jamil got up and walked to the window of Shock's Hummer.

"Ain't shit for real. I was thinking about heading out here to the little mock Color Run they're holding for lupus tomorrow. You trying to roll?"

Jamil shook his head. "Nah. I'm good. Where it's supposed to be?"

"It's right at the high school around the corner. I'm only going out there for my sister. You know what she be going through with that lupus, so I try to make sure I donate a li'l something every year. If time permits, I slide through and jog a few laps."

Jamil frowned slightly. "Oh, damn. I forgot Lisa had lupus." He checked the time on his watch. "I guess I can slide through for a minute. Hit the track a few times with you."

Jamil walked around the back of the truck and slid into the passenger seat. Once he was in and comfortable, Shock pulled off. He turned the music down some as he sped down the highway.

"You still ain't hit your girl Gee up?"

Jamil shook his head. "Why you ask?"

"I saw her yesterday. Still pretty as ever, but she has sad eyes these days."

Jamil's mind went left upon hearing that Gia was still hurting behind him. He hadn't ever wanted to be the cause of her pain, but clearly that was inevitable. What was done, was done. He could easily hit her up and try to make amends, but it was better this way.

The longer they went without talking, the easier it would get for her, and by the time she was set to fly home, she could go back to her regularly scheduled program. No him, no them, just her. The way it needed to be.

"She's a good girl and I really think you should hit her up."

"Nah. Gee's different. She needs a nigga who can match the

shit she has going on. I knew before I started fucking with her that we wouldn't work. I should have left well enough alone. What I look like being at the Olympics and can't even read her damn name when she wins?"

"Nigga, fuck that. You love that damn girl and she loves your yellow ass. I don't know why you're being so difficult. Nobody gives a fuck about all that other shit."

"Just leave it alone, man. It's done." Jamil ended the conversation.

He wasn't really in the mood to talk about Gia. Neither his heart nor his mind was strong enough at the moment. Hopefully once they got to the track and he ran a few laps, he would feel a little better, because right then he felt awful.

All he wanted to do was go back home, sit on his stoop, and chill. Well, in his mind that's what he wanted to do. In his heart he wanted to be wrapped up in Gia's body, her legs around his waist, with her arms circling his neck.

"Milli Rock." Shock was looking at him. "You ain't hear me?"

Jamil looked around. They were parked at the back of the school. There were purple banners and various signs with pictures of women on them.

"I said we're here, nigga. Get out."

"My fault." Jamil opened the door and met Shock around the front of the Hummer.

They were dressed similarly in gym shorts and tank tops as they walked toward the track. There were throngs of people in various spots talking, sitting, and running, while others were parading around the grass holding pictures of their family members who were suffering from or who had passed away from lupus.

"My mama and Lisa out here somewhere. Let me know if you see them." Shock looked all around the open field as Jamil did the same.

"Ain't that them over there?" Jamil pointed toward the group of women that had just finished running around the track.

"Hell yeah. Come on." Shock walked toward them with Jamil in tow.

Once they caught up with them, they exchanged hugs and greetings. After seeing how happy Lisa and Shock's mom, Margaret, were to see them, Jamil was glad he had come. They even walked around the track a few times before the announcer announced that they were getting ready to start the fund-raising relays and asked everyone to clear the track. Since Lisa had her own tent set up in the corner with chairs and drinks, Jamil and Shock relaxed for a few minutes with Shock's family.

"When they started doing this part?" Jamil asked Shock as the runners lined up on the track.

"They do it every year the day before. Tomorrow is the real thing. Tonight is just where they collect donations and shit."

Jamil nodded as the gun sounded and the first set of runners took off in a light jog around the track.

"Oh, that's what's up. How much you normally donate?" Jamil asked.

"A few stacks." Shock looked past him at the people who were lining up on the track. "Depending on what my pockets looking like."

Jamil nodded again and turned his attention back to the parade of people that had packed the park out. The cool breeze and the constant activity were a welcome distraction for Jamil. He had been in such a bad head space since leaving Gia that even the simplest thing had begun to take too much effort.

"Dang, that girl is fast," Lisa told Shock as she handed him a soda. "Did they say who she was?"

"Nah. I think they say their names at the end," Shock said.

"Well, I'm sure I'll hear it, because she's about to beat all them people out there," Lisa said before sitting back in her chair.

"Oh shit. Milli Rock, is that Gee?" Shock pointed.

Jamil's head popped up at the speed of lightening. "Is that Gee where?"

"On the track. The dark-skinned girl in the front with the red shorts on."

Jamil stood so that he could get a better look at the girl who was leading the race. When he felt the familiar thumping of his heartbeat speeding up, he knew it was her. She was the only person to ever have that effect on him.

The long black locs with the different color ends swayed against her back as her ponytail swung from side to side. Her arms pumped by her side as every muscle in her sexy legs popped out when she passed where they were sitting. The tight blue top hugged her body as she ran to the finish line and slowed her pace.

It took her a minute to slow down even after she'd finished running, but that was all Jamil needed to get to her. He hadn't even realized he was moving toward her until he was only a few feet from her. She was on the side of the red track with her hands resting above her head.

He could see from the way her back was moving that she was breathing hard. Jamil tried everything he could to stop his hands from shaking, but he couldn't. He was nervous and he didn't know why. This was his Gee. There was no way she could have stopped loving him in three weeks.

"And the winner of the first-place prize of five hundred dollars is Miss Gianna Ellis. Ladies and gentlemen, give her a round of applause, please. Gianna has kindly decided to donate her winnings back to the Lupus Foundation."

The crowd went wild as Gia stood at the end of the track smiling. Her head was tilted back and she was smiling at someone in the stands. Instinctively, Jamil turned around to see whoever it was that had her attention. There was a tall, burly man around her color with a shirt on it that had "Gia" written in purple.

Jamil wanted to run to her and ask who the man was, but he could tell by the matching smile and the same round eyes that he had to be her father. He watched the two of them smile and wave at each other and only made himself feel worse.

Gia didn't look like she had been missing him half as much as he had been missing her. The sad eyes that Shock had spoken of didn't look to be anywhere in sight. All he saw right then was a winner. A beautiful conqueror who was deserving of the happiness she looked to be basking in at the moment.

Jamil watched her for a few more minutes before he prepared to head back to Lisa's tent. Just as he was about to turn around, he caught her eyes. That fast his feet became cement and his heart melted into a puddle in his chest.

The vibrant smile that had just brightened her face was now gone, replaced with a sullen look that dampened her entire appearance. The beautiful scowl that she shot toward him had him back in the same slump he'd been in for weeks.

For a long time they stood there just staring at one another, neither of them willing to look away first. However, Jamil hated the way she was looking at him now. It was nothing like the way she normally did. This was a look of distance and hurt, something he most definitely was not accustomed to getting from her. Anytime she had looked at him in the past, it was as if he was the sun to her earth, the stars in her sky, the knight in her favorite fairy tale. Now all of that was gone. Pain and loneliness took its place.

Jamil stood stuck in a trance just looking at her until he realized that she had indeed looked away and was now walking farther out of his life. Like a bolt of lightning, Jamil took off in her direction.

With legs much longer than hers, he caught up with her instantly. Already knowing that his words were going to fail him, Jamil didn't even bother with them. Instead, he wrapped her in his embrace like he'd done many times before.

With her back to his chest and his arms resting tightly around her chest, Jamil pressed his face into her neck. Her damp skin was slick against his lips as he kissed one of the spots he'd been missing like crazy.

"Get off me, Jamil."

Jamil?

"Gee . . . baby."

"Don't baby me. Just let me go, and you go back to wherever you've been for the past few weeks."

Jamil tapped her chest where her heart was supposed to be. "I've been here, Gee." He tapped it again and held her tighter. "I've been right here. I miss you so much."

"Not enough for you to return my calls though, huh?" Gia tried to walk away, but he held her tighter, if that was even possible, and took a few steps with her until she stopped trying to pull away. "Milli, please let me go." She sighed.

"Why, Gee? You don't love me no more?" He kissed down the side of her face. "Was it fake to you? Huh? What we had, was it fake to you?"

"Hell fucking no, it wasn't fake to me. Why do you think I want to kill you right now?"

Jamil closed his eyes and inhaled her scent. "Don't kill me unless you're dying with me. I can't make it another day without you."

Gia held her head forward and released a deep breath. With the back of her neck exposed, Jamil took advantage and placed kisses there as well. The more he kissed, the more she relaxed. When he felt her hands on the arm he had thrown across her chest, he nearly fainted.

His entire stance got weak at the smallest touch from her. He hadn't known he missed her this much until he saw her walking away. While sitting at home on his stoop, he'd made himself believe that was what he wanted, when in reality it was the exact opposite.

"I don't want to want you, Gee, I don't." He sniffed. "I just can't help myself. Every time I try to take my mind off you, it goes right back. I told you I was fucked up, Gee."

"And I told you I didn't care." Gia laid her head back so that it was resting against his chest. "Still don't, Milli. I didn't then, and I still don't right now."

Jamil felt his throat getting tight, so versus saying anything, he simply held on to her. He was almost positive that if he opened his mouth to talk he would cry, so he just held her instead. When no more words came from him, Gia spun around in his arms so that she was facing him.

She pushed the locs that had fallen in his face away before placing a kiss on his chin. She did this a few times before tilting her head back so that she could look at him.

"Why you crying, Milli?" She wiped one of his tears away.

"Because, Gee, I can't read." He sniffed to keep his tears at bay. "And you deserve better, but I want you. I don't want nobody else to have you."

Gia kissed his chin again before wrapping her arms around him. "I'll teach you."

"How? You're leaving in a few weeks."

"We'll find a way."

Jamil didn't see how they were going to be able to make that happen, but he nodded and pulled her close to him anyway. He honestly didn't care about reading. He hadn't known how to thus far. All he cared about was being with Gee.

"What you doing here?" he was finally able to ask once he'd gotten himself together.

"My aunt, Oni's mom, has lupus. She asked me to run in the race for her."

"That's what's up. Shock's sister has lupus too."

"I know. Oni told him we'd meet him out here."

Jamil thought about what she'd just said for a minute before pulling away from her. "That nigga set me up."

Gia looked confused. "What you talking about?"

"I was at the house chilling and he came and scooped me talking about chilling out here with Lisa and his family for a little while."

Gia smiled and shook her head. "Oni told that nigga last night that I was running today." Gia chuckled to herself. "He's such a busybody."

Jamil smiled as he looked down at her. "Nah, that nigga was exactly what I needed him to be today." He kissed her forehead. "I love you, Gee."

"I love you too, Milli."

"Your dad is here?"

Gia's eyes widened as if she'd forgotten. She quickly pulled away from him and nodded.

"Oh my God, yes. He's going to kill me!" Gia's eyes were huge as she covered her face momentarily.

"Why?" Jamil didn't like the sound of that, daddy or not.

"I can almost guarantee you he's somewhere watching us right now."

Jamil shrugged because he honestly didn't give two fucks about her daddy. However, judging by the way Gia was acting, she sure as hell did.

"What you doing when you leave here?" Jamil asked.

She was still looking around for her dad. "Don't know, why?"

"I want to be with you."

Gia's mind was back onto him that fast. "I'll come to you. My daddy is staying at my aunt's house, so once we leave there and head back to Oni's house, I'll have her bring me to you."

Jamil didn't know if he liked that plan because it didn't sound definite, but he agreed anyway. They stood there talking for a few more minutes before parting ways. Though being set up wasn't something he was too fond of, Jamil was definitely thankful for Shock in this instance.

Jamil lay flat on his back staring at the ceiling in his room. He'd made his last play of the night about an hour ago and had come straight home after that. Lying up with Gia had been the only thing on his mind since leaving her at the track earlier, and he couldn't wait until she got there.

She'd called him a little over thirty minutes ago to let him know things were still on and to wait up for her. Of course he said he would, and that was exactly what he had been doing since then. Even while he was out on the block slanging, he had been waiting.

While he ate his late-night dinner from Krystal, he had been waiting. Even right then while lying in his bed, he was waiting. From the moment she'd told him she was coming, he had been waiting, and he would continue to wait until she got there. He was just that eager.

It had been too long since he'd been covered deep up in her love, and he had every intention of being just that the moment she entered his house. Zanetta and Owen had long ago gone to bed, so that was one less thing he had to worry about.

The only thing on his mind right then was sexing Gee. His dick had been hard since he got out of the shower and didn't look to have any plans of deflating anytime soon. Absentmindedly, Jamil's hand went to his erection and began to stroke it.

The sight of Gia in the red running shorts from earlier was fresh in his mind, and it was only making his wait that much longer. Just as the visuals of her mouth around the girth of his dick popped into his head, his phone rang.

Jamil snatched it from the nightstand and answered it as soon as he saw Gia's name. "Yeah."

"Hey. I'm outside."

"Here I come."

Jamil hung up and walked toward the door, which was extremely awkward given the fact that his manhood was damn near as hard as it could get. He hadn't had sex since the last time he'd been with Gia, and it was definitely showing.

As soon he opened the front door, she was ready to step into the house. Oni waved at him and pulled off once she was sure Gia was in good hands.

"Took you long enough." Jamil closed the door behind them once they were inside.

Gia shrugged. "I'm here now." She left him in the kitchen and headed down the hallway to his room.

She was seated on the edge of the bed kicking her shoes from her feet when he joined her. Her hair was all tied up in a multicolored wrap while she was dressed leisurely in a pair of tights and a fitted shirt.

Her face looked brighter than it had at the track earlier, and he was glad. Maybe that meant she was just as happy to be with him as he was with her. The lime green shoes she had been wearing on the first day he'd ever met her lay on the floor.

It was crazy how much things between them had changed since that day at the gas station. Never in a million years would Jamil have guessed she would have his heart in such a small amount of time.

"What you thinking about?" Gia asked him.

"That day I saw you and Oni in the gas station across the street." He smiled and lay down on the bed behind her.

"It don't even feel like it's been a month already, does it?"

"Nah. Not for real, but it has, and now you're about to dip back to Hawaii." Jamil rubbed his hand down her back. "What's going to happen then?"

Gia lay back and rested her head on his chest. "We're going to keep being together."

"How? Long distance never really works out."

Gia was quiet for a minute. "I don't know. We'll figure it out, though. We have to." There was a long stretch of silence as Gia played with the hair on his stomach. "I think we're going to have a baby, Milli. My cycle is late, and it's never late . . ."

Silence filled the space between them as he tried to make sense of what she'd said. When he didn't say anything fast enough, she sat up and looked at him.

"Jamil, don't just lie there like that. Say something."

Flabbergasted and lost for words, Jamil sat up and pushed himself back against his headboard.

"My fault, Gee, you just caught me off guard, bae. Come here."
He pulled her to him so that she could straddle his lap. "When
did you find out?"

"While we were broken up. It's really early, but if I'm right, we
made this baby during the time we spent in Atlanta at the hotel."
She held her head down. "I thought about getting an abortion
and never telling you anything, but I couldn't make myself do it. I
kept thinking about how you sounded during sex. When you
would tell me you love me, and I couldn't. Our baby was made
out of happiness and love, and I don't want to destroy that."

Jamil wrapped his arms around her waist and held her. She
looked so innocent and pure as she waited for him to express his
thoughts.

"I was really sad at first because all I want to do is run. Being
pregnant will stop that."

"Why will it stop it?"

"Because I'll get huge." She held her head down. "The Colonel
is going to be so disappointed. He's always telling me not to let
boys trick me and ruin my future."

Jamil held her head up so that he could look at her face clearly.
"You think I tricked you?"

Gia shook her head. "No. We did this together. I gave myself
to you willingly, knowing I wasn't on birth control."

Even though she tried her hardest to make everything sound
all right, he could tell she was really bummed out. It was all in her
tone and the way she looked. He hated to have put her in such a
fucked-up situation, because her life was about to change drasti-
cally.

His life wasn't shit. It didn't matter if he had a kid or not. Hell,
having a baby might actually make things better for him. He'd finally have a purpose. Something other than waking up every day
supplying the hood with poison.

Jamil stared at her flat stomach before placing his hand on it.
"Everything will be okay, Gee. Just keep running, baby. Run until

you can't anymore, and as soon as you give birth, I'll be there with you. Every step of the way. Don't worry."

"How, Jamil? How will you be there?"

Jamil looked away for a moment. "I don't know yet, but I'll take these next couple of months to map it out and set some things up for us." Jamil grabbed Gia's face so that they were looking at each other. "Don't give up on your dreams, Gee. And don't give up on me. I promise I'm going to make something happen."

Gia looked like she believed him. That was all he needed for now. As long as she had faith in him, then he would do whatever he had to do in order to get where she needed him to be.

"You sure you want to keep it? I understand your position, so I wouldn't be mad at you if you chose not to."

Gia leaned her head to the side and closed her eyes. "I don't know. Let's just make love, Milli. That's all I want to do right now."

Nothing further needed to be said. As gently as he could, Jamil laid Gia back on the bed and undressed her. Once she was completely nude, he pulled her head free of her wrap. Anytime he made love to Gee, he liked to see her hair. She reminded him of an African goddess, and he reveled in the thought that she'd chosen him.

With her legs still thrown across his thighs, Jamil lifted her butt from the bed and dove face first into her love box. It was wet from anticipation and dripping with desire she felt for him.

As soon as she arched her back and grabbed the back of his head, Jamil went harder. Her moans fell persistently from her lips, getting louder by the second. Before long, Gia was bucking the bottom half of her body into his mouth as he held her up.

Moments later what he'd been working for came full force. She was shivering and closing her thighs around his head as her orgasm took over her body. Jamil allowed her to ride her orgasmic wave with the help of his tongue until she'd completely stopped shaking.

"You ready for me?" He scooted her back so that he had room to lie on top of her.

As soon as Gia nodded, he pushed completely in and just held it there. Her legs and arms wrapped around his body as they always did. Since it had been such a long time since he'd had sex, Jamil literally had to think of something other than what he was doing right then, or else he was going to bust.

He tried to focus on the clock on his wall for another few minutes before moving his body. With Gia beneath him breathing onto his chest, focusing was becoming extremely difficult. Her breath alone was heightening his awareness of her presence and what they were doing.

"Gee, I don't want to nut, baby."

"What should I do?"

He chuckled, and that gave him all the help he needed. Gia could be so innocent when it came to sex sometimes that he had to make himself remember that she wasn't as experienced as he was.

"Don't do nothing, baby. You and that wet pussy are doing enough. This pregnant stuff got me loving my baby already."

He could feel Gia's smile against his chest as he lay a little closer to her. He had to find a comfortable rhythm before he began sliding in and out. Once he found it, and was able to get Gee to stop tightening her muscles around his dick, he was able to make love to her properly.

"Gee, I'ma take care of you and my baby, okay, bae?"

Gia didn't say anything. She just kept looking at him with weary eyes.

"Daddy got y'all."

"I know," finally found its way out of her mouth. "I love you."

"I love you too, girl."

Jamil kissed and touched all over Gia's body that night, making love to her in every position he could think of. He wanted to make sure that just in case his words failed him like they always

did, his dick wouldn't. He wouldn't be able to rest without knowing that she trusted him to be who she needed.

Once she finally obliged and gave all of her worries to him
fully, they relaxed in each other and made love until the sun came
up. By the time their session was over, both of them were drained
mentally, physically, and emotionally—but they were there together, as they would always be.

Chapter Fourteen

"To have love and to lose it has to be one of the worst things in the history of falling in love. Maybe I was stupid to think that Gee and I were different. That our love was real and that it wasn't like everybody else's. Maybe I really was a fool to fall for a girl I knew I could never have permanently. But then again, maybe I wasn't. Maybe I was just a fool to think I was the type of nigga who deserved a happily-ever-after." —Milli

Gia sniffled for the thousandth time that morning as she sat at the gate for her flight. Her time with Jamil had finally come to an end, and it was time for her to head back home. She'd done all she could to stay until the very last minute, but with workouts with her Olympic trainer starting in three days, she had to get back home.

Why had she never dreaded going back to such a beautiful place as Hawaii before? Gia looked out the window, trying to make herself feel better, but she couldn't. Even with Hawaii being one of the nicest places she'd ever had the privilege of being, it didn't have Jamil.

He wouldn't be there, so she wouldn't be happy. She had spent the entire day at his house, then the entire night with him at Oni's, but that still wasn't enough. Words couldn't begin to explain how happy she'd been when he told her he was staying the night with her.

Gia thought she was going to shoot through the roof with happiness when Oni had led him in, but all of that quickly went away again. A few hours passed before it was time for him to head back out, and ever since then Gia had been a basket case. One tear after the other.

Why hadn't she chosen a trainer on the mainland? Someone close to her family? That way she could see Jamil as much as she wanted, but with her in Hawaii, that was impossible. Had she known she would meet the love of her life and it wouldn't be Kainoa, she would have left Hawaii and never looked back. But because she thought the Colonel and Kainoa were her life, now she was doomed. Doomed to sadness until the moment she was back in Jamil's arms.

Gia wiped her eyes again with the tattered pieces of tissue she'd gotten from the airport employee. She had been leaning against the coffee shop crying when the lady offered her a small pack of tissues.

Knowing she would probably be shedding more and more tears, she'd happily taken it. From that moment to Gia's current one, it had been two hours, and she was on her last tissue. She wiped her face again and was about to stick the tissue in her backpack when her phone began to ring.

She snatched it from her bag in a hurry, hoping it was Jamil. She smiled when she saw his name.

"Hey, Milli." She sniffled.

"Don't leave me, Gee."

Gia closed her eyes and laid her head back. He'd hinted at it plenty of times in the weeks prior, but that was his first time actually saying it.

"Milli, please don't make me feel worse."

"I'm not trying to. You can stay and train here. I'll take care of you."

"No, I can't, Jamil. I've already committed to this opportunity. They're giving me media coverage while I train and everything."

"None of that matters, Gee. You told me yourself that some of the trainers here are offering you the same thing. Just pick one here." He sighed. "Please."

Gia rubbed her hand across her forehead, trying to ease the tightening in her eyebrows. "What then, Milli?"

"I'll take care of you. I'll come see you every weekend. We can be together, Gee. Like we've been doing. You don't have to go, baby."

Gia was silent for a long time. The things Jamil was saying sounded good, but she couldn't depend on that. Suppose they broke up and she'd altered her entire life for him—what would she do then? As much as she wished there was a way they could do this, there wasn't.

"We're just going to have to try the long-distance thing, Jamil."

"What about the baby? What are we going to do when it comes?"

Gia's head began to get tighter as she added more pressure. That was another thing she'd been thinking about all night. What was she going to do when she started showing, or even worse, when it was time to give birth? She was nervous and scared out of her mind, but she didn't want to think about that right then. She couldn't or she'd be even more depressed.

"We'll figure it out," she said.

"Stay here and let me take care of y'all. I know I can do it. I have a lot of money, Gianna. Way more than enough. Just stay. You'll be fine."

"I can't," she whispered.

"Gianna, I don't want you to go!" he yelled desperately.

His tone brought about more tears, and before she knew it, Gia was full-out crying again. She held her phone to her ear, crying to herself, until she heard the announcement that it was time to board. Apparently Jamil had heard it too.

"So you're leaving?" he asked.

Gia sat still in her chair, holding her head in her hands. "Yes."

Jamil cleared his throat. "Cool. Just holla at me if you need me." His voice broke at the end of his sentence.

Gia wanted to say something else, but she couldn't. He'd hung up and her line was dead. Tears clouded her eyes again, and this time they stayed. Not falling, just sitting there as a reflection of the pain she was feeling on the inside. Her entire flight home was a painful yet so beautiful recollection of her summer and the love she'd found by chance.

Two months later

"Faster, Gianna," Coach Sims yelled at her.

Gia had just run past him and a few of his other clients at full speed. Like the fastest girl in the nation that she believed herself to be, she beat everyone. As soon as she passed the mock finish line, she bent over trying to catch her breath.

It was nearly ninety degrees outside, and she was drenched in sweat. It was Thursday and the last day of workouts for the week, thank God. She was so ready to go to her apartment and stay for the weekend, she didn't know what to do. She had been training nonstop since returning from Georgia, and it was definitely taking a toll on her. Not to mention the little human she had growing inside her. Three months and not showing at all was a blessing that she wasn't taking for granted. She was so happy because her secret was still safe. No one other than Jamil and Oni knew, and that was the way she planned to keep it for now.

"That was amazing, Gianna. You're going to do great next Saturday." Coach Sims rested his hand on her back.

Still sweating and trying to catch her breath, all Gia could offer right then was a smile.

"Now, I want you to get some rest this weekend and get ready for training on Monday. I'll have you ready for that race if it's the last thing I do."

"Thanks, Coach. I will."

He patted her shoulder softly before walking away. Gia watched him and all of his other clients finish their training as she headed for the locker room. Next Saturday was the day she had been waiting on for months, and now it was finally here.

Her running coach as well as *Sports Illustrated* had done everything they could to sway the Colonel, and he'd finally given in. After tons of advertising and press interviews, Gia would be racing Stacy Dunlap, the number one runner in the country and the only person who was just as fast as she was.

When her coach had given her the news, she was ecstatic. The first person she wanted to tell was Jamil. She'd called him as soon as she got to her phone, and he hadn't answered. She called back two more times before he finally answered.

She was prepared to tell him all about it but couldn't because as soon as he'd picked up, he told he that he would call her right back and still hadn't. That was almost two weeks ago. Gia had called and texted him since then, receiving no reply.

At first it had bothered her so badly she could hardly focus on her workouts, but she eventually got herself together. Barely, but together. Together enough to carry on her daily routines of healthy eating and training. Anything outside of that was still falling apart.

All she wanted was him, and it was as if her going back to Hawaii had ended it all for him. Some nights she wondered if the love was real or if he was just faking it to get sex, but then she would remember his voice and his words. The way he sounded when he expressed himself to her, she knew it had to be real. It had to be.

It took her a little over twenty minutes to get from the track to her apartment. She talked to her father on her cell phone the entire way there. When she got inside her front door she told him she'd call him back later before hopping into the shower. After getting herself some lunch and a few snacks, she went into her room and locked the door.

She had no plans of doing anything other than eating and resting her body over the weekend. The only thing that would get her out of her apartment would be if Jamil told her he was outside, and she already knew that wasn't happening.

Her TV was on and she had a spoon of vanilla ice cream hanging from her mouth when she heard her phone ringing. At first she'd thought it was the Colonel, since she still hadn't called him back yet, but it was Oni.

"Hey, best friend," Gia said into the phone receiver.

"Hey, baby mama. How you feeling?"

Gia sighed. "Girl, tired as ever and frustrated. Do you know that nigga still hasn't called me back?"

The phone was quiet for a minute before Gia heard Oni sigh. "Um, Gia."

Gia sat up in her bed, afraid of what Oni was about to tell her. She could tell by the way Oni had said her name that it was about Jamil. Her voice was soft and sympathetic. So not only was it about him, it was bad.

"What, Oni?"

"Jamil moved to Miami."

"He did what? Why? When did he do that? Why didn't anyone tell me?" She had so many questions she could barely get them all out.

"Shock just told me today. That's why I was calling you. He said he's doing some work down there."

Gia began to feel light-headed, so she lay back on her pillow again. "Work?"

"Yeah. You know what they do. He's supposed to be getting some more stuff started for their supplier. Whatever it is, it's big, and it's going to make him a lot of money. From what I understand, he's been there since like a week after you left."

Gia's eyes rolled. That explained why he hadn't been talking to her or responding to any of her calls. "No wonder he's been missing in action."

"I'm sorry, boo. I was just as shocked as you."

Tears welled up in Gia's eyes as she lay in her bed thinking about all of the pretty women he might be encountering. Tears began to cascade down her cheek at the thought that he might have already hooked up with one. After all, he hadn't been talking to her for weeks. Really not in the mood to torture herself, Gia decided to switch subjects.

"So how's Shock and the elderly?"

Oni giggled. "Well, Shock and I are cool. He's like a really cool friend for now. We haven't tried to make it anything more. Just chilling. I like him, though, and Isaac . . . well, you know how we are."

"You still love that old man?"

"Yes, I still love that old man. You're killing me with the old jokes."

Gia laughed for the first time since they'd been on the phone. "You know I can't help it."

"Well, he's cool. I'm cool. Shock's cool. All of us are doing fine right now. I miss you, though. You need to come back."

Gia stuffed another spoonful of ice cream into her mouth. "I wish I could."

"I know, boo. If it makes you feel any better, Jamil's supposed to be in town tonight for the party at their supplier's house. I can slap him if you want me to."

"No, it's okay. If he doesn't want me anymore, then so be it. You just have fun. You going with Shock?"

"I sure am, but that doesn't mean I won't slap his friend."

Gia wanted to laugh, but she was too exhausted. "No, it's okay. Thank you, though. Their supplier, that's that dude Little Monty or something, right?"

"Yeah, that's him."

"Oh, okay. I think I heard Milli say his name a few times before." Gia got quiet for a moment. "Thanks for checking on me, boo."

"Anytime."

The line was quiet for a while as neither of them said anything.

"Well, get some rest, girl, and I'll call you later. I'm supposed to meet with Isaac for a few minutes."

"Okay. Love you, and take it easy on Isaac tonight. People go to jail for killing old people."

The girls shared a quick laugh before ending their call. Gia was still so caught off guard by Jamil moving that she felt compelled to call him again. Just like all of the times before that, he didn't answer. Deep into her feelings and seeing no way out, Gia stared at her stomach and cried. What was she going to do?

Sweat beads were building up across his forehead as he fanned himself with the lapel of his jacket. Iverson was seated in the driver seat of his car headed to the party. All day he had been going back and forth in his mind about whether he wanted to go through with his plan, and he'd finally come to a conclusion.

He didn't. Even for all of the money in the world, he couldn't turn his back on Jamil, let alone help someone plot his demise. They had been friends for years, and the more he thought about going through with his and Little Monty's plan, the worse he felt.

Jamil didn't deserve this, even if he was still a little salty about the things that had happened between them. He was a cool dude who stayed to himself. After all, it was Iverson's fault anyway. Had he never let his anger and greed get the best of him, he and Jamil would still be friends. Not once since they'd been friends had Jamil ever crossed him. As embarrassing as it was, he had been the only snake in his and Jamil's friendship.

Even if Little Monty did think Jamil had something to do with his daughter getting killed, which he didn't, there was no reason for Iverson to be in on it. He was supposed to be Jamil's best friend. Going behind his back plotting with the enemy was wrong on so many levels.

The air was blasting, and it still wasn't calming Iverson down. He didn't know if he was really that hot, or if he was simply feeling too nervous to contain himself. Once they went to the party tonight, there was no turning back.

Little Monty had called him late the night before, letting him know that he would be killing Jamil at the party. He'd thought about doing it in Miami, but changed his mind after giving it some thought. He claimed he didn't want the opportunity to slip away again. Iverson had tried everything he could to change Little Monty's mind without giving himself away but he couldn't. Little Monty's mind was made up.

Iverson wiped another bead of sweat with the back of his hand. He pulled into the winding driveway of Little Monty's house. It was packed with cars already, so he had to be quick.

After speaking with Little Monty last night, Iverson came up with a plan of his own. He would first try to talk Little Monty out of it. If that didn't work, he would go to Jamil and inform him of what was going on, omitting his involvement in any of it.

If it happened to come out, which he hoped it didn't, he would accept his part and move forward, even if that meant the two of them never talked again. He would be okay with that, as long as that meant Jamil would be alive.

Iverson took a deep breath before sticking his gun into the back of his pants and getting out of the car. He walked briskly up the driveway and was headed up the stairs when he heard Shock call his name. Upon turning around, he was surprised to see Oni there too.

She wore a form-fitting red dress and a tall pair of heels. She was so breathtaking he almost regretted not doing right by her. He had been so focused on sex, he'd neglected to get to know her. He would regret that forever.

"Why you walking so fast, nigga?" Shock looked Iverson up and down. "And where the hell you coming from sweating like that?"

Iverson gave him his signature sly smile. "Come on, man, you know me. I just got done bussing down a li'l freak I fuck with."

Shock shook his head and smiled. "I should have known."

Iverson slowed his stride and allowed Shock and Oni to catch up to him. Once they were next to one another, he nodded to Oni and she waved. With nothing else to be said, they all walked into Little Monty's house.

"I'm about to go grab me something to eat real fast. I'll check back in with y'all," Iverson said as soon as they got into the main room where everyone was.

He dapped Shock up and walked away as smoothly as he could, in search of Little Monty. He needed to get to him before Jamil got there. He was sure it would be any minute because Milli Rock was a very punctual dude. Tell him a time and he was coming.

As he ascended the stairs, he noticed Daisy coming out of their bedroom. She was looking sexy as usual, but he had to tame his eyes as he did every other time he saw her. The dress that she wore hugged her body in the most undignified way, and he was more than positive every nigga in attendance was going to have to check themselves when she walked past.

"Hello, Iverson. Looking for Monty?"

"Yes. Is he up here?"

She smiled and pointed over her shoulder with her thumb. "In the bedroom."

"Appreciate that." Iverson headed toward the door she'd just come through and pushed it open.

Little Monty was standing in the mirror buttoning up the shirt he was wearing when his eyes darted toward the door. He paused for a moment, probably surprised that it was Iverson coming through the door and not Daisy.

"What you need?" He skipped all pleasantries.

"I just came to see was you still going through with everything."

He turned toward Iverson and continued fixing his clothes. "Why would my plans change?"

Iverson fidgeted with his phone as he tried to think of something to say. "I was just thinking maybe you should hold off on that for a minute. I mean, you have a house full of people. That shit could go terribly wrong." Iverson took a seat on the bed.

Little Monty watched Iverson. Though sweat was dripping profusely from his head, Iverson held his own and stared Little Monty right back down. He didn't want this to happen, and he wouldn't let it if he could help it.

"I think you should do it the way I told you to and just let me set him up myself. We're boys. It would be a lot easier for Jamil to trust me than it is for him to trust you."

"I don't need that muthafucka to trust me for shit. Jamil Rock is going to get what he deserves, and it's going to be on my terms and at my hands. End of fucking story. If you got something to say about the shit, then your ass can get the same shit."

Iverson's blood began boiling as he fought to keep himself under control. Everything in him wanted to jump up and punch Little Monty in his face for talking all that shit, but he kept a cool head. All that meant was he was about to go into plan B. If that didn't work . . . well, he would just have to see what was next.

"Bet." Iverson stood and walked out of the room.

The party was in full swing, and he stood on the top of the stairs to survey the crowd. He needed to find Jamil. He finally spotted him standing near the table where the drinks were laid out. Iverson took a deep breath and took off in his direction.

He hadn't talked to Jamil since the day they fought at Shock's house, so hopefully he would listen to him. Maybe he too would see past the fact that they'd had a brief falling-out and remember they'd been friends for years. The closer he got to Jamil, the faster his heart beat.

By the time he was standing in front of him, his heart was nearly beating out of his chest. The look on Jamil's face didn't help the matter any.

"The fuck you doing in my face?" Jamil's voice sounded just as cold as it did when they were in the streets.

"Listen, I know we're on some other shit right now, but I need to holla at you real quick on some real shit."

"You can say it right here."

Iverson shook his head. "Nah, man, I can't. It's some shit about Little Monty."

Jamil made eye contact with Iverson again. He held it for a minute, obviously trying to gauge the seriousness of his words.

"I can't talk out here." Iverson looked around nervously. Though he wanted to warn Jamil, he didn't want to risk being seen by Little Monty. "Follow me to the balcony outside by the fountain."

Iverson turned and walked away, hoping Jamil would follow him. He moved through the crowd of people as smoothly as he could until he was in the back of the house. He followed the lights down to the small fountain. It was secluded and the perfect place for him to talk to Jamil without being seen.

The large green trees all around the fountain were lit up by the ground lights. The scenery was beautiful, and it was actually calming Iverson down. He had gotten his breathing and his heart rate under control by the time he noticed Jamil's tall body coming down the walkway.

Immediately, he began to sweat again. He hoped like hell Jamil took heed of his warning the right way and just left the party without causing a scene that would end up getting them both killed, but all he could do was hope.

"What's up?" Jamil wasted no time once he'd stopped in front of Iverson.

"Okay, man, it's like this. Little Mont—"

PEW!

In the middle of his sentence blood shot from the side of Iverson's neck. He stood still for barely a second before dropping to the ground. Instinctively, Jamil reached for him and caught him midair. He wasn't exactly sure where that shot had come from, but he snatched his piece out and aimed it anyway.

When he noticed the shadowy figure approaching him, he prepared himself to pull the trigger. Once he saw who it was, he was glad he hadn't shot.

"Bruh, what the fuck?" Jamil asked Shock as he eyed the black gun in his hand.

The silencer was still attached to it, letting Jamil know that he was indeed the one who had killed Iverson.

"Why you do that shit?" Jamil was still dumbfounded as he watched Shock walk over to Iverson's body and check his pulse.

"That trading-ass nigga had it coming." Shock unscrewed his silencer and stuck it into his pocket while shoving his gun back into the waistband of his pants. "Iverson was on some other shit, Milli Rock. That nigga was plotting to kill you. I heard him saying some shit about setting you up a minute ago when I went to take a piss. I don't know who he was talking to, but I know what the fuck I heard."

Jamil fell to the ground and sat flat on his butt. He needed a second to process what he'd just heard. His best friend, his brother, was plotting to set him up? That couldn't be right. But what reason did Shock have to lie?

"You didn't see who he was talking to?"

Shock shook his head. "I just heard him. I would have burst in and blown his head away right then, but I wanted to check that nigga on it first. When I saw him coming out here, I followed his ass. When I saw you down here with him, I went ahead and handled him before he could try some sneaky shit."

Jamil took a few deep breaths as he looked at Iverson's now-lifeless body bleeding on the ground. His eyes were still open and his hands were splayed out next to him.

"So what should we do now?"

Shock stood fixed his clothes. "Go back to the party. Let Little Monty figure this shit out."

Jamil's head was spinning as he blinked rapidly. Too much was happening. "Wait, that nigga was out here just now trying to tell me some shit about Little Monty. You don't think that's who he was talking to, do you?"

Shock looked confused. "Why would he want you hurt? He was just bitching about meeting you a little while ago." Shock shook his head. "I don't think so. I mean, not with all the money you be making that nigga. He would be a fool to do some shit like that."

Jamil's mind was boggled as he rose to his feet and fixed his clothes as well. When he went to check his jeans, he noticed some of Iverson's blood was on them.

"Man, you go ahead. I can't go back up in there like this. I'm about to just dip."

"You sure?" Shock asked. "You came all the way down here just to meet this nigga, only for you to end up not meeting him?"

"I don't leave until tomorrow evening. I'll fuck with y'all in the morning or something."

Shock could tell Jamil was serious, so he nodded and dapped Jamil up. They both took one last look at the friend they'd considered their brother before walking away.

Back in the party Oni stood near the table of food waiting for Shock. He'd told her he was going to talk to his boss for a minute and would be right back. That was almost ten minutes ago. Whatever they had to talk about couldn't have been that important.

She leaned against the wall in her heels, watching all of the people dance around happily. To keep herself from getting angry, she chose to bask in other people's happiness. She wouldn't waste her time being angry even though she hated to be left alone in unfamiliar places. That was one of her biggest pet peeves, not to mention she was at a drug supplier's house. There was no telling who the people were who were lurking around her.

"Why you standing here looking all mad." Shock's voice caught her attention.

She looked at him only long enough to roll her eyes before turning away again.

"I know you don't call yourself mad." He stood in front of her so that she couldn't look away from him.

"Yes, I do. You left me here for too long."

"I told you I had business to handle."

Oni rolled her eyes again. "Well, go handle it, then."

She was trying her hardest to keep a straight face, but she couldn't. For one, he was staring directly in her eyes while rubbing his hands all over her small hips.

"Don't be mad, Oni."

She cleared her throat. "Too late." She watched as the other partygoers crowded the dance floor.

"You want to leave?"

She finally looked at him and nodded.

"Cool. Let's go." He grabbed her hand and they headed for the exit.

"I have to use the restroom first."

Shock showed her where it was and told her he would wait for her by the bar. Oni excused herself and walked as gracefully as she could to the restroom. When she reached it, there were two other women waiting as well, so she stood behind them.

She was fixing her nails when her nose caught a familiar smell. She immediately began looking around, and as soon as she did she got the surprise of her life. Isaac. What was he doing there? He was standing down the hall from her talking to some man.

Oni wanted so badly to call his name, but she didn't want to run the risk of getting caught up with him and Shock. Shock had told her he would wait for her to leave the restroom, but that was still playing with fire. On top of that, she didn't know who Isaac was there with, so there was no reason to make a fool of herself.

She stared at him until it was her turn to go in the restroom. Just as she was walking in, he looked at her. It was as if the world had stopped and no one was around but him and her. The surprised look on his face made her giggle just a tad. He was clearly just as shocked as she was.

Instead of acting like she didn't see him like she'd planned, she waved and entered the bathroom. Oni hurried to handle her business so she could get out of that house and go home. She could already tell by the look on Isaac's face that he would be calling her as soon as he could, and she didn't want to be with Shock when he did.

She had just opened the door to the restroom when Isaac bumped into her, pushing her back inside. He kicked the door closed and locked it before grabbing her arm and pulling her to him.

"What are you doing here?" He sounded angry but still somewhat shocked.

Oni didn't like the tone he was using with her, but she answered anyway. "I'm here with a friend. Why?"

"You and I don't have any of the same friends."

"Clearly we do." Oni rolled her eyes.

"Don't be smart. Who's your friend?"

"Who is yours? Why are you here?"

Isaac got quiet as he stared at her, a silent staring match between the two of them. She could tell by the look on his face he was battling with what to say next, so she waited.

"I was invited by a friend."

Oni's eyebrow raised. "A woman?"

He nodded.

Her heart sank. It ached. This was bad. He was bad. She'd known all along that he might be seeing other women, but to hear him say it made it real. In the back of her mind she'd assumed she would be able to handle it, but clearly she had fooled herself.

"Oni." He sighed and reached for her, but she walked away.

"Excuse me. I have to go." Oni squeezed past him and left the bathroom.

She sniffled continuously as she tried to keep her tears in. When she saw Shock, she latched on to his arm and pulled him toward the door.

"Damn, why you running?"

"I'm just having really bad cramps and I need to go."

Clearly engaging in a conversation about her cramps wasn't on his "to do" list, because he followed her quickly from the house and to his car. The entire ride home she lay with her head on the seat with her eyes closed. For emphasis, she wrapped her arm around her stomach.

By the time she got home, she had three missed calls and two text messages from Isaac. "I'm sorry I ruined your night," she told Shock once she was out of the car.

"It's cool, shawty. Just feel better." He smiled and so did she.

Oni told him she would see him later before walking toward her house. She had just passed her truck when he pulled off. Co-incidentally, her phone rang again as soon as he turned down her street. Oni stared at it trying to see whether or not she wanted to answer, and decided she'd might as well. Couldn't run forever.

"What?"

"Please let me see you tonight. I promise she means nothing to me."

"You lied to me. You said I was the only woman you were seeing."

"You are, Oni. She and I are just friends. She asked me to go out, and I accepted. Nothing more. Now, will you please meet me at the house?"

Oni leaned against her truck and sighed. "Okay."

She could hear him release a sigh of relief before telling her he would be there shortly. After hanging up, Oni decided she wouldn't even go into her house. Instead, she hopped into her truck and headed for Isaac's house.

When she got there, he wasn't home, so she used her key and let herself in. She kicked her heels off and took a seat on the sofa.

Before she had the chance to turn the TV on, she saw a pair of headlights turn into the driveway. Isaac hopped out and jogged to the door.

As soon as he was inside, he rushed straight to her. "Look, Oni, I know you're younger than me and you probably feel like we aren't going to make it, but that's not true. We really can do this. All we have to do is put in the work. Your age doesn't bother me. It's mine that bothers you. If you tell me right now that you don't want me to be with anyone else, then I won't."

Oni watched the way his sexy lips moved over his teeth as she listened to him. She knew right then wasn't the time to be thinking of sex, but she couldn't help herself. Before she could stop herself, she'd leaned forward and taken his lips with hers.

The kiss started off slow but eventually turned into a full-blown freak show. He was on top of her, ripping her dress from her body while she savagely tugged his belt buckle open. They fought for each other's clothes until they were both naked and panting.

"This young pussy got me gone, Oni. I don't want nobody else." He breathed into her ear as he placed himself at her opening.

Oni's legs went around his waist, pulling him closer to her. "Give it to me," she growled as she reached down to touch his hard pole.

He waited no longer before plunging deep into her valley. He grunted so loud, Oni thought maybe he was in pain, but that was definitely not it. He was fucking her like the grown man he was. One pump after the other, each one harder than the last.

He was going so hard Oni thought that he was going to slide into her stomach at any moment, but he didn't. Instead, he stroked her spot until she was shivering and shaking all over his dick.

"How you make me love you? Huh? How you do that shit?" he asked her just before stiffening his body and moaning loudly. "Fuck! I wasn't supposed to love you!" His body shuddered above hers.

His climax was a long, hard one, and she enjoyed riding it with him. When he finally came down from his high, he rolled off her and onto the floor.

"I don't care what you say, you're staying with me tonight."

Oni giggled. "Okay."

"Let's go take a shower." He stood from the floor and picked her up.

They washed each other's bodies before round two began. He worked her out hard just the way he had a few moments prior in the living room before releasing inside her. Oni was so tired after their shower, she nearly collapsed into the bed. She was asleep in no time.

Oni tossed and turned until finally her eyes popped open. She frowned, trying to figure out where she was until she realized she was at Isaac's house. For a moment she lay still, just enjoying the feeling of waking up in his bed.

She was about to call his name to see where he was, but she didn't because she could hear him talking. She rolled over and pushed the covers from her head so that she could hear him. From the sound of it, he was on the phone speaking in a hushed tone. Being the nosy person that she was, Oni eased out of bed and got closer to the door.

"The fuck you mean you couldn't do it? You ain't no different than them other niggas. If I say handle that nigga, that's exactly what I mean for you to do. Y'all muthafuckas are killing me. Y'all act like that nigga Milli Rock is untouchable or something. Do I need to do it myself? Huh? Y'all must have forgotten who I am. I'm muthafucking Little Monty, nigga. I do this shit."

Milli Rock? Little Monty? The fuck?

Oni ran back to bed as quickly as she could. She lay back down for a moment, trying to figure out what to do next. She didn't want him to know that she'd heard him; however, she didn't want to stay there with him. When she finally made up her mind, he was coming through the door.

"I have to go," Oni said quickly. "My mom just called. She needs to go the emergency room."

His face softened a little. "Damn. For real?"

Oni nodded.

"Just stay for a few more minutes. Please. I need to be next to you."

Oni smiled and hugged him quickly. She even pecked his lips for good measure. "I'm sorry, baby, but I have to go."

He sighed but held her tighter, keeping her pressed against his chest for a few minutes before following her into the living room. He watched her get dressed before walking her to her car. He tried a few more unsuccessful times to get her to stay, but she dodged them all and headed home. She needed to call Gia.

Chapter Fifteen

"In life sometimes it seems like it's so hard to choose, like making the right decision is impossible. It's even worse when you're in love. How do you be with a person for so long and still not know them? I've been with Isaac for a while now and no matter how right things are for us, it still seems like we're not meant to be. I wish I knew why." —Oni

"Come on, papi, don't be like that. It's hot outside and I don't want to swim alone," Alira purred in Jamil's ear.

It was a little after two o'clock in the afternoon and it was already blazing hot outside. It was Saturday, so that meant the two of them had the day off, but that didn't mean Jamil wanted to spend it with her. It was bad enough he had to follow her around watching her every move during the week, the least she could do was let him have his weekends.

"I'm good. I'ma just chill right here for a minute," Jamil said.

The white bikini she was wearing barely covered any of her assets and was, in fact, making Jamil's dick jump. But this was business. Alira was business. Nothing more. She had been trying nonstop since he'd gotten there to seduce him, but he wasn't that type of nigga.

Pussy had never been his weakness, even when it was between a pair of the thickest caramel-colored thighs. He could say a lot of things about Alira and mean it, but saying he wasn't attracted to her wasn't one. She was a badass Puerto Rican chick with shoulder-length hair that she wore curly every day.

Her sultry red lips and beautifully slanted eyes made Jamil

hard every time she came in the room, but he knew how to check himself. Being around beautiful women wasn't something that was new to him. Even with her being stacked in all of the right places, he wasn't taking it there with her.

Alira sucked her teeth. "You never want to have any fun with me."

Jamil watched her ass bounce as she stomped toward the pool. She was famous for pouting when she didn't get her way. That was probably why any and every man who circulated around them was at her beck and call, aside from the fact that she was sexy as hell. Her workers did whatever she told them to.

It was sickening to Jamil because he wasn't used to shit like that. In his hood you pulled your own weight. It didn't matter if you was a nigga or a bitch, if you was assigned some work to put in, then that's what you did.

"Please, papi." Alira licked her full lips as she floated near the edge of the pool.

Jamil looked at her for a moment before standing up and shaking his head. "I have a few things I need to take care of. I'll be right back."

He could hear her behind him yelling at him in Spanish, but he didn't care. She had been doing that shit since he'd gotten there. Anytime he rejected her or defied what she said, she would go off on him. He found it quite comical, to be honest.

The cool air from their small beach house hit him in the face as soon as he stepped inside. Jamil instantly felt better than he had sitting outside on the patio. It was hot as hell out there. He had intended to chill outside and think for a while, but once Alira brought her thirsty ass out there, he knew that wasn't happening.

For the past few weeks he'd been living in a nice beach house near the water. It had maids, chefs, and anything else he could think of. To many men the way he was living would be considered paradise, but to Jamil it was just torture. A constant reminder of what he didn't have. The grass was green, the sky was blue, and his bitch was bad, but that meant nothing to him. Alira was a good girl and an even better pretend wife, but she wasn't his Gee. If he had to live like this for the rest of his life, he would have rather it been with Gianna.

She was gone and he was sick, and had been since she'd left. As hard as he tried to push her out of his mind, it was impossible. She had a hold on his heart, and for the life of him, he couldn't let go. Even with a beautiful woman throwing pussy at him every time he turned his head, he couldn't focus. Gia had left and hadn't considered his feelings once, so even though it hurt, he saw no reason to continue their relationship. He'd been ignoring her attempts at communication since her plane took off into the sky that night.

The arrangement upon coming to Miami was that he would team up with Alira and set up shop with a few new distributors. So far things had been going pretty good, minus the fact that they continued to throw paperwork at him every other deal.

That was the part he didn't understand. He had given Shock strict guidelines to be the enforcer and the money man while Alira handled negotiations and paperwork, but somehow it seemed as if that had been forgotten.

He'd made a call twice to Shock to have Little Monty look into that shit, but he still hadn't. Jamil was starting to think something was up, which was another reason why he couldn't focus.

Due to Shock's swift trigger finger, Iverson hadn't been able to tell him whatever it was he needed to know about Little Monty, and that shit was haunting Jamil. He knew for a fact it had to be something, being that he'd gone out of his way not to be heard inside the house. That meant nothing now, though. They'd cleaned his ass up, sent his body to his mama, and moved on like it never happened.

Iverson's behavior was still crazy to him, though. Disappearing, lying, and hiding shit. On top of that, Jamil and Iverson hadn't talked in weeks. For him to just approach him out of the blue was alarming, but there was nothing he could do about it now. Iverson was gone, and Jamil was clueless. Many nights since he'd been in Miami, Jamil had tried to think of what could be up, but he never could single anything out.

His money and shipments were always on time, Little Monty had given him another promotion, and Shock was making sure the block in Georgia was good. Everything was just good, nothing out of place and nothing that stuck out. So why did he have this nagging feeling that something was about to go wrong? He had no clue.

The vibrating from his phone brought him out of his thoughts. When he looked down and noticed it was Gia, he pressed Ignore. He couldn't talk to her right then. He was still angry. She'd left and hadn't bothered to look back. Sure he knew she'd had a life before him, but that didn't ease the pain in his chest upon her departure.

His phone began ringing again, and again it was Gia. Jamil fought with himself about whether to answer and decided he might as well.

"Hello," he said.

"Damn, Jamil, you're so busy with your new bitch you can't answer the phone for me now?"

He sighed and rubbed his hand across his forehead. "I don't have no new bitch, Gee. I've just been busy working."

"So busy you can't call and check on me or at least return my calls? I mean really, Jamil. What did I do to you?"

Jamil looked over his shoulder to see where Alira was before taking the stairs to his room two at a time. When he was inside, he closed the door and lay out across his bed.

"Gee"—he released an exasperated breath—"you didn't do anything to me, baby. I miss you so much. I miss your ass like crazy, and talking to you will only make it worse. So I don't answer. I don't communicate." He stretched his legs out in front of him. "If I don't talk to you, then I don't think about you."

The line was quiet, minus the sniffling he heard from her.

"That's not fair, Milli. You can't do what's best for you and not think about me. I have feelings too."

Hearing Gianna cry made him feel worse. "Don't cry, Gee. It's the best I can do right now. If I talk to you every day knowing I can't be with you, it'll only make things worse for me down here, and I don't need any more complications right now." Jamil's eyes were closed as he listened to her on the other end. "Just be patient with me, a'ight?"

She sniffled again. "Okay."

Silence hung in the air as they both held in things that needed to be said. Jamil especially. He wanted so badly to ask her how the baby was and if she'd kept it, but that would only trouble him even more. Not knowing whether she was still carrying his baby had been weighing on his mind since she left. He was just too afraid of what she might say.

In the back of his mind, her keeping his baby would signify she hadn't moved on, or at least had no plans to do so as yet. However, if he asked her and she had indeed aborted it, that might be it for them, and he couldn't handle that right then. He needed to keep the little hope he had for them while he was in Miami. That was pretty much all he had to keep him going.

"How's track?" he asked her.

"Good. I have a race this Saturday at Howard University against Stacy Dunlap. We're finally going to see who's really worthy of that number one spot."

Jamil could hear the anxiousness in her voice, which in return made him a little hyper as well. "That's what's up, Gee. I know you're going to do great. Is it going to be on TV?"

"Yeah, it is, but I was hoping that maybe you could come."

Jamil sat up so on the side of his bed. "You really want me to be there?"

"If you're not, I don't know if I'll win."

Jamil smiled. She still loved him too. "Of course you're going to win. You're the best."

She paused. "Does that mean you'll come?"

Jamil didn't know how he was going to make it work, he just knew he had to. "Hell yeah, I'ma be there. When you fly in? Let me pick you up."

"I get there Friday. My coach is coming with me, so you don't have to pick me up, but I'll send you my hotel information and you can stay with me."

Jamil could feel himself getting happier by the second. The thought of seeing his Gee had him on cloud nine. Her lips, her thighs, that smile, and her gorgeous face—all of those things bum-rushed his thoughts at once. It had been so long since he'd been wrapped up in her love, and to know it was only a few days away had him feeling different. So different that he spoke without thinking.

"What about my baby, Gee? You still got it?"

He could hear her clearing her throat, and it made him nervous. He could feel it. She was about to break his heart.

"Gee . . . my baby . . ." He didn't want to ask again, but now that it was out, he needed to know.

"Yes, Milli, I have it. Check your phone. I just sent you a picture."

Jamil snatched his phone from his ear quickly and went to his messages. When he pulled up Gia's name, there was a picture of a black-and-white ultrasound. He could see the baby's long legs and arms, and he couldn't stop himself from smiling.

"Aww, man, Gee."

She giggled. "I know, right. It's amazing. I just got that one yesterday."

"This baby got some long-ass legs already."

Again, Gia's laughter floated through the phone. "Like Daddy."

"Damn." Jamil sighed as he lay back on the bed staring at the picture. "Thank you, Gee. Thank you for keeping it."

"I told you I couldn't get rid of something this amazing. It's a product of me and you, the love we share. Even though you been acting like a butthole to me, I still wouldn't do something like that."

"My fault, Gee. For real, I'm sorry about all of this. It's just a lot going on right now."

"I guess, but I'll see you next weekend. I have to go now."

"Why?"

"I'm sleepy."

Jamil really didn't want to let her off the phone, but he understood, so he did. After she told him she loved him and he reciprocated, he tossed the phone onto the bed next to him and closed his eyes. He couldn't wait to be with Gee, even if it was only for a few hours.

He had to think of something to get out of town for the weekend without Alira trying to tag along. He really didn't want to hurt her feelings, but he most definitely would if he had to. Gee came before anyone, and that was law.

"You left me outside to come and lie down?" Alira's voice came from the door of his room.

"I'm tired."

"From what? Georgia to here is not that far."

Jamil kept his eyes closed so that she would know he wasn't listening. He knew the drive from Columbus to Miami wasn't a bad one, but he was still tired. The fuck did it concern her for anyway? He'd gone home to check on his parents and meet up with Shock for a few days and had just returned earlier that day.

That was his problem with her right then. Outside of her being thirsty, she was always being nosy. Worrying about shit that had nothing to do with her.

"Milli." His name rolled off her tongue seductively.

Jamil hated when she called him that. For some reason it only sounded right coming from Gia, and every time Alira said it, it made him angry.

"Get out. I'm about to take a nap."

He could feel her presence at his door for a few minutes before she sucked her teeth and left. The door slammed so hard one of the pictures fell off the wall, but he didn't care. This wasn't his shit.

"You sure you don't want to ride with us, sweetheart?" Oni's father asked her.

When she turned around he was standing at her front door with her mother next to him. They were going to a cookout at one of his friends' house. He had been asking her to come along all day.

"I'm sure. Y'all go ahead. I'll be here when you get back." She gave them a reassuring smile to let them know that she was fine and they could leave.

"Okay, baby. Just call me if you need anything," her father said as he and her mother headed for the stairs.

Oni was sitting on the small bench beneath her window staring outside. She had so much on her mind that she had no desire to do much of anything. All she wanted to do was figure out what was next for her so that she could get some sleep at night.

Ever since the night she'd found out who Isaac really was, she hadn't been able to rest. It was heavy on her mind because she didn't know what to do. Initially she'd thought maybe telling Gia was the right thing to do, but now she wasn't so sure.

In no way, shape, or form did she want any harm to come to Jamil, but she didn't want any to come to Isaac either. She was so torn. On the one hand, she was in love with a man and would be devastated if something happened to him. On the other hand, so were her cousin and best friend.

Gia loved Jamil just as much as Oni loved Isaac. If something were to transpire between the two of them, then surely she and Gia would be inconsolable. She had been driving herself crazy trying to figure out what to do next, but she was lost.

The only thing that was pushing her a little more toward telling

Gia was the fact that Gia was pregnant. Oni didn't want her to have to go through life raising her baby alone because something had happened to Jamil. She sighed and held her head in the palm of her hand.

"How did I get myself into this?" Oni pulled at her hair lightly as she rocked back and forth.

It was all so much. Almost too much. She had to make a decision. She wasn't too involved with the scheme of things and how Little Monty—or Isaac, as she knew him—conducted business, but she was sure whatever she decided, she needed to act fast.

She had been going over and over in her mind trying to figure out what would happen if she told Isaac she knew who he really was. What if he hurt her? What if he hurt her, Gia, and Jamil? Oni wanted to scream as she laid her head back against the wall. She was so overwhelmed.

After taking a few deep breaths, she decided she would get out of the house and go shopping. Maybe some retail therapy would do the trick. Isaac had been calling her nonstop, and it was becoming harder and harder for her to resist. Busying herself in the mall would definitely do the trick.

Once she'd gotten herself dressed in a cute little dress and some sandals, she grabbed her things and headed for the mall. She needed to get something for Gia's trip anyway. She had called her the night before to make sure she was still meeting her in Washington.

As soon as she got into the mall she almost regretted it. It was so packed that she could hardly move, but she was there now, so she'd might as well do what she had to do. One store after another, Oni shopped until she'd found exactly what she was looking for; a cute little romper and something for them to hit the clubs if Gia wanted to. All she had to do now was grab a pair of heels for her nighttime wear and she would be set.

"Those are so comfortable. I have that exact pair in red."

Oni looked to the side to see a beautiful dark-skinned lady

standing next to her. She was so pretty Oni almost neglected to speak back to her.

"These?" She held up the tan pair of heels.

The lady touched her shoulder and nodded. "Yes. So comfortable. I can wear them all night with no problems. They're so comfortable I've even worn them to the club and kept them on for hubby once I got home." She winked at Oni.

"Oh well, I definitely need to get these." Oni turned the shoe over and checked the price. "Damn. Never mind. These are out of my budget."

Oni and the lady laughed before the lady nudged her shoulder. "That's why you get a man with money like I did. Girl, I don't pay for shit. We've been together for years, and it's the same old thing. He gives me that weak dick, I take it, act happy, and spend all of his money whenever I want."

The lady was being so forward. She was definitely Oni's type of woman. "I like you." Oni smiled.

"Girl, I'm just being real. You give these niggas your heart and they do what they want. I learned a long time ago to never love a man more than he loves me. The moment you show signs of genuine feelings for their asses, they do you dirty. That's why you always have to be smarter than them. Beat them at their own games."

"Even if you love them?"

"Especially if you love them. Men aren't good for nothing but money and kids. Don't be a fool, sweetie."

"Well, I'm good on kids for now." Oni shook her head.

A faraway look appeared in the lady's eyes. "I had one. She died, so now I just live for me."

Oni immediately felt bad for saying she didn't want any. You never knew what people were going through.

"I'm sorry," Oni said.

The smile was back on her face. "It's fine, sweetie. I'm over it. Now I just use her daddy for his money."

"I want to be just like you when I grow up."

Oni and the lady both started laughing. They laughed together as the lady slowly moved toward the register.

"Don't be like me, baby. Be better."

Oni nodded and went back to looking at the shoes. They were the cutest pair in the store, but they were so expensive. She was just going to have to find something else. Since she was done shopping, Oni headed out of the store and bumped right into the man who was coming in.

"Excuse me. I'm so sorry." Oni looked up as the man tried to steady her.

"Oni." Isaac looked down at her. "You've been ignoring me."

Oni looked away and stepped out of his grasp. "I have to go. Sorry for bumping into you." She walked away and he followed her.

"Oni, wait!" He grabbed her. "You don't love me anymore?"

She took a deep breath, trying to her hardest to remain calm. She had no intention of crying in the middle of the mall, but being close to him brought back everything she'd been thinking about.

"Of course I love you."

"Well, come see me tonight. Please. I have something I want to talk to you about."

Oni thought about telling him no but felt herself nodding instead.

His lips brushed against her cheek quickly before he stepped away. "I love you."

Oni was about to tell him she loved him too, but the pretty lady from the store caught her attention. "See you later." Oni waved at her as she neared.

She smiled back. "Remember what I told you, sweetie." She winked at Oni and turned her attention to Isaac. "Ready, baby?"

If at all possible, Oni died right there in the middle of the mall.

Baby? Isaac was the man the lady had been talking about in the store? How could that be? Was this the lady who had invited him to the party? All kinds of things floated through Oni's head as she smiled at the lady and nodded again.

"I remember. It was nice to meet you all." Oni cleared her throat and walked away.

When she looked back over her shoulder as she rode down the escalator, she saw Isaac still watching her. He looked like he wanted to say something so badly, but couldn't. And to be honest, it was best that he didn't. Oni didn't know how much more she could take.

She thought about everything the lady had told her, everything she'd heard Isaac tell her, and the constant pressure of needing to make a decision about it all. By the time she got home, she was too tired to do anything except fall into her bed and go to sleep.

When she finally woke up, she had ten missed calls from Isaac and a few text messages. All of them were begging her to come over. She tossed her phone down just as it began ringing again. She stared at Isaac's name before pressing the Answer button.

"Oni, please," he begged.

"What do you want, Isaac?"

"Please come over and let me explain. I'll tell you everything, I promise."

"Why should I believe you? You're nothing but a liar."

She could hear him sighing dramatically. "Please, Oni, just give me a chance."

"Maybe some other time. I'm a little busy right now." Oni hung up before he could say anything else.

She just needed some time. Just a little bit of time to get her thoughts together, then she would handle it all. Hopefully she wouldn't wait until it was too late.

Finally, the day Gia had been waiting for was here. She and her coach had just landed in Washington and were preparing to check into their hotel rooms. She'd talked to her parents and Oni, and all of them were already in their rooms and waiting for her.

Due to her coach's strict orders, she was only allowed to see them for a few minutes before it was time for bed. He told her he wanted to make sure she was ready for her big day tomorrow. Like the understanding people they were, her parents and Oni all agreed.

"Get some rest, Gianna. I'll see you in the morning," her coach told her as he headed down the opposite end of the hallway.

"I will." Gia used her key card to get into her room and set her bags down.

As soon as she got settled, she grabbed her pajamas and headed for the bathroom. She couldn't wait to shower after all of her traveling. The hot water felt just as good as she knew it would as she stood beneath the stream of it.

Gia bathed quickly and wrapped herself in her towel. As soon as she stepped out of the bathroom, her eyes landed on Jamil. He was laid back on her bed in nothing but a pair of gym shorts. His chest was bare, showing off all of his tattoos. His long legs and long orange hair were spread out all over the bed as he lay perfectly still with his eyes closed.

"Come here," he told her without even opening his eyes.

Gia's heart smiled as she walked to him and straddled his lap. His hands went to both sides of her body immediately. He rubbed her up and down, squeezing in certain places and rubbing in others.

"I missed you." He finally opened his eyes.

"I missed you more." She leaned over and kissed his lips. "I didn't think you were still coming."

Jamil reached up and pulled her towel away. "I wouldn't have missed it for anything in the world." He took a deep breath. "Getting an extra key to your room was hell, but I made it happen." He chuckled.

He stared at her naked body as he groped her breasts. He massaged and twirled her nipples as he began to harden beneath her.

"You ready to give me some pussy?"

Gia nodded and eased up so that he could pull his shorts off. The two of them maneuvered until he was completely undressed. When she was comfortably back on top of him, she lifted some so that he could slide in. They both moaned upon connection.

"Oh, Gee." Jamil's eyes rolled to the back of his head. "Damn, baby." He continued to moan beneath her.

Gia watched him as he pumped up toward her body with his hips. She might have been the one on top, but he was most definitely doing all of the work. She wanted to muffle her moans, but he felt too good. She was riding him as he slid inside her continuously, both of them relishing the feeling of being with one another again.

"Move your hands and let me see your stomach, Gee." Jamil moved her arms so that she was no longer blocking his view of her midsection. "It's still flat."

"I know. That's a good thing."

"Lift up." Jamil sat up and laid her back down so that he was on top.

Before sliding back in, he leaned over and placed kisses all over her stomach. Gia smiled as she rubbed her hands through his hair.

"I love you, Milli."

"I love you too, Gee." He plunged back into her, causing her to cry out.

Gia didn't know how much she had loved or missed this man until this moment. She watched as he pushed his locs from his face. The way he held his bottom lip between his teeth while he sexed her crazy. All of it was a dream, and she never wanted to wake from it.

"Look, baby." Jamil tapped the side of his rib.

Gia's eyes went to the bold letters in a neat bold script written across his rib. *GIANNA*. Gia smiled big as she realized he'd tattooed her name on him just like he'd told her he would.

"I told you." He smiled.

Her eyes misted with tears as she nodded. For at least another few hours, the two of them went at it, making up for lost time. By the time they showered and prepared to get some sleep, it was almost two in the morning. Jamil snuggled up behind her before resting his face in her neck.

"What now, Milli?"

"What you mean, Gee?"

"Are you going to go back to Miami and keep ignoring me?"

Jamil kissed the side of her face. "No. I'm going to go back to Miami and talk to you every day until you find a trainer closer to me so we can be together."

Gia smiled to herself because he sounded like he had it all thought out. "I love you."

"Love you too. Now, go to sleep so you can beat Stacy Dunlap's ass tomorrow."

Her eyes closed but her smile remained. She was finally back in Jamil's arms. Right where she belonged.

Chapter Sixteen

"Even when I thought my life couldn't get any worse, it did. I stay awake so many nights trying to figure out what I've done to deserve what I go through, and I have yet to find an answer. Hopefully one day it'll all make sense, but until then, I'm left to put the pieces together on my own." —Oni

The crowd went wild as Gia passed Stacy Dunlap on the last turn and ran straight across the finish line. Everyone who had been in their seats were now on their feet as the announcer screamed Gia's name. It was crazy how the crowd reacted to Gia finishing first.

It was like everyone at the stadium was rooting for her. Sure, there were people there for Stacy as well, but it looked to Oni like Gia had won the crowd over. People from all over the place were rooting and yelling for her as she took her spot on the winner's podium.

Oni watched with a large smile as cameras flashed all around Gia as she received her medals and certificates. The race had been a tough yet amazing one, and Gia had won. Everything she'd been working for and waiting for had finally paid off.

Oni jumped up and down screaming as she watched the news cameras and reporters swarm Gia. Oni was so loud she couldn't tell who was worse, her or her aunt and uncle. Gia's parents were out of their seats and on their way to her the moment she crossed the finish line. Oni was so wrapped up in Gia's success that she had forgotten about her own problems.

This was the most peace she'd had since the night she found out about Isaac. Little did she know that it was all about to come to an end.

"I didn't know your cousin was that fast." Isaac's voice came from behind her.

Oni almost jumped out of her skin when she saw him. "Oh my God. What are you doing here?"

He smiled at her and grabbed her hand. "You told me last night you were coming here, and since you act like you can't talk to me at home, I figured I could surprise you." He looked so handsome and sweet she almost forgave him right there on the spot. "I thought maybe you and I could use this weekend to get our relationship back on track."

Oni wanted to be mad at him. She wanted to ignore everything he stood for, but she loved him. So when he pulled her to him for a hug, she obliged.

"Please stop ignoring me, Oni."

"Okay." Nothing more was said as her head rested against his chest.

Maybe being in Washington with him would give her time to get everything together. She didn't have to worry about anyone seeing them or causing problems. It would just be them. They could actually go on a real date and figure their world out, because as of right then, it was upside down. He had a lot of explaining to do, and she couldn't wait to hear it.

"I can't believe you're here." Oni looked at him again once she'd pulled out of his embrace.

He wiped his hand over his head and shrugged. "I honestly can't either."

"Well, I have to go congratulate Gia. I'll meet back up with you later?"

"Yeah, we can do that. Just call me as soon as you leave your family."

Oni smiled. "I will."

He hugged her once more before walking away. Oni stood in her same spot, a little dazed by the fact that he had come all the way to Washington just to be with her. Even though he had flaws and the two of them had a lot to figure out, he'd come.

He loved her enough to come. No man she had been with had ever put forth that much effort, and for that she would hear him out. Initially she had planned to just break things off with him, warn Gia, and never look back, but now she didn't know anymore.

Maybe after they talked he could help her figure out what to do. Something that would benefit her and Gia. When the crowd began to roar again, Oni looked for Gia. She was in the middle of the field with her parents on both sides of her smiling.

With a new burst of energy, Oni took off toward her. She pushed through people the best she could without being rude until she was in the middle of the field as well. Though she could see Gia, she was still relatively far from her. By the time she got to where they were standing, they were walking off again.

"Gia!" Oni yelled.

Gia turned around and gave Oni a large smile before moving in her direction. As soon as she got to Oni, they embraced.

"You did it! I'm so proud of you," Oni screamed in Gia's ear.

"I know. I'm ready to go now, though. My stomach is so upset."

Oni gave her a sympathetic look before nodding. "Let's go, then."

Gia looked around in exhaustion at all of the people surrounding her and the other runners. "I wish it were that easy." Gia gave her an exhausted smile before grabbing her hand and pulling her through all of the flashing cameras and celebrating fans.

Jamil stood in the middle of the parking lot with a large bouquet of balloons and flowers. He'd made sure to grab them before coming to the race that morning. Gia had left pretty early, leaving him plenty of time to get her goodies without her seeing.

Now he was in the middle of the parking lot waiting for her to come out. The stadium had been crazy, so he sure as hell wasn't about to drag all of the balloons and flowers through a crowd. The moment he'd watched Gee cross the finish line, his heart surged through his chest.

One would have thought he won the race by the way he jumped and screamed. Soon after, he rushed to the car and grabbed her stuff. It had been almost thirty minutes, and people were now pouring from the stadium. Because of all of the publicity she was getting at the moment, he knew he would be able to spot her the moment she emerged.

"Yeah." Jamil answered his ringing phone.

"When you coming back?" Alira's voice sounded urgent.

"In a few days. Why? What's up?"

"I have to go out of town tonight to do some work with one of my distributors. I was just checking in to see what you had planned."

"Well, you good. I'll just hit you when I get back. Everything is pretty much set until Thursday, and I'll definitely be back by then." Jamil noticed the flashing cameras exiting the gates, so he figured Gia was on her way.

"Okay. Hit me up if you need to. I'll check in later."

"Bet." Jamil hung up his phone and stuffed it into his pocket.

As more and more people began to disperse, he caught a glimpse of Gia. She was smiling and waving, but she looked a little weird. Her face didn't look right or something. Almost like she was on the verge of throwing up.

He wanted to rush to her and pull her away from everyone, but this was the moment she had been waiting for, and he didn't want to be the one to interrupt her shine. However, watching her look so miserable was making it hard for him not to move.

He shifted from one foot to the other, trying to make himself stay put, but it was getting harder and harder by the second. It was baffling him that even with all of the people around her, no one noticed that she didn't look well. When she covered her mouth with her hand and closed her eyes for a second, that was it.

Jamil set the bouquet down on his rental car and took off running toward her. "Gee!" he yelled as he neared her.

As soon as she saw Jamil, she took off running in his direction. Everyone's attention turned to him as she made her way over to him. She was only a few feet away when he grabbed her in one of his arms and pulled her to him. Her smaller body was wrapped up in his immediately.

"You not feeling well, Gee?"

"No. I need to throw up." She barely got the words out of her mouth before she pulled away.

As soon as she bent down beside him, he grabbed her ponytail and held it. People stood around watching her empty the contents of her stomach as if she was some sort of freak show, which only angered Jamil.

"Can y'all give her some privacy?" he yelled.

For a moment people stood around unsure of what to do next, but when he yelled it a second time, they began to move away. The only remaining people were her parents and Oni. He nodded at Oni, but she didn't look so well either. She almost looked like she was on the verge of passing out. What the hell was wrong with her and Gia?

"You feeling better?" he asked Gia when she stood, feet wiping her mouth.

Versus saying anything, she simply nodded.

"And who are you?" A tall burly man looked Jamil up and down.

He could tell by the man's eyes and skin color that he was Gia's father. She looked exactly like him.

Jamil stuck his hand out for a shake. "Jamil Rock. Gia's boyfriend."

"Boyfriend?" the lady beside him asked.

"Yes, ma'am."

"This is Milli, Colonel," Gia said weakly as she leaned against Jamil. "The one from Georgia."

Her father looked him up and down with a hard stare while her mother simply smiled. Jamil, not one to be easily intimidated, stared him right back down. The two of them participated in a full-out staring match until her father cracked a smile.

"Nice to meet you, young man."

Jamil nodded. "Likewise, sir." He then looked down at Gia. "You did awesome, Gee. Like I knew you would." He kissed her forehead. "I'm so proud of you."

Gia was smiling from ear to ear. Even with her tired posture and sad face, she looked beautiful. "Thank you. I was looking for you."

"I wanted to give you your moment. Plus I had some stuff for you." Jamil turned her toward the car where all her balloons and flowers were.

Gia smiled and took off running toward it with everyone else in tow. After smelling the flowers and grabbing the large silver balloon that was shaped like the number one, she ran back to Jamil.

"I'm so happy you're here."

He wrapped one arm around her neck and kissed her ear. "I told you I wouldn't miss it." He kissed her again before whispering into her ear, "We need to go check on my baby. Can you get away?"

Gia shook her head. "No, we don't. I always get sick after I run. The doctor said it's normal," she whispered before turning back toward her parents. "I'm starving."

Everyone agreed to go eat except Oni. She told them she wasn't feeling well and needed to go lie down. Jamil wasn't too sure about that, but Oni wasn't his girl. She was probably going to trick off and didn't need them following her.

Once they decided where to go, they all got in their cars and left, Gia riding with Jamil. The two of them were so in love, and it was so obvious. Jamil was most definitely glad that he'd shown up. Seeing Gia as happy as she was right then was all he wanted out of life. Her, him, and their baby.

After a long lunch, Gia's parents told her they would see her later and to enjoy her friend while she was in town. Jamil was more than happy to hear that. They were cool people and treated him nicely, but he was ready to be alone with Gia.

"So where are we going?" Gia asked Jamil as they walked hand in hand down the street.

"To get dessert and to go to the park. You okay with walking or are your legs tired?"

Gia shook her head. "I'm fine. As long as I'm with you I'm good."

Jamil nodded and kissed the back of her hand. He wasn't too sure about where they were going either, he just knew there was a small ice cream shop up ahead. He'd spotted it the night before on his way to the hotel. After grabbing their ice cream, they headed to the park.

"What made you want to come to the park?" Gia asked as they took a seat on one of the park benches.

"It's calming and I figured we needed time to talk."

There were people all around them. Some were running, some walking, others playing with their kids or having small picnics. The spot was relaxing—the perfect place for them to hash things out.

"I want you to move to Georgia with me, Gianna."

Gia lay her head against his shoulder and sighed. "I don't know, Jamil. That's such a big step."

"I want to be with you, Gee. I want to see you every day. I want to help you raise our kid. I can't do that with you being all the way in fucking Hawaii." He sounded a lot more irritated than he'd wanted to, but it was the truth. He had been thinking about having a family with Gia since she'd left, and he wasn't about to let it pass him by without a fight.

"I know, Milli, and I want to do all that too, but I have the Olympics coming up. I don't want to lose focus."

"I promise I got you. You won't lose focus. I'll take care of the baby while you're working out and shit. Then we can help each other when you get there."

"That sounds easy, but what will we do about money and stuff? I don't want to be with you if you're going to be selling drugs all night and day. That's not safe for the baby."

"I'll stop," he said before he knew it. He was desperate.

Gia sat up and looked at him. "Will you for real?"

Jamil nodded. "I mean, not immediately, like tomorrow or anything. But give me at least until the baby comes to get some stuff in order, then I'll stop."

"You'll get a regular job?"

Jamil's face frowned and he shook his head. "Gee, do you know how much money I have?" He chuckled. "I don't need a job right now, baby. Neither do you." He chuckled again.

Like Shock had said, Jamil might have been illiterate, but he was a self-made millionaire. He'd been slanging dope and getting paid for years, each deal making more money than the last. He and Gia would be straight forever if he did right by his funds, which he knew he could.

"That's drug money, though. How long do you think it'll last?"

Jamil sat in deep thought because he knew for a fact it would last for years to come, but he was sure she needed something more concrete.

"As long as you make it last. You're smart, Gee. You can take all my money and do whatever you want to do with it to make it grow. I'm not the smartest nigga, as we both know, but as long as you help me, we can make it."

Gia laid her head back against his and closed her eyes. Her

hands rested across her flat abdomen as she breathed quietly. Her
silence was unnerving, but he didn't want to crowd her thoughts.

"I still don't know about that, Jamil. That's a lot to ask with
nothing solid to stand on."

"Nothing solid? What else do you need me to do?"

Gia shrugged and looked away.

"I always thought I would be married before I started having
kids and living with a man. Not like this."

"I'll marry you, Gee. We can get married tomorrow before we
leave," he rushed to say.

This made Gia sit up out of her seat. She frowned and raised
one eyebrow. "You're serious?"

"As hell."

"Okay." She giggled. "I don't know why you haven't said that.
I would have moved back. I have an offer to train at UGA. I could
work out there."

Jamil felt so good, he wanted to fly. He smiled so hard it could
have lit up the park. There was nothing anybody could do to
bring him down from this high. Or so he thought.

They sat at the park for another hour or two, ironing out specifics, before heading back to her hotel room. It had gotten dark
outside and they were in an unfamiliar place, it was time to go.

"Let's stop and see Oni real fast so I can tell her the good news.
Her room is downstairs from mine."

Jamil nodded and followed her lead. They were in the parking
lot when he remembered he had a surprise for Gia in the car.

"You go ahead. I'm coming. I need to grab something out of
the car."

"I'll wait for you on the sidewalk."

Jamil nodded and darted to his car. He looked up as he dug
into his armrest and noticed Gia was talking to someone. Though
he couldn't see who it was because of the wall of the hotel, he was
sure it was Oni. Perfect timing, he thought.

Jamil stuck his gift behind his back and locked the doors to his car before heading toward her. She was smiling at him when she saw him coming but turned back around to talk. As he got closer, he recognized the girl's voice to be Oni's. However, there was a male voice too. Jamil shook his head. Just like he'd thought, Oni had skipped dinner to trick off.

"Hurry up, babe." Gia waved him over.

"You're not alone?" The sound of Oni's voice didn't sit right with him, but he couldn't figure out why. "You should have told me."

"What's the big deal? It's only Jamil," Gia said.

There was a brief silence as he approached before he heard the male voice.

"Jamil as in Milli Rock?"

Milli Rock?

That alerted Jamil, so he immediately stuck Gia's gift into his pocket and snatched his gun from his waistband. There weren't any niggas in DC that should know him by Milli Rock.

"Yeah, why? You know him?" Gia asked skeptically.

The man chuckled. "Yeah, we go way back."

That was the last thing he said before Jamil rounded the corner. When his eyes landed on the man, he knew he recognized him, he just couldn't remember from where.

"You think you know me?" Jamil asked with his gun by his side. He didn't trust niggas and he didn't take chances.

The man smiled deviously before nodding. "Hell, yeah. Me and you go way back, Milli Rock." His tone was taunting.

"What's going on?" Gia looked afraid.

"Isaac, let's go back inside," Oni told him.

"I don't have time for guessing games, nigga. Who are you?" Jamil raised his gun.

Gia and Oni both shrieked.

"Milli, no." Gia touched his side. "Put your gun away. That's just Isaac. He and Oni have been dating."

Jamil shook his head. "Nah, this nigga think he knows me, so I'm waiting on him to tell me how." He cocked his gun.

"I'm surprised you don't remember me." Isaac stepped forward a little more. "If I was the reason behind a man losing his only child, I would remember his face forever."

That statement hit Jamil like a ton of bricks.

Lauren.

Jamil looked at the man, and he was right. It was Lauren's daddy. But what the fuck was he doing with Oni, and how in the hell was he in Washington with his people?

"You know how long I've been waiting for this?" Isaac smiled at Jamil as he too raised his gun.

"Y'all stop. Please stop," Gia pleaded. "People are going to see you. Milli, I don't want you to go to jail. Please don't do this." Her cry fell on deaf ears.

Both men stood with guns pointed at each other. Jamil didn't know if Isaac was going to use his, but he most definitely would let his hammer fly if necessary.

"It's crazy how you can work for a nigga for years and never see his face." Isaac chuckled. "Then out of nowhere you finally come face-to-face and you're both pointing guns."

Jamil found no humor in what Isaac was saying. Nothing about it made any sense to him. "I didn't get Lauren killed. I told her not to go to that fight and she went anyway. That shit ain't on me," he said.

"Yes the fuck it is!" Isaac's shout startled Gia and Oni.

Jamil, on the other hand, didn't budge. He wasn't afraid of this nigga. If he really wanted to kill him, he'd be dead already.

PEW!

Isaac's body dropped to the ground with a thud. Oni and Gia both screamed as Jamil jumped back in shock.

"The fuck?" he said as he searched the darkness.

He didn't see or hear anyone for a moment due to Gia's and Oni's cries, but then Shock appeared from the darkness. He was accompanied by a sexy dark-skinned lady, and Alira.

The fuck? Jamil wondered as the three of them approached him.

"Bruh, what the fuck is going on?" Jamil asked as soon as they got close to him.

"He had it coming. He's too weak," the dark-skinned lady said. "I've allowed him to play hard long enough. I'm tired of it." She walked over to Isaac's dead body and spat on it before grabbing Oni's arm.

Oni jumped back and fell against the wall. "No! Don't touch me," she shrieked.

Everyone watched as the lady kneeled next to Oni. "You remember what I told you in the mall that day, sweetie?" She paused. "It applies to any man. Even the ones you think you love." She gave Oni a sympathetic smile. "I've been married to Isaac for almost fifteen years, and he's been cheating every one of them. I know you probably think you were special, baby girl, but you weren't.

"Ever since our daughter was killed he's been chasing you young girls. I don't know why, but he has. Since he took such good care of me, I turned the other cheek and did my own thing, but I'm tired now. He played me for the last time when he chased you all the way up here."

Oni listened to the woman speak while tears rushed down her face. She was shaking and could hardly keep her head held up. The pain she felt in that moment was nothing like she'd ever felt before, and the continuous sobs escaping her lips relayed that. In an effort to console her, Gia rushed to her side and held on to her.

Her arms were wrapped tightly around Oni's shoulders as she tried to help her control her agony. Oni's weeping was so violent that it was shaking Gia as well.

"He probably had no idea that I've known about his cheating all these years, but I have. I just didn't care. I gave that bastard my name and everything that came with it, and he was still ungrateful." The lady stood and looked down at Isaac's lifeless body before looking back at Oni. "You're young, you'll love again, sweetie. Just make sure next time it's the right man."

Jamil watched her walk over to where Shock and Alira stood before she turned toward him. "Milli Rock, my sincerest apologies, sweetheart. I've been telling him to let it go, but he refused. I tried everything in my power to keep you away from him, even sending you to Miami, but he continued to be an ass. Forgive me for his foolishness. I hope that you and I can still work together in the future."

"Who are you?" Gia's voice gained all of their attention.

The beautiful lady smiled at Gia, still holding Oni, before blowing her a kiss. "Daisy Monty. Daughter of the infamous Big Monty. I run a drug cartel that your man works in. A very well-connected and a pretty-ass bitch who's getting paid." She winked before looking over at Shock. "Thanks for everything."

Everyone sat in stunned silence watching Daisy walk away. She had this alluring aura about her that commanded attention, yet she was still as graceful as a butterfly. Jamil tried to turn his eyes away from her to focus on what had just happened, but was caught off guard again by the team of men that converged around them to gather Isaac's body. They moved quickly and efficiently, cleaning the blood before hopping into a white van and leaving.

"Bruh, what the fuck just happen?" Jamil looked over at Shock.

He smiled at him and shrugged. "Exactly what needed to happen."

"Nigga, I see that, but tell me something. I'm confused as hell."

"Daisy is Big Monty's daughter. She's been letting this nigga run everything for her because he was her man, but I guess she just got tired and decided to off his ass. He's been on your trail like hell these past few years, but you were too good for that nigga and he was too much of a hoe to catch you slipping. Which is why he tried to get at me and Iverson to help him. I started to blow that nigga's head off right then, but I had to play smart. That nigga Iverson, well . . . you saw what he was on."

"Damn." Jamil sighed, trying to make sense of it all. "So you've been working with her all this time?"

Shock nodded. "Right after Iverson got knocked, that nigga propositioned me too, and I went to her to see what was up. When I saw she was G, I stuck with it. You my li'l brother. I had to make sure you was straight."

Jamil stuck his gun in his waist and walked over to Shock. He dapped him up before giving him a brief hug.

"Appreciate that, my nigga, but you could have given me a heads-up or something."

"I couldn't. You're too smart. You would have killed that nigga before I could get Daisy on our team. I wanted him dead, but I had to make sure the streets didn't dry up because of it."

"I know that's right." Alira giggled.

"Damn, so you knew too?"

She nodded. "Why you think I was always trying to keep you in Miami when you would say something about Georgia? I was trying to look out for your country ass, but you was making it hard. That's why I hit you up earlier. Daisy told me this nigga was here, and I knew you were too. We all got on the first flight out and been following his ass ever since."

Jamil took a deep breath because he really couldn't believe what was happening around him. It was all so crazy, but oddly enough, it made sense.

"Baby." Gia's voice brought Jamil back to reality.

He spun around and went right to her. He kneeled down next to her and pulled her from the ground. "What's wrong?"

"I just need to go lie down. This is too much."

Jamil understood completely, so he didn't fight it. "Y'all, I appreciate all this, but I got to jet."

"Bet. I'll see you around, Milli Rock," Alira said before walking away.

"I'ma stay with Oni tonight, so we'll link up in the morning," Shock told Jamil before going over to a weeping Oni.

She was still in the same place and looked to be really distraught. She looked so bad that Jamil actually felt sorry for her. Her face was swollen and stained with tears as he watched Shock lift her from the ground. Jamil and Gia followed them until they were in her room before walking off. Had anyone told him that today would pan out the way it did, he wouldn't have believed them. However, he did believe that everything happened for a reason. Even with so much unfolding and falling out, he was positive that there had to be a reason why. Hopefully, one day he would find out what it was.

Epilogue

"Milli Rock is my heart. The love of my life and the man of my dreams. It's crazy how when you're a little girl you dream of your Prince Charming or your knight in shining armor. I had no idea that mine would turn out to be a tall dreadheaded thug who would give me more passion and street than I could ask for, but I'm glad he did. I wouldn't trade him or our love for anything in the world." —Gee

"My best friend, my girlfriend, my baby mama, my wife, my soul, and anything else she could be, that's my Gee. My li'l chocolate baby has changed me in so many ways that I hardly recognize myself anymore, but in my case, that's a good thing. Gorgeous and beautiful in every way possible. Whoever said that thugs needed love too must have been talking about me and Gee. It's still surreal to me that I actually lived a life without her, because now that seems like the most impossible thing in the world to me. I love her, she loves me, that's all I need." —Milli

"Nine pounds, six ounces," the nurse called out across the hospital room. "All ten toes and all ten fingers, Mom. He's a whopper."

Gia smiled as she watched them clean her son. He was indeed a whopper. His cheeks were so fat she could see them from where she lay. It had been a long, tiring journey, but she'd made it. Baby Jamil Rock Jr. was here and she could finally rest.

"Oh thank God." Gia's head fell back against her pillow.

"You did amazing, baby girl." Her mother wiped the sweat from her forehead before kissing it.

"I'm so glad it's over."

Her mom chuckled. "Oh no, baby. It ain't over yet. It's actually just beginning."

Gia wanted to roll her eyes because the way she felt at that moment, she couldn't fathom having to do anything else. After sixteen hours of labor, her body was tired and she couldn't wait to just go to sleep.

"He's a beautiful baby." Jamil finally left the baby and came to Gia's side. "He looks just like me."

"What color is his hair?" Gia asked.

Jamil smiled big. "Orange."

Both of them shared a laugh as everything continued to move around them. It took at least another hour before the doctors had gotten Gia and Baby Milli ready for visitors. Once the room was clean and everything was back in place, they allowed the rest of her family in.

The first people to enter were Oni, Shock, Zanetta, and Gia's aunt and uncle. Everyone came in either kissing her or grabbing Baby Milli. It was a sea of emotions as they crowded around her bed, congratulating her and cooing at the baby.

"Hey, auntie baby." Oni kissed all over his round cheeks. "I love you."

"You love him enough to give me one?" Shock asked her.

Oni blushed as she shied away from him. "I told you I'm still thinking about it."

Shock kissed her and grabbed the baby from her hands. "Well, give me my nephew until you decide."

Everyone in the room laughed at them as they bickered back and forth, Gia being the main one. She was so happy for her cousin. After all she'd been through, she hadn't folded. It had been seven months since Isaac's death, and Shock had been there every step of the way for her. Helping her get back to herself.

It had taken a while, but with his help, Oni had made a much quicker recovery. From the moment they'd met, Gia had known Shock would be the one for Oni. Oni just didn't know. Now that he'd helped her realize it, they were inseparable. If you saw Oni, you saw Shock, and vice versa. Gia was truly happy for the both of them.

Her family stayed for another few hours before everyone left her and Jamil alone. He was lying on the pullout sofa with the baby on his chest when Gia walked back into the room. She had just taken a little sponge bath and was preparing for bed.

"You feeling okay, Gee?"

"I'm fine, baby. You good?"

Jamil smiled at her. "Happier than I've ever been."

"Happier than when we got married?"

He looked at her then down at their son, then back at her before nodding. He laughed and so did she.

"Let me find out he's already stealing all your love from me."

"There's no one on earth that could do that. He's just sharing it with you."

Gia blew Jamil a kiss before climbing into her bed. Once she got comfortable, she turned so that she was facing him. His eyes were closed again and he looked to be on the way to sleep, which was fine with her. Gia was more than positive he was just as tired as her.

From the day they left Washington, they'd been doing everything they could to get their lives in order for when the baby came, and it was finally done. They'd gotten married and bought a house, Gia had begun training at UGA, and Jamil was finally learning how to read.

After investing some of his money in stocks that were constantly growing, they put the rest in the bank and were sitting pretty nicely. The two of them had worked hard for their happiness and would fight anyone who thought they were going to take it away.

Once Jamil finally made good on his promise and stopped moving drugs, the couple had extra time to do a lot more things, the main one being teaching Jamil how to read. Gia had begun teaching him, but once he became too embarrassed to allow her to help him anymore, she hired him a teacher.

The teacher had been coming to the house to help him for the past few months, and he was improving tremendously. He told Gia all the time how proud of her he was, but the truth be told, she was proud of him. He had stepped up to the plate in a major way, unafraid of becoming a man and leaving his childish behavior behind and evolving into the husband and father that she and Baby Milli needed. It was an amazing sight to see, and Gia felt honored to be the one chosen to see it.

"Take your ass to sleep, Gee, and stop staring at me."

Gia giggled. "I can't. You're better than any dream I could ever have."

He shook his head with his eyes still closed. "Nah, that's you, Gee. I told you the first night we ever made love that you were going to be everything to me. I could see it then." He looked over at her. "But I can feel it now. This forever, Gee."

"I can feel it too, Milli . . . I will forever."

DON'T MISS
Collusion
by De'nesha Diamond

Framed for a high-profile murder, Abrianna Parker finds herself
hurtling down a conspiracy rabbit hole in a desperate attempt to
clear her name. Her only way out is to go after the most powerful man in the country. But the powers that be play dirty. . . .

Enjoy the following excerpt from *Collusion*. . . .

The Bunker

In an unknown place in an unknown location along the bowels of Washington DC, Douglas "Ghost" Jenkins, lifelong political hacktivist, pulled open the metal door of his underground bunker to see his old friend.

"Well, if it ain't Bonnie and Clyde," Ghost said, blocking the entrance to his hideout. "Or should I say Clyde and Clyde?" He cocked his head at Abrianna and took in her outfit. "Nice disguise."

"Thanks."

Ghost's gaze darted to Julian and Draya. "Damn if every time I see you, man, your ass don't multiply. What kind of place do you think I'm running here?"

"Really? You're going to do this now? I have an injured woman. She's been shot."

Ghost straightened and glanced at Abrianna. "What? Again?"

"Not me this time."

Draya raised her good arm. "It's me."

Interest lit Ghost's eyes. "Well, hello."

Draya frowned.

"You're hitting on an injured woman?" Kadir asked.

"Is it my fault that women are always getting shot around you?" Ghost stepped back, allowing the small group to enter.

Hunkered down behind a row of terminals sat a skeletal crew of millennial hackers. Ghost introduced them as "the fellas" to Draya.

"Uh, nice to meet you," she said and then looked to Abrianna like, *Who is this clown?*

"C'mon." Abrianna led Draya toward the bunker's cot room. "I'll fix you right up."

Ghost smiled as he watched them walk away.

Arms crossed, Julian stepped forward to block Ghost's view.

"Oh. My bad." Ghost looked to Kadir. "Just how many people are you planning to tell about this place?"

"Chill. They're cool," Kadir said. "So what happened to you the other night? I thought you'd still be waiting to post bail."

"C'mon, playa. Am I the sort of person to give the cops my *real* ID?"

"They were putting you in the back of a squad car."

"Just some rookie busting my chops. You know how they do. Of course, I hope you got rid of the van. I had to report it stolen."

"Yeah. We traded that one in for another one and then filled that one with bullet holes too."

Ghost chuckled. "That straight and narrow path you swore that you were on isn't looking too damn straight, if you ask me."

"You don't know the half of it." Kadir looked around and leaned in close. "What do you know about . . . telekinesis?"

"What?"

"You know . . ." Kadir shrugged, inched closer. "The ability to move shit with your mind. Have you ever known anyone who could—"

"*Kadir!*"

At Abrianna's shout, Kadir and Ghost took off toward the back.

In the cot room, Draya and Abrianna stood in front of a nine-inch TV.

When the guys couldn't see what was the emergency was, Kadir asked, "Is everything okay?"

Abrianna shook her head and pointed at the news broadcast on the screen.

"Federal Judge Katherine J. Sanders will be sworn in tomorrow as the eighteenth chief justice of the United States Supreme Court, enabling President Daniel Walker to put his stamp on the court for decades to come. Sanders's nomination had been slow-walked while Senate Republicans waited to see whether the new Speaker would pursue impeachment of the president. But with Speaker Reynolds's death, the Senate majority leader decided to move ahead with the confirmation."

Abrianna stared transfixed at the image in the corner of the screen. "That's her!"

"That's who?" Kadir asked.

She pointed. "That's the other woman from the hotel. That's Kitty!"

"Judge Katherine Sanders?" he thundered. "*She's* the one you think framed you for murder?"

"Yes! I'd know that face anywhere. It's her!"

"But why?" Kadir asked, puzzled.

"Didn't you hear the reporter?" Draya asked. "That Speaker guy was going to impeach the president. An impeachment meant no confirmation. No Supreme Court."

Ghost slapped a hand across his forehead and whistled. "Holy shit. The same judge who sent you to the clink," he said. "The *new* chief justice of the Supreme Court. Ha! Good luck taking her down."

"We're going to need more than luck," Kadir grumbled, ripping off his fake mustache. "We're going to need a miracle."

Ghost shook his head. "Yo, dawg. That road you are on just got as crooked as a muthafucka."

"No shit," Kadir hissed, staring at Judge Sanders's image on the screen until the telecast cut to a commercial.

Defensive, Abrianna glanced around the eclectic group and read doubt and disbelief. "You guys believe me, don't you? I'm not making it up. She's Kitty—the other woman at the hotel that night."

Draya pressed a hand against Abrianna's shoulder. "I believe you."

"Yeah. I believe you, too," Julian added, curling up only one corner of his lips. His eyes, however, avoided her gaze.

Abrianna's jaw hardened.

Julian explained, "It's just that . . . well, this is *huge*, Bree. The fucking *chief justice* of the Supreme Court? What the fuck are we going to do?"

Abrianna's body slumped. "I have no idea."

"Well. How about that?" Ghost said. "We're all on the same page with our heads up our asses. Great!"

Kadir cut his friend a hard look. "Chill."

"What? I'm just stating facts. It's a miracle that every Uncle Sam soldier isn't pouring into this bitch and hauling our asses to jail right now. You're wanted for bombing the damn airport and your new chick here is wanted for killing the third most powerful man in America. Firing squads were made for terrorists like you two." He held up a hand and added, "I'm just telling you how the media *is* going to spin it."

"And don't forget the dead bitch we left back in the van," Draya reminded them.

Shut up, Abrianna mouthed.

"Come again?" Ghost cupped his ear and leaned toward Draya. "Dead body? What dead body?" He looked to Kadir. "What the fuck is she talking about?"

Kadir hedged.

"Mutha—come here! Let me holler at you for a moment." Ghost spun his boy by his shoulder and shoved him out the door.

Sighing, Kadir went along. Deep down he knew that he was wrong for springing this situation on Ghost. If the roles had been reversed, he would have gone apeshit.

Ghost jostled Kadir to the bunker's break room and slammed the door. It took another minute to calm down and choose his words carefully. "There is no point in my asking whether you've lost your damn mind because I already know that since you laid eyes on that suicidal stripper, you've completely checked the fuck out of reality."

"Ghost, calm—"

"Ah, ah, ah." Ghost held up a finger and shook his head. "You've lost any right to tell me to calm down. I'm not the one whose face is plastered on the news as a domestic terrorist."

"Hold up," Kadir interjected. "You're wanted by the federal authorities too for political hacking."

"For *questioning* . . . and for something that they can't prove, *and*, more importantly, my mug shot hasn't debuted on a single wanted poster or news broadcast."

Kadir cocked his head. "Are you jealous?"

"Jealous? Who? Me?" He waved the notion off. "Don't be ridiculous."

Kadir squinted and read the truth in his face.

Ghost swung the conversation back to the matter at hand. "Who is the corpse?"

Kadir sighed.

"Please, please tell me it's not *the* president of the United States."

"Don't be ridiculous," Kadir said.

"Then who?"

"Remember the madam we raced across town to *talk* to?"

"You're shitting me," Ghost said. "She killed her?"

"No. Abrianna didn't kill her," Kadir snapped. "We just . . . sort of *kidnapped* her."

"Oh. Well. That makes more sense. What's a little kidnapping every now and then?" Ghost shrugged with a straight face. "What the fuck, man? Snap out of it!"

"We didn't have much of a choice since the woman cleared out of her estate. A friend of Abrianna's was catering a party for the woman's boyfriend, so her other friend, Draya, created these disguises and we crashed the joint."

"To kidnap the madam?" Ghost clarified, following along.

"Right. Only . . . there was a hiccup."

Ghost crossed his arms. "That tends to happen when committing *federal* crimes."

Kadir glared.

"What happened?" Ghost asked, rolling his hand, wanting to get the end of the story.

"Bruh, I'm still not sure. This guard showed up when we were loading the body up, and I think . . ." Kadir glanced at the closed door and then crossed over to stand in front of it, to make sure that no one entered. He lowered his voice. "I think . . . Abrianna threw this four-hundred-pound guy up against the side of the house—*without* laying a finger on him."

Ghost stared.

"You think I'm crazy, don't you?" Kadir tossed up his hands. "I don't blame you. If I hadn't seen the shit for myself, I wouldn't believe it either, but . . . there's no other explanation. I saw what I saw."

"Catering?"

"Yeah. We—"

"Never mind. Finish the story."

"Like I was saying, the guy startled us, and when he approached the van to see for himself what we were doing, Draya slammed the van door into his face and his gun went off."

"So that's how she got shot?"

"Right. But when the gun went off," Kadir's voice went even lower, "Abrianna screamed and . . . this huge guy *flew* backward. I mean literally up in the *air* and slammed into the side of the house, knocking him out cold. I've never seen anything like it."

Silence.

Kadir's hands fell to his sides. "You don't believe me."

"Believe what? That your hooker girlfriend out there has superpowers? Sure. Of course I believe you. Why wouldn't I?"

Kadir's gaze leveled on his friend. "I'm not bullshitting you, man."

Ghost evaluated Kadir and then took a deep breath. "Okay."

"Okay? So you believe me?" Kadir checked, surprised.

"I believe that *you* believe what you thought you saw."

Kadir ran that sentence back through his head. "But . . . you don't believe it happened?"

"Is it important that I believe it? Does it change anything?"

Kadir sighed. "I guess not."

A few minutes later, they returned to the cot room where the group waited.

"I'm not crazy," Abrianna Parker insisted.

Ghost folded his meaty arms while his black gaze centered on her. "I've only known you for a few days, I hope you don't take offense, but I personally think you're batshit crazy and I don't want anything more to do with this nonsense." His lethal gaze sliced toward Kadir. "Look, bruh. We go *way* back, but this mess right here? I want no part of it."

Kadir squared his shoulders at the curt tone. Emotions warred across his face, and despite his own visible doubt, he defended Abrianna. "Why don't we just hear her out?"

"Hear her out? She just said that the new chief justice of the Supreme Court—and your mortal enemy, I may add—*murdered* the Speaker of the U.S. House of Representatives, the second man in line of succession to the presidency. Do you know how fucking *crazy* that shit sounds?"

"No crazier than half the conspiracy theories that you've entertained over the years. All of which has you huddled down here in this underground bunker, hiding from the feds in the first place. Is what she's saying really that hard to believe?"

Ghost opened his mouth, but the words never tumbled out.

Kadir arched a brow and cocked his head.

Finally, Ghost closed his mouth and speared Abrianna with a look. "What happened to the madam? Wasn't she supposedly behind the conspiracy theory when y'all left here the last time? Who is it going to be next? The president?"

"Hey!" Kadir shoved Ghost, sending him careening into the nearest wall.

"Yo, dude!"

"Watch it," Kadir warned.

Julian crowded behind Kadir, ready to tag into the fight.

Tension layered the room while everyone else held their breath.

Ghost backed down. "All right, man. My bad." He clamped his mouth shut.

Kadir glanced back over at Abrianna. "Please. Continue."

Abrianna battled her pride to get the rest of her story out. "Look, you guys already know the rest. It was my first night as an escort working for Madam Nevaeh. That woman showed up and introduced herself as Kitty. My john was happy when she arrived up. They knew each other. We . . . partied . . . and when I woke up, my client was missing part of his head and that Kitty bitch was nowhere to be found. I got out of there, but then gunmen showed up at my apartment. My best friend Shawn, who's still laid up in the hospital right now, took a hit, but I kept running until I jumped into your car, Kadir."

"Where they shot up my car and I brought you here the last time." Kadir finished the story for her.

"Right." She huffed. "Now, what are we going to do?"

Everyone's eyeballs ping-ponged around the room again. Clearly, none of them had a clue to what to do next.

Ghost sighed. "Great," he moaned.

Their gazes shifted around the room again.

Roger, one of Ghost's hackers, cleared his throat and drew everyone's attention.

Ghost's brows climbed to the center of his forehead. "You got something to say? Speak up."

Nervous, Roger cleared his throat. "Well . . . I take it that the media received the image of Abrianna from the Hay-Adams Hotel security surveillance."

Ghost shrugged. "Yeah, and?"

"Then Kitty, er, Judge Sanders should be on surveillance, too," Abrianna said, grinning.

Roger smiled. "Exactly."

Hope, the last emotion in Pandora's box, filled the room.

"But how are we going to get our hands on their surveillance footage?" Draya asked.

Kadir's handsome grin stretched. "How else? We *hack.*"

However, hacking the luxury hotel turned out to be a difficult job. Ghost and Kadir ascertained that it would require physical access to the hotel's security server.

"How are we going to manage to do that?" Abrianna asked.

"My guess is that someone is going to have to pose as an employee and break into their security department. Once in there, upload a custom malware to give us access to their digital files."

"That sounds simple, which means it's anything but," Abrianna said.

Ghost smiled. "Smart girl. I'd imagine posing as an employee would be difficult. Something as small staffed as a hotel, everyone would know everybody. Don't you think?"

"Well, it's a pretty big hotel with shops and restaurants—but getting near security . . ." Abrianna shook her head.

"Right."

Julian spoke up. "What if someone was applying for a job?" He had everyone's attention and continued, "I worked security once at a hotel, and our security department was near the human resources office. New hires passed by our department every day."

Ghost and Kadir smiled. "You're hired."

Julian blinked. "Me?"

"Yep. You're not on anybody's radar. And you have the expertise to get in the door." Kadir slapped Julian on the back. "First thing tomorrow, you're applying for a job."

Julian looked sick.

DON'T MISS
Stiletto Justice
Camryn King's sizzling debut novel delivers an intriguing tale of
three resourceful women with a ruthless senator in their sights—
and even more explosive ways to take him down. . . .

Enjoy the following excerpt of **Stiletto Justice**. . . .

Prologue

"Is he dead?"

"I don't know, but seeing that lying trap of a mouth shut is a nice change of pace."

Kim Logan, Harley Buchanan, and Jayda Sanchez peered down at the limp body of Senator Hammond Grey of Kansas.

"I agree he looks better silent," Kim mused, while mentally willing his chest to move. "But I don't think prison garb will improve my appearance."

"Move, guys." Jayda, who'd hung in the background, pushed Harley aside to get closer. She stuck a finger under his nose. "He's alive, but I don't know how long he'll be unconscious. Whatever we're going to do needs to happen fast."

"Fine with me." Harley stripped off her jacket and unzipped her jeans. "The sooner we get this done, the sooner we can get the hell out of here."

"I'm with you," Kim replied. Her hands shook as she unsnapped the black leather jacket she'd borrowed from her husband and removed her phone from its inside pocket. "Jayda, start taking his clothes off."

"Why me?" Jayda whispered. "I don't want to touch him."

"That's why you're wearing gloves," Harley hissed back. "Look, if I can bare my ass for the world to see, the least you can do is pull his pants down. Where's that wig?"

Kim showed more sympathy, as she pointed toward the bag holding a brunette hair transformer. "Jayda, I understand completely. I don't even want to look at his penis, let alone capture it on video."

Harley had stripped down to her undies. She stood impatiently, hand on hip. "I tell you what I'm not going to do. I'm not going to get buck-ass naked for you two to punk out. It's why we all took a shot of Jack!"

"I'm too nervous to feel it," Jayda said as she wrung her hands. "I probably should have added Jim and Bud."

"Hold this." Kim handed Jayda the phone and walked over to the bed. After the slightest of pauses, she reached for the belt and undid it. Next, she unbuttoned and unzipped the dress slacks. "Jayda, raise him up a little so I can pull these down."

Harley walked over to where Kim stood next to the bed. "Don't take them all the way off. He looks like the type who'd screw without bothering to get totally undressed."

Kim pulled the pants down to Hammond's knees. The room went silent. The women stared. Kim looked at Harley. Harley looked at Jayda. The three looked at each other.

"Am I seeing what I think I'm seeing?" Jayda asked.

Harley rubbed the chill from her arms. "We're all seeing it."

"Star Wars? Really, Hammond?" Kim quickly snapped a couple pics, then gently lowered the colorful boxers and murmured, "Looks like his political viewpoint isn't the only thing that's conservative."

She snapped a few more. Harley donned the wig, looked in the mirror, and snickered. "Guys, how do I look?"

"Don't," Kim began, covering her mouth. "Don't start laugh—"
The low rumble of muted guffaws replaced speech.

The liquor finally kicked in.

"Come on, guys!" Jayda's whisper was harsh though her eyes gleamed. "We've got to hurry."

"You look fine, Harley. As gorgeous a brunette as you are a blonde."

Harley removed her thong and climbed on the bed. "Remember . . ."

"I won't get your face, Harley. What the wig doesn't cover, I'll clip out or blur. You won't be recognizable in any way."

"And you're sure this superglue will work and hide my fingerprints?"

Jayda nodded. "That's what it said on the internet."

"I'm nervous." Harley straddled the unconscious body and placed a fisted hand on each side.

"Wait!" Kim stilled Harley with a hand to the shoulder. "Don't let your mouth actually touch his. We don't want to leave a speck of DNA. I'll angle the shot so that it looks like you're kissing."

"What about . . . that." Jayda pointed toward the flaccid member.

"Oh yeah. I forgot. Look inside that bag." Harley tilted her head in that direction. "With the condom on, it looks like the real thing."

Jayda retrieved a condom-clad cucumber and marched back to the bed as though it were a baton. "He won't like that we've filmed him, but he'll hopefully appreciate that we replaced his Vienna sausage with a jumbo hot link."

The women got down to business—Jayda directing, Harley performing, Kim videotaping. Each job was executed quickly, efficiently, just as they'd planned.

Finally, after double-checking to make sure her work had been captured, Kim shut off the camera. "Okay, guys, I think we've got enough."

Harley moved toward the edge of the bed. "Pictures and video?"

292 / CAMRYN KING

"Yep. Want to see it?"

"No," she replied, scrambling into her jeans. "I want to get the hell out of here."

"That makes two of us," Jayda said, walking toward the coat she'd tossed on a chair.

"Three of us." Kim took another look at the footage. "Wait, guys. I have an idea. Jayda, quick, come here."

"What?"

"No time to explain. Just take my phone . . . please?"

Five minutes later they were ready to go. "What should we do about him?" Jayda asked, waving a hand at his state of undress.

"Nothing," Kim replied. She returned the phone to its hiding place in her pocket. "Let him figure out what may or may not have happened."

They'd been careful, but taking no chances, they wiped down every available surface with cleaning wipes, which they then placed back in the bag that once again held the condom-clad cucumber. Harley almost had a heart attack when she glimpsed the wineglass that if forgotten and left behind would have been a forensic team's dream. After rinsing away prime evidence, she pressed Grey's fingers around the bowl, refilled it with a splash of wine, and placed it back on the nightstand. After a last look around, sure nothing was left that could be traced back to them, the women crept out of the bedroom and down the stairs. Harley turned off the outside light and unbolted the side door.

Kim turned to her. "You sure you don't want to come with us?"

Harley shook her head. "I have to leave the way I came. Don't worry. The car service is on the way. See you at the hotel."

After peeking out to make sure the coast was clear, Jayda and Kim tipped out the back door as quietly and inconspicuously as they'd arrived. A short time later Harley left, too.

Once down the block, around the corner, and in the rental car, Jayda and Kim finally exhaled. The next day, as the women left the nation's capital, hope began to bloom like cherry blossoms in spring. Until now their calls for help and cries for justice had been drowned out or ignored. Maybe the package specially delivered to his office next week would finally get the senator's attention and get him to do the right thing.

Connect with Us

Visit us online at
KensingtonBooks.com
to read more from your favorite authors, see books
by series, view reading group guides, and more.

for sneak peeks, chances to win books and prize packs,
and to share your thoughts with other readers.

facebook.com/kensingtonpublishing
twitter.com/kensingtonbooks

Tell us what you think!

To share your thoughts, submit a review,
or sign up for our eNewsletters, please visit:
KensingtonBooks.com/TellUs.